# 串流追劇宅英文

## BINGE WATCHING ENGLISH STREAMING SERIES

# 音檔
# 使用說明

## 立即註冊

👤 **帳號** 限3-21碼小寫英文數字

✉️ **信箱**

🔒 **密碼** 限8-24碼小寫英文數字

再次輸入密碼

**完成**

───── 或 ─────

社群帳號註冊

**f** 使用Facebook註冊

**Google** 使用Goole註冊

👤 **帳號** 請輸入電子郵件

🔒 **密碼** 請輸入密碼

**登入**

快速註冊 ｜ 忘記密碼

───── 或 ─────

**f** 使用Facebook登入

**Google** 使用Gooole登入

| 掃描書中 QRCode | 快速註冊或登入 EZCourse |
|---|---|

### 請回答以下問題完成訂閱

**一、請問本書第65頁，紅色框線中的英文＿＿＿＿是什麼？**

**答案** 請注意大小寫

**二、請問本書第33頁，紅色框線中的英文＿＿＿＿是什麼？**

**答案** 請注意大小寫

**送出**

| 回答問題按送出 | 完成訂閱 | 點選個人檔案 |
|---|---|---|

答案就在書中（需注意空格與大小寫）。

該書右側會顯示「**已訂閱**」，
表示已成功訂閱，
即可點選播放本書音檔。

查看「**我的訂閱紀錄**」
會顯示已訂閱本書，
點選封面可到本書線上聆聽。

各大串流平台如 Netflix、Apple TV+、HBO GO 隨選隨看的方便性改變觀眾收視習慣。全球受到疫情影響，許多人改由在家遠端上班，追劇防疫變成很多人生活的一部分。本期《串流追劇宅英文》嚴選三大串流平台 15 部強檔影集，陪伴讀者追劇的同時，兼顧語言學習，並且解析影集背後的時事議題，在不出國的時候也能拓展國際視野。

本期總編嚴選除了慣有的單字句型、文法大師，最大的特色就是從強檔影集台詞、梅根哈利、Lady Gaga 等名人經句中學習道地流行「口說英語」，包含英國、美國犀利俚語、慣用語、雙關語、網路縮寫，都是一般在課堂學習不到的英文，卻又是聽懂老外幽默不可或缺的關鍵。此外，介紹多元樣貌的英語，在影集《王冠》有很 posh 的王室貴族英語、《艾蜜莉在巴黎》浪漫的法語外來字、造成誤會的「假朋友」。與來自世界各地，不同生長背景的族群交流時，要特別注意文化差異、語言細節，才能達到有效溝通。此外，在劇情閱讀部分也加入 EZpedia 關鍵字說明，讓讀者一目瞭然特殊專有名詞的意義。

現今歐美影集注重種族、性別、語言、題材多元，並且透過影音娛樂視角，加入社會議題喚起大眾意識。《性愛自修室》多元性別 & 校園霸凌、《晨間直播秀》探討職場性騷擾 #MeToo 運動、《核爆家園》綠色替代能源等。EZ TALK 除了致力語言教學，這期《串流追劇宅英文》更加入延伸英文閱讀，探討每部劇背後的時事、歷史議題。此外，我們也專訪了台灣最大的本土串流平台《GagaOOLala》LGBTQ+ 原創題材、YouTuber Jonas 分享瑞典環境保護、Podcaster 賓狗性平教育、高中法語教師浪漫巴黎專欄。在學習英文同時，真正關心全球社會時事。

解憂雜貨店《正念冥想指南》、《安眠指南》、《怦然心動的人生魔法》，陪伴你防疫充電，滿滿正能量度過這艱難時期。希望全球能平安度過這波疫情，再次和朋友家人團聚，一起到戶外散步、世界旅遊。

EZ TALK
本期責任編輯

*Yushen*

目次頁
**Table of Contents**

tv+　NETFLIX　HBO GO

▶▶

PART **1** 串流強檔影集

Megahit Original Streaming Series

🔵 Drama 劇情

*The Crown* 《王冠》

*The Morning Show*

《晨間直播秀》

🔵 Comedy 喜劇

*Sex Education*

《性愛自修室》

# Emily in Paris 《艾蜜莉在巴黎》

🎞 Thriller 懸疑驚悚

# You 《安眠書店》

🎞 Sci-Fi 科幻

# Stranger Things
## 《怪奇物語》

# Black Mirror 《黑鏡》

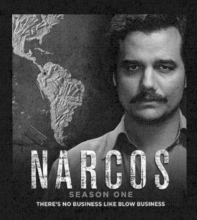

# Gossip Girl 2021 《花邊教主》

## GOSSIP GIRL

▶▶
## PART 2 串流解憂雜貨店 Stress Relief Streaming Series

# Tidying Up with Marie Kondo

## 《怦然心動的人生整理魔法》

# Headspace Guide to Meditation

# Headspace Guide to Sleep

▶▶
## PART 3 串流 KOLs 訪談 Interviews with Content Creators

# 串流強檔影集

## Megahit Original Streaming Series

---

串流平台隨選隨看的方便性，改變了全球觀眾收視習慣。加上疫情影響，在家
追劇變成許多人生活的一部分。看影劇學習時下流行道地口語之外，我們可以
發現劇情題材、角色、性別都越來越多元，並且能結合時事，提供娛樂享受同
時帶入議題。因此這期《EZTALK 總編嚴選》也希望帶給讀者多元的主題，除
了影劇閱讀、經典台詞，還有延伸議題閱讀，並邀請 Podcaster 賓狗單字、泰山
高中法語教師 Laëtitia 撰寫專欄，深入解析讓你看懂影劇。

# tv+

2019 年 11 月 1 日蘋果推出自家串流平台，執行長庫克（Tim Cook）強調，重播舊片不符合蘋果的原創精神，Apple TV+ 將專注於原創內容。原創影集包含：《晨間直播秀》、《你看不見的我》。

Apple TV+ 的訂閱價格：(1) 購買 Apple 裝置即贈 Apple TV+ 三個月免費訂閱服務。 (2) 每月訂閱費用 NT$170。透過「家人共享」功能，可讓六位家庭成員共享 Apple TV+ 訂閱方案。Apple TV+ 僅可收看串流平台上影集，若要收看 iTunes 電影，必須以單次租片或珍藏購買等方式額外付費。

# NETFLIX

Netflix 是目前世界最大的線上影音串流平台，包含台、日、韓、歐洲、拉丁美洲等多國影集，原創電影也多次獲奧斯卡獎肯定。Netflix 的原創影集包含：《艾蜜莉在巴黎》、《性愛自修室》、《安眠書店》、《黑鏡》等。

Netflix 每一部影集都能切換原文字幕，如需要雙語字幕，可在 Chrome 瀏覽器上使用外掛插件，除了英文還提供其他多國語言，非常適合看劇學習外語。

Netflix 共有 4 種方案：(1) 基本方案月費為 NT$270，可在一個裝置觀看 SD 畫質，(2) 標準方案月費 NT$330，可同時在 2 個裝置觀看 HD 高畫質 (3) 高級方案月費 NT$390，可同時在 4 個裝置觀看 UltraHD 超高畫質。

# HBO GO

華納媒體（Warner Media）串流平台，提供 HBO 與 HBO Asia 原創影集，原創節目包含：《新版花邊教主 Gossip Girl》、《核爆家園 Chernobyl》與 HBO Asia《我們與惡的距離》等。

與美國 HBO Max 不同，HBO Max 提供華納媒體旗下的電視頻道，包括：TNT 特納電視網、CW 電視網、CNN、Cartoon Network 卡通頻道。疫情開始後，HBO Max 更同步上映 DC 與華納兄弟影。然而 HBO Max 目前尚未開放台灣地區收看。

HBO GO 的訂閱方案：(1) 每月訂閱費用 NT$150，可同時在 2 個裝置觀看 (2) 每季訂閱費用 NT$380 (2) 搭配有線電視業者方案，每月最低 NT$99 起。

# THE CROWN

**#thecrown #poshenglish**
**#britishroyalfamily #queen**

全文朗讀 ♫ 001    單字 ♫ 002

## *The Crown*《王冠》
### 揭露英國皇室神秘面紗

**NETFLIX**

### Vocabulary

1. **roughly** [ˋrʌfli] *(adv.)*
   大約地 = approximately, about

2. **episode** [ˋɛpəˏsod] *(n.)*
   （影劇、廣播）集數

3. **costume** [ˋkɑstum] *(n.)*
   道具服

▲ 伊莉莎白女王

Queen Elizabeth II is one of the most well-known figures in the world, but do you know how she came to be queen? What better way to find out than by watching the big-budget Netflix historical drama *The Crown*, which tells Elizabeth's life story from her marriage in 1947 all the way to the 21st century, with each of the show's six seasons covering ¹⁾**roughly** a decade. At $130 million per ²⁾**episode**, *The Crown* is one of the most expensive shows ever made, and it shows in the ˡ**lavish** ³⁾**costumes** and set design—⁴⁾**recreating** ⁵⁾**locations** like **Buckingham Palace** and **Windsor Castle** isn't cheap!

伊莉莎白二世女王是世界上最著名的人物之一，但你知道她是如何成為女王的嗎？觀賞 Netflix 鉅資歷史劇《王冠》是最好認識英國王室的方式。該劇講述女王的一生，從 1947 年結婚一路到 21 世紀，該劇預計播出六季，一季大約涵蓋十年的故事。每集 1.3 億美元的《王冠》是有史以來最昂貴的影集之一，展現奢華的服裝與場景設計，要重現白金漢宮和溫莎城堡所費不貲！

The story begins in 1947 at Buckingham Palace. It's two years after the end of World War II, and King George VI (Jared Harris) is in the bathroom coughing up blood. When he's done, he [6]**casually** [7]**flushes** it down the toilet. If he doesn't seem too concerned, it's because he has more important matters to [8]**attend** to: the wedding of his daughter Elizabeth (Claire Foy) to her distant cousin, Prince Philip of Greece and Denmark. As George arrives downstairs, Philip (Matt Smith) has just finished **renouncing** all of his foreign titles and is waiting for the king to give him his new royal title: Prince Philip, Duke of Edinburgh.

故事開始於 1947 年的白金漢宮。二戰結束兩年後，英王喬治六世（傑瑞德哈裏斯 飾）在浴室中咳血。事後，他隨意將血衝下馬桶。看似不太擔心的他，是因為有更重要的事情要處理：女兒伊莉莎白（克萊兒芙伊 飾）與她的遠房表親——希臘與丹麥王子菲利普的婚禮。當喬治國王下樓後，菲利普（馬特史密斯）剛放棄所有外國頭銜，正等著國王授與新的英國王室頭銜：愛丁堡公爵菲利普親王。

The following day, we join Elizabeth and Philip for their royal wedding at **Westminster Abbey**, where we meet more of the show's characters. There's former **Prime Minister** Winston Churchill (John Lithgow), still loved by the country for his wartime leadership, who arrives at the last minute to **upstage** current PM Attlee. Then there's King George's wife Elizabeth and his mother Queen Mary, who both 🔊 look down on Philip's foreign family. And we also meet George's [9]**attendant**, Peter Townsend (Ben Miles), a married man who 🄖 can't help sharing 🔊 stolen glances with the bride's younger sister, Princess Margaret (Vanessa Kirby).

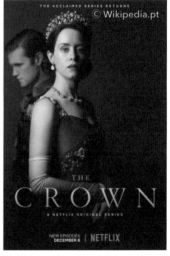
© Wikipedia.pt

▲ 《王冠》海報

4. **recreate** [ˋrikrɪˌet] (v.)
   重現

5. **location** [loˋkeʃən] (n.)
   地點，拍攝現場

6. **casually** [ˋkæʒjuəlɪ] (adv.)
   隨意地

7. **flush** [flʌʃ] (v./n.)
   沖水

8. **attend (to)** [əˋtɛnd] (v.)
   處理，照顧

9. **attendant** [əˋtɛndənt] (n.)
   侍從，服務者

**Grammar** Master

● **can't help but + 原形動詞** 忍不住，不禁
I couldn't help but cry when I watched the movie.
當看我這部電影時，我忍不住哭了。

● **can't help + Ving** 忍不住，不禁
I couldn't help crying when I watched the movie.
當看我這部電影時，我忍不住哭了。

## Vocabulary

**10. honeymoon** [ˋhʌniˏmun] *(n.)*
蜜月，蜜月旅行

**11. promotion** [prəˋmoʃən] *(n.)*
升遷，促銷

**12. pass away** *(phr.)*
過世

### 補充單字

**lavish** [ˋlævɪʃ] *(a.)*
鋪張的，奢華的

**duke** [duk] *(n.)*
公爵，（公國）君主

**renounce** [rɪˋnaʊns] *(v.)*
宣布放棄

**upstage** [ˏʌpˋstedʒ] *(v.)*
佔風頭，搶走焦點

**Commonwealth**
[ˋkɑmənˏwɛlθ] *(n.)* 大英國協

▲ 伊莉莎白女王與菲利普親王

第二天，我們一起見證了伊莉莎白和菲利普在西敏寺舉行的皇室婚禮，認識更多劇中的人物。前首相丘吉爾（約翰李斯高 飾）因戰時領導能力，仍受英國人民愛戴，他在最後一刻趕到，搶占了時任首相艾德禮的風頭。還有喬治國王的配偶伊莉莎白王后，與他的母親瑪麗王后，她們都看不上菲利普的外國身世。我們還見到了喬治英王的侍從武官彼得湯森（班邁爾斯 飾），他是一位已婚男子，但情不自禁地與新娘的妹妹—瑪格麗特公主（凡妮莎柯比 飾）偷偷眉來眼去。

▲ Claire Foy 飾演伊莉莎白女王

▲ Matt Smith 飾演菲利普親王

After their [10]**honeymoon**, the young couple moves to Malta, where Philip ❶ <u>rises through the ranks</u> of the Royal Navy, and Elizabeth gives birth to their first two children, Charles and Anne. But just as Philip is receiving a [11]**promotion**, they're called back to London, where King George—a lifelong smoker—is having a lung removed. When George learns there's cancer in his remaining lung and he doesn't have long to live, he asks Elizabeth if she and Philip would be willing to go on a tour of the Commonwealth in his place. On their first stop in Kenya, the news arrives: King George has [12]**passed away** in his sleep, and Elizabeth is now Queen Elizabeth.

蜜月後，這對新婚夫妻搬到馬爾他，菲利普在在皇家海軍一路晉升，伊莉莎白生下了他們的頭兩胎孩子，查爾斯和安妮。但就在菲利普升等之際，他們被召回倫敦，長期吸煙的喬治國王正接受肺切除手術。當他得知所剩的肺部裡有癌細胞，能活的日子不多時，他問伊莉莎白是否願意與菲利普代替他出訪大英國協。在出訪第一站肯亞傳來消息：喬治國王在睡夢中去世，伊莉莎白成為伊莉莎白女王。

**rise through the ranks 一路升遷，晉級**
Martha rose through the ranks to become VP. 瑪塔一路升遷為副總。

**look down on sb. 瞧不起某人**
You shouldn't look down on people just because they're poor.
你不能因為對方窮就瞧不起他們。

**steal a glance/look (at) 偷看**
That cute girl stole a glance at you when she left the room.
那個美女離開房間時，偷看你一眼。

# E Z pedia

**Buckingham Palace 白金漢宮**
英國君主位於倫敦的主要寢宮及辦公處。1703 年至 1705 年，白金漢公爵（Duke of Buckingham）在此建造白金漢屋（Buckingham House），為白金漢宮前身。1837 年，維多利亞女王登基後，白金漢宮成為英王正式宮寢。現今白金漢宮的女王畫廊（Queen's Gallery）對外開放參觀，每天清晨白金漢宮外都會進行著名的禁衛軍交接典禮，成為英國王室的文化景點。

**Windsor Castle 溫莎城堡**
位於倫敦近郊的溫莎鎮，是英國王室溫莎王朝的家族城堡，也是現今世界最大、最古老且目前仍有人居住的王室城堡。從威廉一世 1070 年開始創建至今，溫莎城堡已有千年歷史。溫莎城堡現今仍是英國王室的行政官邸，若看到圓塔上掛著皇室旗幟，則表示女王正在裡面辦公。

▲ 溫莎城堡

**Westminster Abbey 西敏寺**
位於倫敦市中心西敏市區的大型哥德式建築風格教教堂，minster 在英文是「大教堂」，abbey 則是「修道院」。西敏寺是英國君主舉行登基加冕、王室葬禮的地點，黛安娜王妃的葬禮、威廉王子和凱特王妃的婚禮也是在這舉行。此外，許多偉大的英國詩人、科學家都埋葬於此，例如：詩人喬叟、科學家達爾文、牛頓、史帝芬霍金等。1987 年被列為世界文化遺產。

▲ 英國首相 Boris Johnson

**prime minister 首相**
常縮寫成 PM，是國家的政府首腦，負責統領政府的行政工作，在英國翻作「首相」，加拿大、澳洲翻成「總理」，可通用於君主立憲國（如：英國、日本）或有總統（president）又有總理的共和雙首長國（如：法國、俄羅斯）。每個國家首相、總理使用的英文職稱不一定相同，如：德國總理 chancellor，台灣其實也是雙首長制，行政院長使用 premier。

〔菲利普獲得新頭銜，正要離開時，在大廳看到伊莉莎白在等他〕

Philip　I think they'd have preferred a nice, 1)**pink-faced ˈmarquis** with a **ˈgrouse ˈmoor** in the Scottish Borders. *[lights cigarette]* Are you sure you wouldn't have preferred one of those? Someone with a grand title, rather than a homeless **ˈCharlie Kraut**?

Elizabeth　No, that would have all been very 2)**antiseptic**. Must you really smoke? You know how I hate it.

Philip　Pity, because I love it so very much. But like a great many other things, I'm going to give it all up for you.

Elizabeth　Well, you still have 24 hours to change your mind.

Philip　You think I can change my mind after all that? No, too late. I've ❶ <u>signed myself away</u>.

Elizabeth　Or won the greatest prize on Earth.

Philip　That's 3)**certainly** what they think. *[pauses to put out cigarette, kisses Elizabeth]* It's what I think, too.

---

## Vocabulary

1. **pink-faced** [ˈpɪŋk.fest] *(a.)*
   害羞的，天真的

2. **antiseptic** [ˌæntəˈsɛptɪk] *(a.)*
   冷淡缺乏熱情的，抗菌的

3. **certainly** [ˈsɝtənli] *(adv.)*
   無疑地，當然地

### 𝓣ongue-tied 𝓝o 𝓜ore

**sign sth. away 簽字放棄**
Martin had to sign his house away during the divorce.
馬丁離婚時必須簽字放棄房屋。

菲利普　他們應該比較喜愛個性溫和害羞的侯爵，在蘇格蘭邊界擁有松雞狩獵場的那種人。〔點煙〕妳確定真的不喜歡那種擁有高貴頭銜的對象？而不是無家可歸，混有英德血統的笨蛋傢伙？

伊莉莎白　我不喜歡。那樣日子就太單調了。你真的要抽煙嗎？你明知道我很討厭。

菲利普　可惜，因為我愛死抽煙的感覺。不過，如同其他美好的事物，我也會為了妳而放棄。

伊莉莎白　呃，你還有 24 個小時可以考慮。

菲利普　事情已走到這一步，妳以為我還能改變心意？不行，太遲了，我已簽字放棄自己。

伊莉莎白　或是，已贏得世上最棒的獎品。

菲利普　他們正是這麼想，〔熄煙後親了伊莉莎白〕而我也有同感。

## 加冕下跪

〔菲利普被要求在加冕典禮上向伊莉莎白下跪〕

Philip　　It's released an [4]**unattractive** sense of [5]**authority** and [6]**entitlement** that I have never seen before.

Elizabeth　In you, it's released a weakness and [7]**insecurity** I've never seen before.

Philip　　Are you my wife or my Queen?

Elizabeth　I'm both.

Philip　　I want to be married to my wife.

Elizabeth　I am both and a strong man would be able to kneel to both.

Philip　　I will not kneel before my wife.

Elizabeth　Your wife is not asking you to.

Philip　　But my Queen commands me?

Elizabeth　Yes.

Philip　　I beg you ☎ make an exception for me.

Elizabeth　No.

---

菲利普　　這樣讓妳散發一種我從未見過、令人厭惡的威信和特權感。

伊莉莎白　你則是散發一種我從未見過的懦弱和不安全感。

菲利普　　妳是我的妻子還是女王？

伊莉莎白　我兩者皆是。

菲利普　　我要娶的是我的妻子。

伊莉莎白　我兩者皆是，而堅強的男人，能對我這兩個身分下跪。

菲利普　　我不會跪在妻子面前。

伊莉莎白　妻子沒有要求你這麼做。

菲利普　　但女王命令我下跪？

伊莉莎白　是的。

菲利普　　我求妳讓我成為例外。

伊莉莎白　不行。

---

### Vocabulary

4. **unattractive** [ˌʌnəˈtræktɪv] (a.)
   無吸引力的，不可愛的

5. **authority** [əˈθɔrəti] (n.)
   權力，威信

6. **entitlement** [ɪnˈtaɪtəlmənt] (n.)
   權利，特權

7. **insecurity** [ˌɪnsɪˈkjʊrəti] (n.)
   沒安全感

#### 補充單字

**marquis** [ˈmɑrkwɪs] (n.) 侯爵

**grouse** [graʊs] (n.) 松雞

**moor** [mʊr] 高沼，曠野

**Charlie Kraut** 混英德血統的笨蛋
Charlie 在英式英語是「愚笨的」，kraut 是「德國酸菜」即「德國佬」的蔑稱，兩字加起來指「混英德血統的笨蛋」，菲利普的母親有德國血統，四位姐妹也都嫁給德國貴族。

---

### *Tongue-tied No More*

**make an exception 破例**
I know you don't accept late papers, but could you make an exception?
我知道你不接受遲交報告，但可以請你破例一次嗎？

## 她才是你的職責

[ 英王喬治與菲利普王子登船去獵鴨 ]

George    *[seeing Philip almost lose his balance]* We'll be all right. My [8]**son-in-law's** a [9]**naval** man.

Philip    We will. If I can handle a **frigate**.

George    You understand, the titles, the **dukedom**. They're not the job. She is the job. She is the [10]**essence** of your duty. Loving her, protecting her. Of course, you'll miss your career. But doing this for her, doing this for me...there may be no greater act of [11]**patriotism**. Or love.

Philip    I understand, sir.

George    Do you, boy? Do you really?

Philip    I think so.

©Wikicommons

▲1953 年伊莉莎白女王加冕典禮

---

### Vocabulary

8. **son-in-law** [ˋsʌnɪn.lɔ] *(n.)* 女婿
9. **naval** [ˋnevəl] *(a.)* 海軍的
10. **essence** [ˋɛsəns] *(n.)* 本質，精髓
11. **patriotism** [ˋpætrɪə.tɪzəm] *(n.)*
     愛國主義，愛國精神
12. **overlook** [.ovəˋluk] *(v.)*
     忽視，俯瞰

喬治     〔看到菲利普差點跌倒〕我們沒問題的，我的女婿可是一位海軍軍官。

菲利普   沒錯，我都能駕駛巡防艦了。

喬治     你知道這些稱號、爵位並非你的工作。照顧她才是你的工作，她才是你真正的職責，愛護她、保護她。當然，你會想念自己原本的職涯，但是為了她這麼做，也為了我這麼做……也許就是最偉大的愛國表現，或是愛的表現。

菲利普   我了解，閣下。

喬治     你了解嗎？孩子，你真的了解嗎？

菲利普   我想是的。

# 姊姊的光環

〔伊莉莎白告訴瑪格麗特她不被允許與彼得湯森結婚〕

Margaret　 ˈ**Admonishing** your ˈ**unruly** young sister. Have you ever thought how it must be for me?

Elizabeth　Many times. At great length. **Wistfully**.

Margaret　 You have a role, a clear set of rules. All you have to do is follow them.

Elizabeth　Margaret, you have freedom. All you have to do is enjoy it.

Margaret　 You think that I am free? To ❶ <u>be</u> constantly <u>in your shadow</u>. Constantly the ¹²⁾**overlooked** one.

Elizabeth　It looks like heaven to me.

Margaret　 What you have looks like heaven to me. Two sisters who envy one another.

Elizabeth　We wouldn't be the first.

### 補充單字

**frigate** [ˈfrɪɡɪt] (n.) 巡防艦
**dukedom** [ˈdukdəm] (n.) 爵位
**admonish** [ədˈmɑnɪʃ] (v.) 責備，告誡
**unruly** [ʌnˈruli] (a.) 難控制的
**wistfully** [ˈwɪstfəli] (adv.)
渴望留戀地，望眼欲穿

### *Tongue-tied No More*

**be/live in sb.'s shadow**
**活在某人的陰影下**
He's always lived in his successful brother's shadow. 他一直活在成功哥哥的陰影下。

---

瑪格麗特　責備妳難管束的妹妹。妳是否想過我的感受？

伊莉莎白　很多次，仔細思量，望眼欲穿。

瑪格麗特　妳有自己的角色、一套清楚的規則，妳只需要遵守就好。

伊莉莎白　瑪格麗特，妳有自由，妳只需要享受就好。

瑪格麗特　妳以為我自由？我一直活在妳的陰影下，一直被人忽視。

伊莉莎白　對我而言那是天堂。

瑪格麗特　妳的生活才是我的天堂。姊妹嫉妒彼此的生活。

伊莉莎白　不只有我們這樣。

© Wikicommons
▲ 1943 伊莉莎白（左）、瑪格麗特公主（右）

Travers Lewis / Shutterstock.com

## Vocabulary

1. **reign** [ren] (n./v.) 統治（時期）
2. **certificate** [sə`tɪfəkɪt] (n.) 證明，證書
3. **mourn** [mɔrn] (v.) 哀悼，哀痛
4. **funeral** [`fjunərəl] (n.) 葬禮
5. **generation** [ˌdʒɛnə`reʃən] (n.) 代，世代
6. **reasonably** [`rizənəbli] (adv.) 還算是
7. **bloody** [`blʌdi] (a./adv.) 【英俚】天殺的，極度地
8. **bugger** [`bʌgə] (exp.) 【英俚】該死

### 補充單字

**consort** [`kɑnsɔrt] (n.) 君王的配偶

**Highness** [`haɪnɪs] (n.) 殿下

**chapel** [`tʃæpəl] (n.) 禮拜堂，小教堂

**condolence** [kən`doləns] (n.) （多用複數）哀悼

**ghastly** [`gæstli] (a.) 可怕的，恐怖的

# The Death of Prince Philip 菲利普親王辭世

On April 9, 2021, Prince Philip, husband of Queen Elizabeth II, died at the age of 99, just two months short of his 100th birthday. The Duke of Edinburgh, the longest-serving royal \***consort** in British history, was at the Queen's side throughout her six decades of ¹⁾**reign**. According to the official statement from the Royal Family, "His Royal \***Highness** passed away peacefully this morning at Windsor Castle." On his death ²⁾**certificate**, the cause of death was listed as "old age."

2021 年 4 月 9 日，英國女王伊莉莎白二世的丈夫菲利普親王去世，耆壽 99 歲，距他 100 歲生日僅差兩個月。愛丁堡公爵是英國歷史上在位時間最長的王室配偶，在女王 60 年統治期間一直陪伴在她身邊。根據皇室官方聲明：「殿下今早在溫莎城堡安詳離世。」死亡證明上，「高齡」為其死因。

❶ **In tribute to** the Duke, Westminster Abbey rang its bell once every minute for 99 minutes to honor each year of his life. After a period of ³⁾**mourning**, Prince Philip's ⁴⁾**funeral** was held on April 17 at St. George's \***Chapel** in Windsor Castle. National leaders around the world sent their \***condolences** to the Queen.

為了向公爵致敬，西敏寺每分鐘響一次鐘，持續 99 分鐘，以紀念他生命中的每一年。經過一段時間的哀悼，菲利普親王的葬禮於 4 月 17 日在溫莎城堡的聖喬治教堂舉行。世界各國領導人向女王表示哀悼。

### 𝒯ongue-tied 𝒩o 𝒨ore

**in tribute to sb. 向某人致敬**

The mayor made a speech in tribute to the firefighter who died fighting the blaze. 市長發表演說向殉職的打火消防員致敬。

## 菲利浦親王語出驚人 英式幽默、俚語

菲利普親王生前幽默風趣，尤其諷刺（irony）、自我解嘲（self-deprecation），正是所謂的英式幽默（British humor）。不過他也常在公共場合直率地表達個人意見，甚至開毒舌玩笑，總讓大眾瞠目結舌。回顧菲利普親王生前語出驚人的名言，學習英國俚語，感受英式幽默。

▶ "My [9]**generation**, although [6]**reasonably** well-schooled, is probably the worst educated of this age."

「我們這一代雖然算是受過良好教育，但在這個年頭，我們應該是教育水準最低的一代。」

▶ "When a man opens a car door for his wife, it's  either a new car or a new wife."

「如果一個男人會幫他老婆開車門，如果那不是新車，就是新老婆。」

▶ To Elton John: "Oh it's you that owns that [7]**ghastly** car is it? We often see it when driving to Windsor Castle."

對艾爾頓強：「喔那輛可怕的車（沃特福德足球隊塗裝）是你的嗎？我開車去溫莎城堡時常常看到欸。」

▶ To Nigerian President dressed in traditional robes: "You look like you're ready for bed." 對穿著傳統長袍的奈及利亞總統：「你這身穿著看起來要準備上床睡覺了。

▲ 奈及利亞總統 Olusegun Obasanjo 穿著傳統長袍

▶ To a Cambridge student who didn't recognize him: "[7]**Bloody** silly fool!"

對不認識他的劍橋生：「你這該死的笨蛋！」

▶ At a royal dinner party in 2004: "[8]**Bugger** the table plan, give me my dinner!"

在王室晚宴：「管他什麼餐桌座位，我要趕快吃晚餐！」

▶ To a Scottish driving instructor in 1991: "How do you keep the natives 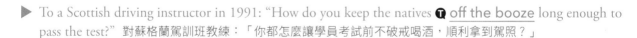 off the booze long enough to pass the test?" 對蘇格蘭駕訓班教練：「你都怎麼讓學員考試前不破戒喝酒，順利拿到駕照？」

**either A or B 不是 A 就是 B**
Either Mom or Dad will pick you up at the airport. 不是媽媽就是爸爸會去機場接你。

**off/on the booze 戒酒／酗酒**
Every Friday night Richie would go out on the booze. 每週五晚上瑞奇都會去狂喝一番。

29 July 1981

25P

© Shutterstock.com

## Vocabulary

1. **fairytale** [ˈfɛriˌtel] *(a.)*
   童話故事般的

2. **resume** [rɪˈzum] *(v.)*
   恢復，重新開始

3. **disorder** [dɪsˈɔrdə] *(n.)*
   失調症

4. **air** [ɛr] *(v.)* 播送，播放

5. **essential** [ɪˈsɛnʃəl] *(a.)*
   基本的，必要的

6. **destiny** [ˈdɛstənɪ] *(n.)* 命運，天命

7. **intolerance** [ɪnˈtɑlərəns] *(n.)*
   無包容心

8. **free spirit** *(phr.)* 自由自在的人

# Charles and Diana 童話幻滅 查爾斯和黛安娜

The ¹⁾**fairytale** wedding of Prince Charles and Lady Diana Spencer in 1981 captured the world's imagination. But, as we find out in Season 4 of *The Crown*, not all fairy tales have happy endings.

1981 年查爾斯王子和黛安娜斯賓塞女爵的童話婚禮擄獲世界眾人的幻想。然而，正如我們在《王冠》第 4 季中看到的，並非所有童話都有美好結局。

Charles first meets Diana while picking up her older sister Sarah for a date. Diana is just 16 at the time, but she catches the Prince's eye. Several years later, after Charles receives a letter from his grand-uncle Lord Mountbatten—who has been killed in a bombing—telling him to find a suitable wife, the two start dating and decide to marry.

查爾斯第一次見到黛安娜，是在接她姐姐莎拉去約會時。黛安娜當時只有 16 歲，但她引起了王子的注意。幾年後，查爾斯收到炸彈攻擊喪生的叔公蒙巴頓伯爵生前寫的一封信，要他找個合適的妻子，於是兩人開始約會並決定結婚。

But Charles and Diana's marriage is an unhappy one from the start. Diana soon finds that Charles has ²⁾**resumed** his affair with the married Camilla Parker-Bowles, and the pressures of royal life become so great that she develops an eating ³⁾**disorder**. Things will only get worse for Diana, as you'll find out in Season 5, set to ⁴⁾**air** in late 2021.

但查爾斯和戴安娜的婚姻從一開始就不幸福。黛安娜隨後發現查爾斯與已婚的卡蜜拉帕克鮑爾斯舊情復燃，王室生活的壓力過大以至於她患上飲食失調症。隨著第 5 季將在 2021 年底播出，你會發現一切對黛安娜更是每況愈下。

## 優雅黛妃經典語錄

黛安娜王妃生前致力於慈善事業，親切優雅的形象深得民心。愛護威廉、哈利兩個小王子的她，曾說過家庭是最重要的一切。遺憾的是，1997 離婚後一年，黛安娜在巴黎為了躲避狗仔追拍，最終車禍離世。

▶ "Helping people in need is a good and ⁵⁾**essential** part of my life, a kind of ⁶⁾**destiny**. Anywhere I see suffering, that is where I want to be, doing what I can."

「幫助別人很美好，在我生命中不可缺少，像是命中註定。只要有災苦的地方，就是我想去的地方，並設法解決。」

▶ "The greatest problem in the world today is ⁷⁾**intolerance**. Everyone is so intolerant of each other. Every one of us needs to show how much we care for each other and, in the process, care for ourselves."

「現今世上最大的問題就是缺乏包容心，每個人對彼此都無法包容。我們每個人都需要關心彼此，在這過程中也關心我們自己。」

▶ "Being a princess ❶ <u>isn't all that it's cracked up to be</u>. I'd like to be a ⁸⁾**free spirit**. Some don't like that but that's who I am."

「當王妃並不是幻想的那麼美好。我嚮往成為自由的靈魂，有些人不能接受這種想法，但這就是我。」

▶ "If you find someone you love in your life, then ❶ <u>hang on to</u> that love, and look after it."

「如果你發現生命中的摯愛，就要緊緊抓住，細心呵護。」

### Tongue-tied No More

**sth. be not all it's cracked up to be** …並非一般認為那麼好
The new phone isn't all it's cracked up to be.
新款手機並非大家說的那麼好。

**hang on (to sth.)** 堅持某事，緊握不放
How long can you hang on to that impossible dream?
你還能堅守那不切實際的夢多久？

# MEGXIT

Perry Correll © Shutterstock

Bart Lenoir © Shutterstock

## Vocabulary

1. **withdrawal** [wɪð`drɔəl] (n.) 退出，撤退
2. **overwhelm** [ˌovə·`wɛlm] (v.) 使壓垮、難以承受
3. **adjust (to)** [ə`dʒʌst] (v.) 調適，適應
4. **intense** [ɪn`tɛns] (a.) 強烈的，激烈的
5. **concern** [kən`sɜn] (n.) 憂慮，疑慮

### 補充單字

**portmanteau** [pɔrt`mænto] (n.) 混合字
**duchess** [`dʌtʃɪs] (n.) 公爵夫人，女公爵
**tabloid** [`tæblɔɪd] (n.) 八卦小報
**mixed-race** [`mɪkst.res] (a.) 混血的
**outspoken** [aʊt`spokən] (a.) 直言不諱的

## Megxit 哈利梅根退出英國王室

A **portmanteau** of *Meghan* and *exit*, Megxit describes the 2020 [1]**withdrawal** of Prince Harry, Duke of Sussex, and Meghan, **Duchess** of Sussex, from their Royal Family duties. When Prince Harry and Meghan Markle got married in 2018, as with Charles and Diana, the event was described as a "fairytale wedding." And as with Diana, Meghan soon became [2]**overwhelmed** by the pressures of royal life. In a 2019 interview, Meghan said [3]**adjusting** to royal life had been hard, and that [4]**intense** attention from the **tabloids** was affecting her mental and physical health.

"Megxit" 是梅根（Meghan）與離開（exit）的混合詞，指 2020 年哈利王子薩塞克斯公爵和梅根薩塞克斯公爵夫人退出王室職責。2018 年哈利王子和梅根馬克爾結婚時，就像查爾斯和黛安娜一樣，被喻為「童話般的婚禮」。梅根與黛安娜一樣，很快就被王室生活壓力所淹沒。在 2019 年的一次採訪中，梅根說適應王室生活一直很艱難，八卦小報的強烈關注正在影響她的身心健康。

But it wasn't until January 2020, after returning from a trip to Canada, that Harry and Meghan announced they'd be stepping away from their royal duties. In a March interview with Oprah Winfrey, Meghan, who is **mixed-race**, said that within the Royal Family, there had been [5]**concerns** about how dark her son Archie's skin might be.

但直到 2020 年 1 月從加拿大旅行回來後，哈利和梅根才宣布他們將辭去王室職務。今年 3 月接受歐普拉溫芙蕾採訪時，非裔混血的梅根表示，王室內部有人擔心兒子亞契的皮膚可能有多黝黑。

## 哈利梅根爆料！歐普拉獨家訪談

今天 3 月哈利梅根接受美國 CBS 新聞台歐普拉獨家專訪，說明兩人退出王室的原因。梅根爆料宮廷種族歧視，一度有自殺念頭。哈利則把兩人婚姻比喻為母親黛安娜王妃，深怕重演歷史悲劇。

DFree © Shutterstock

▶ "I grew up in L.A.—I see °**celebrities** all the time—but it's not the same. This is ❶ a completely different ball game."

「我在洛杉磯長大，與名人見面習以為常。但王室生活不同，根本是完全兩回事。」

▶ "In those months when I was ⁷**pregnant**...we have ❶ in tandem the conversation of, you won't be given security, not gonna be given a title and also concerns and conversations about how dark his skin might be when he's born."

「我懷孕的那幾個月，我們倆被告知孩子將不會被給予保護、頭銜，還有人耳語擔心小孩出生時，皮膚不知道有多黑。」

▶ "I have always been ⁷**outspoken** — especially about women's rights — that's the sad irony of the past four years. I have ⁸⁾**advocated** for so long for women to use their voice and then I was silenced."

「我一直是直言不諱，尤其是為女權喉舌，因此過去四年諷刺而令人難過。我一直呼籲女性站出來發聲，結果我自己卻被滅口。」

▶ "My biggest concern was history repeating itself. I'm just really ⁹**relieved** and happy to be sitting here talking to you with my wife by my side. Because I can't imagine what it must have been like for her [Diana], going through this process by herself all those years ago. It's been unbelievably ¹⁰**tough** for the two of us, but at least we had each other."

「我最大的擔憂就是歷史重演。我很慶幸可以和老婆坐在這跟你說話。因為我無法想像，她（母親黛妃）一個人那些年要經歷這過程會是怎麼樣。對我們倆來說已經極難無比，但我們至少還有彼此。」

---

## Vocabulary

6. **celebrity** [səˋlɛbrətɪ] (n.) 名人，名流
7. **pregnant** [ˋprɛɡnənt] (a.) 懷孕的
8. **advocate** [ˋædvəˌket] (v.) 擁護，提倡
9. **relieved** [rɪˋlivd] (a.) 放心的，寬慰的
10. **tough** [tʌf] (a.) 艱困的，難受的

## Tongue-tied No More

**a different ball game 完全是兩回事、截然不同**

I used to babysit, but having a child of my own is a different ball game.
我曾當過保母，但跟有自己小孩是完全兩回事。

**in tandem 兩人一起**

The director and composer have worked in tandem on several films.
該導演和作曲家聯手合作好幾部電影。

#sexualmisconduct #sexualharassment
#newsnetwork #metoo

© Wikicommons

▲《晨間直播秀》主要演員 Jennifer Aniston（左）、Reese Witherspoon（中）、Steve Carell（右）

全文朗讀 ♫ 011　單字 ♫ 012

# The Morning Show《晨間直播秀》

暗黑新聞台　拒絕職場性騷擾

## Vocabulary

1. **launch** [lɔntʃ] (v.)
   推出，發行

2. **content** [ˋkɑntɛnt] (n.)
   內容

3. **journalist** [ˋdʒɜnəlɪst] (n.)
   新聞工作者

When you're one of the wealthiest companies in the world, and you want to enter the video **streaming** business and compete against big names like Netflix, Amazon and Disney, what do you do? Well of course you open your wallet. So in preparation for the [1]**launch** of its TV+ streaming service, Apple decided to spend $6 billion dollars creating original [2]**content**. For its first big-budget drama, *The Morning Show*, the money went to hiring big stars—Jennifer Anniston, Reese Witherspoon and Steve Carrell, who all play [3]**journalists** in the **cutthroat** world of TV news.

如果世界上數一數二最富有的公司想進入串流影音市場，與 Netflix、亞馬遜和迪士尼等大牌競爭會怎麼做？ 當然就是大開荷包了。因此，蘋果公司為了推出自家 Apple TV+ 串流服務， 決定砸下 60 億美元製作原創節目。首部巨資劇作《晨間直播秀》預算花在聘請大牌明星——珍妮佛安妮斯頓、瑞絲薇斯朋和史提夫卡爾，扮演殘酷無情電視媒體圈的新聞工作者。

*The Morning Show* is [4]**loosely** based on CNN host Brian Stelter's book *Top of the Morning*, which tells the inside story of the battle for [5]**ratings** between America's two top morning news programs, NBC's *Today* and ABC's *Good Morning America*. In the TV+ series, *Today* becomes *The Morning Show* and *Good Morning America* becomes *Your Day, America*. Stelter's

book was written before the Me Too [6]**movement** led to the firing of many powerful men, including *Today* co-host Matt Lauer. But in *The Morning Show*, the theme of sexual [7]**harassment** in the workplace ⊤takes center stage, with Carrell's character, Mitch Kessler, ⊤standing in for Matt Lauer.

《晨間直播秀》大致根據 CNN 主播布萊恩斯特爾特的著作《晨間頭條》，該書講述美國兩大晨間新聞節目 NBC《今日秀》與 ABC《早安美國》為了爭奪收視率的秘辛內幕。在這部 Apple TV+ 影集中，《今日秀》變成了《晨間直播秀》，《早安美國》則化為《今日好美國》。斯特爾特的著作是在 Me Too 運動前寫成的，該運動讓許多位處權力階級的男性被解僱，其中包括《今日秀》共同主持人馬特勞爾。然而在《晨間直播秀》中，職場性騷擾主題成為故事的主軸，史提夫卡爾扮演的角色米契凱斯勒，正是代表馬特勞爾。

It's three in the morning, and the phones of UBA employees are ⊤blowing up with shocking news—Mitch Kessler is being fired from the show ahead of a *New York Times* article [8]**exposing** the network's internal [9]**investigation** into sexual **misconduct allegations** against him. Nobody is more shocked than his co-[10]**anchor**, Alex Levy, who has to go on the air in a few short hours—alone—and explain the situation to audiences across the country. She ⊤nails it, but her troubles are just beginning. Angry at her producer Chip (Mark Duplass) for not telling her about the investigation, and at herself for not realizing that her "TV husband" of 15 years is a sexual **predator**, Alex knows she's going to have to fight to save her career.

現在是凌晨三點，UBA 電視網員工的電話裡響起令人震驚的消息——米契凱斯勒在《紐約時報》曝光新聞網對他不當性行為指控的內部調查前被解僱了。最震驚的莫過於搭檔主播艾莉克絲李維，她必須在短短幾個小時內獨立擔當播出，

4. **loosely** [ˈluslɪ] (*adv.*)
大致上

5. **rating** [ˈretɪŋ] (*n.*)
評價，排名

6. **movement** [ˈmuvmənt] (*n.*)
（政治、社會）運動

7. **harassment** [həˈræsmənt] (*n.*)
騷擾

8. **expose (to)** [ɪkˈspoz] (*v.*)
暴光，暴露於

9. **investigation** [ɪn͵vɛstəˈgeʃən] (*n.*) 調查

10. **anchor** [ˈæŋkɚ] (*n.*)
新聞主播，船錨

©Wikicommons

▲ NBC 著名主播 Matt Lauer
因性騷擾指控遭解僱

11. **protest** [ˋprotɛst] [prəˋtɛst] (n./v.)
抗議，protestor (n.) 抗議者

12. **divide** [dəˋvaɪd]
政治分歧

13. **explore** [ɪkˋsplor] (v.)
探索，探究

14. **issue** [ˋɪʃju] (n.)
議題

15. **entertainment** [ˌɛntɚˋtenmənt]
(n.) 娛樂

### 補充單字

**streaming** [ˋstrimɪŋ] (a.)
串流的

**cutthroat** [ˋkʌt.θrot] (a.)
兇殘的，無情的

**misconduct** [mɪsˋkɑndʌkt] (n.)
不當行為

**allegation** [ˌæləˋgeʃən] (n.)
指控，斷言

**predator** [ˋprɛdətɚ] (n.)
侵害者，掠奪者

**hotheaded** [ˋhɑtˋhɛdɪd] (a.)
暴躁的；魯莽的

**booker** [ˋbʊkɚ] (n.)
預定員

©Shutterstock.com

▲ Billy Crudup 飾演 Cory

並向全國觀眾解釋情況。她辦到了，但麻煩才正要開始。她對製片人奇普（馬克杜普拉斯 飾）發飆，責怪他為何沒告知調查的事，同時也對自己生氣，竟然沒有意識到 15 年的「螢幕伴侶」是個性掠奪者，艾莉克絲知道她必須奮鬥挽救她的職業生涯。

Meanwhile, Bradley Jackson (Reese Witherspoon), a **hotheaded** field reporter at a news network in Virginia, arrives at a coal mine to cover a [11]**protest**. When a protester knocks over her cameraman, she starts screaming at him about the dangers of coal and the country's political [12]**divide**. She doesn't realize someone's filming her, and when the video ❶ goes viral, the head **booker** at UBA invites her to Manhattan for an interview with Alex. ⓖ Seeing her as a threat, Alex attacks Bradley during what was supposed to be a friendly interview. But just as Bradley is ready to return to Virginia, network news head Cory Ellison (Billy Crudup) invites her for a drink so they can talk about her future.

同時，維吉尼亞州一家新聞網個性魯莽的採訪記者布萊德莉傑克森（瑞絲薇斯彭 飾）抵達煤礦報導一場抗議活動。當一名抗議者撞倒她的攝影師時，她開始對抗議者咆哮煤炭的危害與國家的政治分歧。她並沒察覺到此時有人正在拍攝她。後來影片瘋狂轉載，UBA 的採編負責人邀請她到紐約曼哈頓接受艾莉克絲的採訪。艾莉克絲將她視為同業威脅，本來應該是場親切的採訪，艾莉克絲卻攻擊了布萊德莉。但正當布萊德莉準備返回維吉尼亞州時，電視網新聞製作人科瑞艾利森（比利克魯德普 飾）邀請她喝杯酒好好談論她的未來。

### Grammar Master

● 省略主詞的主動分詞構句

"Seeing her..., Alex attacks Bradley.... "
原句為 Alex sees Bradley as a threat so Alex attacks her during the interview. 當主詞相同時，可省略第一個主詞，「see 視為」為主動，動詞改成 Ving 現在分詞，此時的分詞已不是子句，不需要連接詞接續兩個子句，所以刪除 so。以下例句：

例：I got up late so I missed the bus.
我因為晚起床，所以錯過公車。
Getting up late, I missed the bus.

例：She doesn't know what to do so she asks her mom for advice.
Not knowing what to do, she asks her mom for advice.
她不知該怎麼辦，所以問媽媽的建議。

That may seem like a lot of drama for one episode, but the drama is just beginning. And because *The Morning Show*, after all, is about a news program, the series also [13]**explores** important [14]**issues** that have made the headlines in recent years, like mass shootings and climate change. So whether you're looking for [15]**entertainment** or education, *The Morning Show* has you covered!

©Shutterstock.com

以單集來說，看似上演很多衝突戲碼，但好戲才正要開始。《晨間直播秀》畢竟是關於新聞節目，因此影集還探討了近年的頭條新聞重要議題，例如大規模槍擊事件與氣候變遷。因此，無論尋找娛樂或教育題材，《晨間直播秀》都能滿足你的需求！

## Tongue-tied No More

**take center stage 成為關注焦點**
The crime issue took center stage in the elections.
犯罪議題在選舉中成為關注焦點。

**stand in for sb./sth. 扮演代替某人的角色**
I asked my coworker to stand in for me so I could take the day off.
我請同事代替我的業務，所以我才能請假。

**blow up one's phone 鈴聲狂響，奪命連環 call**
My mom always blows up my phone when I stay out late.
當我晚回家的時候，媽媽總會打爆我的電話。

**nail it/sth. 做得好，精湛表現**
I was worried about my job interview, but I ended up nailing it.
我原本很擔心工作面試，但最後我表現超好。

**go viral 網路爆紅，瘋狂轉載**
The singer got a record deal after his YouTube video went viral.
這位歌手的 YouTube 影片在網路爆紅後，獲得唱片合約。

©Wikicommons

▲ Billie Eilish 怪奇比莉《Ocean Eyes》在網路爆紅後獲得唱片合約

〔製作人契普與艾莉克絲討論關於米契被節目解雇的事〕

**Chip**　We had no choice. It was 1)**multiple** complaints of sexual misconduct.

**Alex**　How multiple? Who? When?

**Chip**　I don't know. It's 2)**confidential**. I fucking wish I knew. I'm trying to deal with this quietly. *[pauses]* Shit. OK. **HR** has been looking into it for a few weeks. I didn't want to drag you in.

**Alex**　You knew about this, and you didn't tell me? What am I? Some fucking **PA** from Idaho who doesn't need to know what's going on?

**Chip**　Alex, I was trying to respect your space so that you can go out there every morning and do what you do, what America needs you to do.

**Alex**　Fuck you, Chip. Don't drag America into this. They've got enough shit to deal with. This affects *me*, OK? My on-air partner is a sexual predator now? What part of you thought that I should not have been 3)**involved** in this conversation? You think 4)**chemistry** just comes in a bottle, and we go out and we buy another one?

## Vocabulary

1. **multiple** [ˋmʌltəpəl] *(a.)* 多次的
2. **confidential** [ˌkɑnfəˋdɛnʃəl] *(a.)* 機密的
3. **involve** [ɪnˋvɑlv] *(v.)* 涉入，牽扯
4. **chemistry** [ˋkɛmɪstri] *(n.)* 默契
5. **foremost** [ˋfor.most] *(a.)* 首先，最重要的
6. **sympathy** [ˋsɪmpəθi] *(n.)* 同情心
7. **devastated** [ˋdɛvəs.tetɪd] *(a.)* 受到極度震驚的，重創的
8. **disbelief** [ˌdɪsbəˋlif] *(n.)* 不願相信
9. **option** [ˋɑpʃən] *(n.)* 選擇，選項
10. **uphold** [ʌpˋhold] *(v.)* 堅守，維護

### 補充單字

**HR** 人力資源管理部
= human resources
**PA** 個人助理 = personal assistant

奇普　我們別無選擇。這是多次不當性行為的投訴。

艾莉克絲　有多少？誰投訴？什麼時候？

奇普　我不知道。這是保密的。我他媽的很想知道。我正在努力要私下處理這件事。〔停頓〕該死，好，人資已經調查了幾個星期。我不想牽扯到妳。

艾莉克絲　你知道這件事，卻沒有告訴我？我是什麼？來自愛達荷州鄉下該死的個人助理，不需要知道發生什麼事嗎？

奇普　艾莉克絲，我是尊重妳，給你空間，所以妳才可以每天早上在鏡頭前做好妳的工作，做好全美觀眾需要妳做的。

艾莉克絲　操你媽的，奇普。不要把全美觀眾扯進來。他們已經有一堆鳥事要處理了。這影響到我，好嗎？我的直播搭檔……現在是個性掠奪者？你怎麼會認為我不應該參與這個對話？你以為默契就裝在瓶子裡，用完再買一罐嗎？

# 為後果付出代價

〔艾莉克絲在直播新聞中解釋米契被解僱的原因〕

**Alex** Good morning. I'm bringing you some sad and upsetting news. Mitch Kessler, my cohost and partner of 15 years, was fired today for sexual misconduct. First and ⁵**foremost**, I want to offer our ⁶**sympathy** and support to the women. We are ⁷**devastated** that this happened ❶ <u>on our watch</u>, and our hearts are with you. And to you at home, I understand how you must be feeling because I and the whole team here at *The Morning Show* are feeling the same way. Shock, disappointment, ⁸**disbelief**.

**Mitch** *[watching at home]* She's ❷ <u>throwing me under the bus</u>.

**Alex** And while I don't know the details of the allegations, I understand that they were serious and that keeping Mitch on was not an ⁹**option**. We know he was part of our family, of your families. We will all miss that person. But there are consequences in life. As a woman, I can say there often aren't enough of them. And while I will miss the Mitch I thought I knew with all of my heart...I am proud to work on a network and live in a country that ¹⁰**upholds** consequences.

---

艾莉克絲 早安。我要告訴你們一則令人難過的消息。米契凱斯勒，我 15 年來的搭檔主持人，今天因不當性行為遭解僱。首先，我想對受害的女性表示同情與支持。我們對這件事發生在我們的監督下感到震驚，我們的心與妳們同在。而在電視機前的你們，我理解你們的感受，因為我和《晨間直播秀》的全體團隊也有同樣的感受。震驚、失望、難以置信。

米契 〔在家看新聞〕她出賣我。

艾莉克絲 雖然我不知道這些指控的細節，但我理解事情的嚴重性。我們無法選擇再讓米契留下。我們知道他曾是我們的家人，也曾是你們的家人。我們都會想念這個人。但人生的所作所為是有後果的。作為一個女人，我可以說後果付出的代價總是不夠。儘管我會想念這個我以為自己全心認識的米契……我很自豪自己工作的電視網、居住的國家堅守為後果付出代價的原則。

## Tongue-tied No More

**drag sb. in/into 牽扯某人進來**
Kevin is always trying to drag me into his crazy schemes. 凱文總是想把我扯進他的瘋狂計畫。

**on (one's) watch
在某人監督，在位期間**
The error didn't happen on my watch, so I refuse to take responsibility.
這個錯誤並非發生於我在位的期間，因此我拒絕承擔責任。

**throw sb. under the bus
陷害，出賣某人**
A loyal friend would never throw you under the bus like that.
一個忠誠的朋友是永遠不會像那樣出賣你的。

## 暴走記者 I

[ 布萊德莉與撞倒攝影師的抗議者發生衝突 ]

▲《晨間直播秀》海報

Bradley　I'm fake news? What's the real news then? You tell me five facts about coal and I'll let you go.

Protestor　I don't have to tell you shit, lady.

Bradley　You knocked down my cameraman.

Otherwise I'm gonna have you arrested for [11]**assault**. I bet you don't 🅣 <u>know jack shit about</u> coal. You're just out here trying to 🅣 <u>raise some hell</u>. Go! Tell me!

Protester　Coal is a cheap [12]**fuel**.

Bradley　Wrong! What else?

Protester　I don't know. It's easy to get for people.

Bradley　Wrong! What else?

---

### Vocabulary

11. **assault** [ə`sɔlt] *(v.)* 襲擊，攻擊
12. **fuel** [`fjuəl] *(n.)* 燃料
13. **toxic** [`tɑksɪk] *(a.)* 有毒的
14. **sanction** [`sæŋkʃən] *(n.)* 制裁
15. **liberal** [`lɪbərəl] *(n./a.)* 自由派（主義者）
16. **conservative** [kən`sɜvətɪv] *(n./a.)* 保守派（主義者）
17. **exhausting** [ɪg`zɔstɪŋ] *(a.)* 令人心力交瘁的
18. **exhausted** [ɪg`zɔstɪd] *(a.)* 感到心力交瘁的

布拉德利　我報假新聞？那麼什麼是真新聞？你告訴我五個關於煤炭的事實，我就放你走。

抗議者　我才懶得理妳，這位小姐。

布拉德利　你撞倒了我的攝影師。你不說，我就讓你以攻擊罪名被逮捕。我打賭你對煤炭一無所知。你只是來這裡鬧事。說啊！告訴我！

抗議者　煤炭是一種廉價燃料。

布拉德利　錯了！還有什麼？

抗議者　我不知道。人們很容易取得。

布拉德利　錯了！還有什麼？

| | |
|---|---|
| Protester | It makes jobs for everybody. Everyone's happy. |
| Bradley | Yeah, so does death, OK? You think that's a good idea? If it's so positive, why do you think all these people are out here protesting? |
| Protester | I don't know. Because they think it's dangerous or whatever.... |
| Bradley | Do you think it's dangerous? Do you even know what's in coal ash? Arsenic, copper, lead, mercury, uranium. That is some [13]**toxic** shit. And what about jobs? How many jobs have been lost in the last ten years? |
| Protester | I don't know. I don't know. |
| Bradley | Thousands! Thousands of fucking families ❶<u>knocked on their asses</u>. And it's just a big wheel that goes around. [14]**Liberals** add [15]**sanctions**. [16]**Conservatives** remove those sanctions. And they just keep fighting 'cause all they wanna do is hear themselves talk. And they all want to be right. And they all wanna win. And that's all they fucking care about. And there's a human cost! And it's [17]**exhausting**! I'm [18]**exhausted**! |

---

| | |
|---|---|
| 抗議者 | 它為每個人創造就業機會。皆大歡喜。 |
| 布拉德利 | 對,人死了也創造就業機會,好嗎?你認為那是個好主意嗎?如果煤礦真的這麼好,你認為為什麼這些人都在這裡抗議? |
| 抗議者 | 我不知道。因為他們覺得很危險之類...... |
| 布拉德利 | 你認為這很危險嗎?你知道煤灰裡的成分嗎?砷、銅、鉛、汞、鈾。那些都是他媽的有毒物質。那工作呢?過去十年多少人失去工作? |
| 抗議者 | 我不知道。我不知道。 |
| 布拉德利 | 數千人!數千個家庭家破人亡。這只是極大的惡性循環,自由派實施制裁、保守派取消制裁。他們只會持續惡鬥,因為他們只想聽自己的意見。他們都希望自己是對的,他們都想勝利。他們他媽的滿腦子只在乎這些。這還犧牲人命耶!讓人心力交瘁!我心力交瘁! |

### Tongue-tied No More

**(not) know jack shit about sth.**
**什麼都不懂**
= know nothing at all
People who know jack shit about politics shouldn't be allowed to vote. 什麼政治都不懂的人不應該被允許投票。

**raise hell 大吵大鬧、惹是生非**
The locals like to get drunk and raise hell on weekends.
當地人喜歡在週末喝酒惹是生非。

**knock one on one's ass**
**造成重大衝擊**
Losing his job really knocked Martin on his ass.
失業造成馬丁極大衝擊。

全文朗讀 🎵 015　　單字 🎵 016

▲ January 20, 2018 San Francisco / "Me too"

## Vocabulary

1. **advance** [əd`væns] *(n.)* 搭訕，示愛
2. **unfortunate** [ʌn`fɔrtʃənɪt] *(a.)* 不幸的
3. **stamp out** *(phr.)* 斬除，消滅

### 補充單字

**predatory** [`prɛdə,tori] *(a.)*
掠奪的，侵略的

**hashtag** [`hæʃ,tæg] *(n.)*
# 井字標籤，用於社群媒體關鍵字

### ⟨ Tongue-tied No More ⟩

**shed light on 解釋清楚**
New physics research has helped shed light on the origins of the universe. 新的物理研究幫助解釋宇宙的起源。

**pick up steam 升溫；加速馬力**
With the import of more vaccines, the vaccine effort is finally starting to pick up steam. 隨著疫苗的進口，疫苗接種工作終於開始加速進行。

# The Me Too Movement
## 「#我也是運動」抗議好萊塢大咖淫魔製片

In today's society, women are often faced with unwanted sexual [1)]**advances**. The idea behind "Me Too," which first appeared in 2006, is about 🎧 <u>shedding light on</u> this [2)]**unfortunate** truth. In 2017, the movement really 🎧 <u>picked up steam</u> after media reports of Hollywood producer Harvey Weinstein's long history of [3)]**predatory** behavior. In the years since, millions of women around the world have shared their personal experiences of sexual harassment on social media with the [4)]**hashtag** #MeToo. By doing so, they hope to comfort fellow victims and teach both women and men that such unwelcome advances are never acceptable. With more education and awareness, hopefully sexual harassment can be [5)]**stamped out**.

當今社會女性經常遭受不該有的不當性騷擾，尤其是來自男性的騷擾。2006 年首次出現的「我也是」運動旨在闡明這個不幸的事實。2017 年媒體震撼報導好萊塢製片人哈維韋恩斯坦長期性掠奪行為，該運動才真正升溫。在此期間，世界各地數百萬女性在社群媒體上以 #MeToo 標籤分享她們遭受性騷擾的個人經歷。希望這麼做能安慰受害者，並教導無論女性或男性，如此不當的騷擾永不可行。隨著教育和意識提升，希望性騷擾能因此杜絕。

©Shutterstock.com

◀ 好萊塢製片 Harvey Weinstein 因性侵遭判刑 23 年監禁

# March 4 Justice
## 「#公平正義遊行」性醜聞 澳洲政壇淪陷

全文朗讀 🎵 017　　單字 🎵 018

▲ 澳洲 # 公平正義遊行

The March 4 Justice was a [1]**series** of protests that took place on March 15, 2021 in over forty major cities across Australia. These protests started when the Australian government failed to respond to the [2]**rape** allegations of a government worker, Brittany Higgins. Recent [3]**revelations** that Australian *Attorney General* Christian Porter was [4]**accused** of rape in 1988 also ❶ added fuel to the fire. Tens of thousands of people marched to protest against the sexual [5]**abuse** of women and [6]**demand** that the government do more. Protestors wore black and carried signs with the names of victims. "There is a horrible [7]**acceptance** of sexual violence experienced by women in Australia," Higgins told the crowd gathered in the capital city of Canberra.

「公平正義遊行」於 2021 年 3 月 15 日在澳洲四十多個主要城市發起一連串抗議。引爆原因是澳洲政府未能回應政務職員布列塔尼希金斯的性侵指控。近期揭露澳洲司法部長克里斯蒂安波特在 1988 年性侵的控訴更是火上加油。數以萬計民眾反抗針對女性的不當性虐待，並要求政府積極採取行動。抗議者身穿黑色衣服，高舉有受害者姓名的牌子。希金斯對聚集在首都坎培拉的群眾說：「澳洲社會對女性遭受性暴力的容忍度令人震驚。」

©截圖YouTube ABC News (Australia)

◀ Brittany Higgins 揭露自己曾在澳洲國會大廈遭男同事性侵

## Vocabulary

1. **series** [ˋsɪrɪz] (n.) 一連串，影集
2. **rape** [rep] (n./v.) 強暴，性侵害
3. **revelation** [ˌrɛvəˋeʃən] (n.) 揭發，披露
4. **accuse (of)** [əˋkjuz] (v.) 指控，控訴
5. **abuse** [əˋbjus] (n./v.) 虐待，濫用
6. **demand** [dɪˋmænd] (v.) 要求
7. **acceptance** [əkˋsɛptəns] (n.) 接受

### 補充單字
**attorney general** 司法部長

### Tongue-tied No More

**add fuel to the fire**
**火上澆油，雪上加霜**
The Delta variant is adding fuel to the fire of the pandemic. 印度變種病毒讓疫情雪上加霜。

©Shutterstock.com

▲ Lady Gaga

## Vocabulary

1. **executive** [ɪɡˋzɛkjətɪv] (a./n.)
   執行的;高階主管
2. **psychological** [ˏsaɪkəˋlɑdʒɪkəl] (a.)
   心理的
3. **trauma** [ˋtrɔmə] (n.) 精神創傷
4. **freeze** [friz] (v.) 愣住
   freeze-froze-frozen
5. **numb** [nʌm] (a.) 麻木的,失去知覺的
6. **drop off** (phr.) 開車放下
7. **healing** [ˋhilɪŋ] (n.) 療癒過程

## *The Me You Can't See*: Lady Gaga's Story
## 女神卡卡自爆 19 歲入行遭性侵

In the first episode of the new Apple TV+ series *The Me You Can't See*, pop star Lady Gaga tells the *harrowing* story of how she was raped by a music producer at the age of 19. Now 35, she continues to deal with the *aftermath* of the assault, and in the interview, stresses the importance of getting help and support. The *docuseries*, which is the *brainchild* of [1]*executive* producers Oprah Winfrey and Prince Harry, attempts to remove the *stigma* from the mental health struggles of those like Lady Gaga by discussing [2]*psychological* [3]*trauma*. As Prince Harry notes in the series *teaser*, "To receive help is not a sign of weakness. In today's world, more than ever, it's a sign of strength."

Apple TV+ 新影集《你看不見的我》首集,流行明星女神卡卡講述她在 19 歲遭音樂製作人性侵的悲傷故事。現年 35 歲的她持續面對性侵後的餘波,並在採訪中強調尋求幫助與支持的重要性。這部紀錄影集是執行製片人歐普拉溫芙蕾與哈利王子的心力結晶,試圖透過說出心理創傷,消除那些像女神卡卡為精神健康所苦的污名。正如哈利王子在節目預告說的:「接受幫助並不是軟弱的表現。在當今世界,它比以往任何時候都更像是一種堅強的象徵。」

# Lady Gaga 勇敢說出內心秘密

2015 年女神卡卡推出《Til It Happens to You》，作為校園性侵紀錄片《獵場》（The Hunting Ground）主題曲，歌曲講述性侵的傷痛，並入圍 2016 奧斯卡「最佳原創歌曲」提名。2021 年 Apple TV+《你看不見的我》節目中，女神卡卡道出埋藏在內心深處多年的秘密，但最後她敞開心房走出陰霾。她鼓勵受害者也勇敢站出來接受幫助。

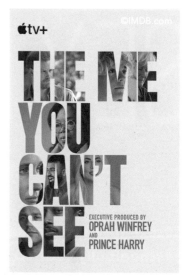

▲《你看不見的我》海報

▶ "I was 19 years old, and I was working in the business, and a music producer said to me, 'Take your clothes off,' and I said 'No.' And I left, and they told me they were going to burn all of my music. And they didn't stop. They didn't stop asking me, and I just **froze** and...I don't even remember.'"

「我 19 歲踏入這個產業，音樂製作人對我說：『脫掉你的衣服』，我說：『不。』離開，然後他們威脅要燒掉我所有的音樂。他們沒有停止，不斷地問我，我就僵住了，然後…我就什麼都不記得了。」

▶ "First I felt **full-on** pain, then I went **numb**. And then I was sick for weeks and weeks and weeks and weeks after, and I realized that it was the same pain that I felt when the person who raped me **dropped** me **off** pregnant on a corner."

「一開始我感到極度悲痛，然後就麻痺了。我病了好幾個星期，一個又一個星期，我意識到這種痛苦和當時強暴我的人讓我懷孕，再把我扔到角落是一樣的。」

▶ "Open your heart up for somebody else, because I'm telling you, I've been through it and people need help. That's part of my **healing**, which is being able to talk to you."

「為他人敞開心扉，因為我告訴你，我經歷過這一切，人都需要幫助。能夠與你交談就是我療癒的一部分。」

© 擷取 YouTube Apple TV 頻道

▲ 2015 年 Lady Gaga《Til It Happens to You》歌詞講述性侵害，並希望受害者勇敢站出來

## 補充單字

**harrowing** [ˋhærəwɪŋ] (a.)
悲痛的，折磨人的

**aftermath** [ˋæftɚˏmæθ] (n.)
（悲劇）後果，（災難）餘震

**docuseries** [ˋdɑkjuˏsɪriz] (n.) 紀錄影集
（documentary + series）

**brainchild** [ˋbrenˏtʃaɪld] (n.) 創作結晶

**stigma** [ˋstɪgmə] (n.) 污名

**teaser** [ˋtizɚ] (n.) 預告片

**full-on** [ˋfulˏɑn] (a.) 極度的

# N SERIES
# SEX EDUCATION

**#sexeducation #sexuality
#schoolbully #LGBTQ**

© Wikicommons

全文朗讀 ♪ 021　　單字 ♪ 022

## *Sex Education*《性愛自修室》
### 英國喜劇聊色　多元性別青春轉大人

**NETFLIX**

### Vocabulary

1. **awkward** [`ɔkwəd] *(a.)*
   尷尬的，彆扭的

2. **embarrassing** [ɪm`bærəsɪŋ]
   *(a.)* 令人尷尬的

3. **therapist** [`θɛrəpɪst] *(n.)*
   治療師

4. **fictional** [`fɪkʃənl] *(a.)*
   虛構的

© Shutterstock.com

What if you were an ¹⁾**awkward** teenager and your mother was a sex ²⁾**therapist**? That would be really ³⁾**embarrassing**, right? That's the ⁴premise of *Sex Education*, a British teen ⁵dramedy that ⁶debuted on Netflix in 2019. The show was created by British-Australian writer Laurie Nunn, who based the story on her own experiences learning about sex—both inside and outside of the classroom—as a teenager. The popular series, set at Moordale Secondary School in the ⁶⁾**fictional** town of Moordale, has run for two seasons, with a third season set to come out sometime in the second half of 2021.

如果你是一個成長尷尬期彆扭的青少年，母親又是性愛治療師會怎麼樣？ 那應該很尷尬，對吧？ 這就是 Netflix 2019 年首播的青少年英劇《性愛自修室》故事前提。影集為英國澳洲編劇羅莉努恩創作，她根據自己青少年時期在課堂、課外學習性教育的經歷寫成劇本。這部廣受好評的影集故事場景為虛構摩爾戴鎮的摩爾戴高中，目前兩季已播畢，第三季將於 2021 年下半年推出。

Just in case the title isn't clear enough, the opening scene lets [5]**viewers** know exactly what the show is going to be about. Adam (Connor Swindells), the [6]**headmaster**'s son and school [6]**bully**, is having sex with his girlfriend Aimee, and fakes an [6]**orgasm**. Next, we meet Otis (Asa Butterfield), who's having sexual problems of his own.

▲ Gillian Anderson 飾演性愛治療師

He's the one whose mother is a sex therapist—Jean, played by Gillian Anderson of *X-Files* [7]**fame**—and listening to too much frank talk about [8]**sexuality** has made him so [9]**anxious** about sex that he can't even [9]**masturbate**. "Sweetheart, I've noticed you're pretending to masturbate," she says, "and I was wondering if you wanted to talk about it." Of *course* not!

為了怕劇名說明不夠清楚，本劇開場讓觀眾確切了解影集主題。亞當（康納斯溫德爾斯 飾）是校長的兒子，也是校園惡霸，正和女朋友艾米發生性關係，並假裝高潮。接著，我們看到歐帝斯（阿薩巴特菲爾德 飾）有自己的性問題。他的母親珍（《X 檔案》成名的吉蓮安德森飾演）是名性愛治療師，因為聽了太多關於性的開放話題，讓他對性太過焦慮導致無法自慰。「寶貝兒子，我注意到你在假裝自慰，」珍說「我在想你要不要跟我談談。」當然不要！

It also doesn't help when his best friend, the openly [10]**gay** Eric (Nkuti Gatwa), tells Otis that everyone in their class, except him, has had sex over the summer. Luckily, Otis' life is about to 🎧 take a turn for the better. But first it takes a turn for the worse. Adam, who bullies Eric by stealing his lunch every day, becomes Otis' partner on a class project, and while working on it at his house, Adam discovers what Jean does for a living after walking into her home office and seeing all the sex toys and [10]**pornography**. When the whole school finds out the next

5. **viewer** [ˋvjuɚ] *(n.)*
   觀眾

6. **bully** [ˋbʊlɪ] *(n./v.)*
   惡霸，霸凌

7. **fame** [fem] *(n.)*
   名聲

8. **sexuality** [ˏsɛkʃuˋælətɪ] *(n.)*
   性，性向

9. **anxious** [ˋæŋkʃəs] *(a.)*
   焦慮的

10. **gay** [ge] *(a.)*
    男同志的

© Shutterstock

▲ Asa Butterfield 飾演 Otis

11. **post** [post] (v./n.)
貼文，刊登

12. **online** [`ɑn.laɪn] (a.)
線上的

13. **flee** [fli] (v.)
逃離 flee-fled-fled

14. **abandoned** [ə`bændənd] (a.)
廢棄的

15. **psychology** [saɪ`kɑlədʒi] (n.)
心理學

### 補充單字

**premise** [`prɛmɪs] (n.) 前提，假設
**dramedy** [`drɑmədi] (n.)
劇情喜劇 = drama comedy
**debut** [de`bju] (v./n.) 首映
**headmaster** [`hɛd.mæstə] (n.)
男校長，headmistress 女校長
**masturbate** [`mæstə.bet] (v.) 自慰
**orgasm** [`ɔr.gæzm] (n./v.) 性高潮
**pornography** [pɔr`nɑgrəfi] (n.)
色情刊物，色情影片
**erection** [ɪ`rɛkʃən] (n.) 勃起
**Viagra** [vaɪ`ægrə] (n.) 威而鋼

day—Adam ¹¹⁾**posted** a video of Jean teaching a hand job class ¹²⁾**online**—Otis ¹³⁾**flees** in embarrassment.

當最好的出櫃同志朋友艾瑞克（舒提加特瓦 飾）告訴歐帝斯班上每個人，除了他，在暑假都有了性經驗時，更是無濟於事。幸運的是，歐帝斯的生活即將好轉。但首先它會變得更糟。每天霸凌、偷艾瑞克午餐的亞當成為歐帝斯課堂報告的搭檔，在他家寫報告的時候，亞當走進珍的辦公室，看到一大堆的性愛玩具、書刊等，發現珍的工作。亞當之後在網路上發布珍教授如何打手槍的課程影片，結果第二天全校都知道了，歐帝斯尷尬地逃跑。

This is where things get interesting. Maeve (Emma Mackey), the school bad girl, follows Otis to see if he's all right, and they 🔁 run into Adam in an ¹⁴⁾**abandoned** building. He's hiding in the bathroom with a painful ˙**erection**, which he got from taking too much ˙**Viagra** in an attempt to solve his performance issues. Using the knowledge of sex—and ¹⁵⁾**psychology**—learned from his mother, Otis manages not only to solve Adam's erection problem, but his orgasm issue as well. Sensing a business opportunity, Maeve talks Otis into starting a sex clinic for the students at their school. Will their business be a success? And what embarrassing sex problems will Otis help solve? You'll have to watch *Sex Education* to find out!

接下來就是劇情有趣的部分了。學校的壞女孩梅芙（艾瑪麥基 飾）跟著歐帝斯看他是否沒事，他們在一座廢棄的建築裡遇到亞當。他為了解決床上表現的問題服用過多威而鋼，導致勃起疼痛而躲在浴室裡。歐帝斯利用從母親那學到的性和心理知識，不僅解決了亞當的勃起問題，還解決了他的性高潮問題。梅芙察覺到商機，說服歐帝斯在學校為學生開設性診所。他們的生意會成功嗎？歐帝斯將幫助學生解決哪些令人尷尬的性問題？你必須看《性愛自修室》才能找到答案！

◄ Nkuti Gatwa（左）飾演 Eric、Emma Mackey（右）飾演 Maeve

**just in case 以防萬一**
I'll take my umbrella too, just in case it rains. 我會帶雨傘出門，以防下雨。

**take a turn for the better/worse 好轉，惡化**
Mary's health took a turn for the worse after her husband's death. 瑪麗的健康在丈夫去世後惡化。

**run into sb. 巧遇某人**
I ran into my friend at the grocery store the other day. 那天我在超市巧遇我的朋友。

## Grammar Master

### 「與現在事實不符」的假設語氣

文中 "What if you were an awkward teenager...? That would be..." 用到假設語氣，假設你現在是誰，「與現在事實不符」或「該事發生可能性極低」，必須用「過去簡單式」。

● 句型 **If S + were ... , S + would/could/might/should + VR.**

例：If I were rich, I would buy a big house in Taipei. 如果我很富有，我就會在台北買一棟大豪宅。〔事實是，我現在很窮一點都負擔不起。〕

例：If I were a boy, I'd be a better man. I'd listen to her.
如果我是個男孩，我會是個好男人。我會仔細聆聽她的心聲。〔事實是我是個女孩，不是男孩。〕碧昂絲 Beyoncé《If I Were A Boy》歌詞

〔歐帝斯與艾瑞克放完暑假，剛回到學校〕

Eric　Oh, this is gonna be such a good year! I can feel it!

Otis　Is that Tom Baker?

Eric　Yup. Captain of the Warhammer Society. His ❶ **balls finally dropped**. Yeah, I keep telling you, man, everyone has had sex over the summer. Everyone except you.

Otis　And you.

Eric　Excuse me, I gave two and a half [1]**hand jobs** to that guy I met in Butlin's.

Otis　Why the half?

Eric　We got interrupted. Stupid surprise karaoke.

Otis　Still, not exactly a [2]**player**.

Eric　Yeah, at least I can touch my own penis. I'm worried about you, man. Like, look around. Everybody's either thinking about **shagging**, about to shag, or actually shagging, and you can't even ❶ **jack your beanstalk**.

## Vocabulary

1. **hand job** (phr.) 手淫
2. **player** [ˋpleɚ] (n.) 花花公子，玩咖

### Tongue-tied No More

**one's balls drop 男生轉大人**
balls 是「睪丸」，使用複數，成熟變大下垂也就是轉大人

**jack one's beanstalk 自慰**
jack off 是「手淫、自慰」，*Jack and Beanstalk* 是童話故事《傑克與豌豆莖》，這裡雙關語把 jack 當動詞，beanstalk 比喻成男性生殖器，即男性自慰

艾瑞克　今年一定會很棒的！我感覺到了！

歐帝斯　那是湯姆貝克嗎？-

艾瑞克　是啊，電玩戰鎚社宅男社長，終於轉大人了。就跟你說吧，這個夏天每個人都做愛了，所有人…除了你。

歐帝斯　還有你。

艾瑞克　不好意思，我可是幫度假中心遇到的男子打了兩次半的手槍唷。

歐帝斯　為什麼有半次？

艾瑞克　被打斷了，白痴的卡拉 OK 意外驚喜。

歐帝斯　那還不能算玩咖。

艾瑞克　至少我敢摸自己的老二。我真的很擔心你，你看看四周，大家不是想著要做愛，即將要做愛，就是正在做愛。你卻連手淫都不會。

# 太大出不來

〔亞當吃太多威而鋼，歐帝斯為他診療〕

Otis     Why did you take it?

Adam     I don't know. Heard it gives you a good [3]**buzz**. Maybe you should try it sometime instead of being such a **joy fucker**.

Maeve     He's having **dick** problems.

Adam     Yeah? What would you know, Wiley?

Maeve     Girls talk, **clodpole**. Aimee said you can't come.

Adam     Everyone knows I've got a giant [4]**penis**.

Otis     So you wanted to make it bigger?

Adam     No. I just wanted it to get hard.

Otis     Well, why do you think it couldn't?

Adam     I don't know. I can't stop thinking about stuff when we're shagging. What if I'm not good at this? Maybe I'm doing it wrong. What if my dad walks in and it's right when I'm ❶ <u>blowing my load</u>, and he sees my **jizz** face?

---

| | |
|---|---|
| 歐帝斯 | 你為什麼要吃藥？ |
| 亞當 | 我不知道，聽說會很爽，也許你該試試看，而不是整天當個掃興的傢伙。 |
| 梅芙 | 他老二有問題。 |
| 亞當 | 是嗎？妳怎麼會知道，威利？ |
| 梅芙 | 女生會八卦，白痴，艾咪說你射不出來。 |
| 亞當 | 壓力太大了。 |
| 歐帝斯 | 什麼壓力？ |
| 亞當 | 大家都知道我老二很大。 |
| 歐帝斯 | 所以你想要它更大？ |
| 亞當 | 不，我只想要它硬起來。 |
| 歐帝斯 | 那你為什麼覺得會硬不起來？ |
| 亞當 | 我不知道，我們打炮的時候就會一直想東想西，如果我表現不好呢？也許我沒弄好，要是我爸在我射的時候走進來？然後他看到我高潮的臉呢？ |

3. **buzz** [bʌz] (n.)（口）興奮愉悅感
4. **dick** [dɪk] (n.)（口）陰莖 = penis

### 補充單字

**shag** [ʃæg] (n./v.)（口）【英俚】性交
**joy fucker** (n.)（口）掃興的人
**clodpole** [ˋklɑd͵pol] (n.)（口）【英俚】笨蛋，白痴
**jizz** [jɪz] (n./v.)（口）射精

### Tongue-tied No More

**blow one's load 射精**
blow 是「爆炸」，load「裝載量」，指男性射精

# 天生性愛的料

〔梅芙來找歐帝斯談性愛治療門診的生意〕

**Maeve**  See those two over there? The one on the right has never been in a **¹lesbian** relationship before. She's **⁵⁾terrified** of her new girlfriend's **⁶⁾vagina**. See her? She believes that ❶ flicking the bean might make her **clit** drop off. She hates herself, but she just can't stop **wanking**. Do you see them? Yeah, he's definitely giving everyone **pubic lice**.

**Otis**  What's your point?

**Maeve**  The students at this school need your help, Otis. And we need their money. I haven't really worked out the details yet, but I'm good with numbers, so I'll deal with the business end of things and you can do the **⁷⁾therapy**. We'll charge for every **⁸⁾appointment** and **⁹⁾split** the cash.

**Otis**  Therapy?

**Maeve**  Yeah, sex therapy. You have a gift. It would be **¹⁰⁾irresponsible** to waste it.

---

## Vocabulary

5. **terrified** [ˋtɛrəˌfaɪd] (a.)
   受到驚嚇的
6. **vagina** [vəˋdʒaɪnə] (n.) 女性陰道
7. **therapy** [ˋθɛrəpɪ] (n.) 療法
8. **appointment** [əˋpɔɪntmənt] (n.)
   看診，預約
9. **split** [splɪt] (v.) 對分，分割
10. **irresponsible** [ˌɪrɪˋspɑnsəbəl] (a.)
    不負責任的

### 補充單字

**lesbian** [ˋlɛzbiən] (n.) 女同志

**clit** [klɪt] (n.) 陰蒂 = clitoris

**wank** [wæŋk] (v./n.)【英俚】自慰

**pubic** [ˋpjubɪk] (a.) 陰部的

**lice** [laɪs] (n.) 蝨子，單數 louse

梅芙  你看到那兩個了嗎？右邊那個女生第一次交女友，她對女友的陰道感到恐懼。看到她了嗎？她相信自慰就會讓陰蒂掉下來，她討厭自己但她又無法停止手淫。看到他們了嗎？他肯定在四處散播陰蝨。

歐帝斯  妳到底想說什麼？

梅芙  學生們都需要你的幫助，歐帝斯，而我們需要他們的錢。我還沒想好細節，但我對數字很在行，我來管錢，然後你來治療。我們收門診錢，然後平分。

歐帝斯  治療？

梅芙  對，性治療。你有天分，浪費它就太不負責任了。

©Shutterstock.com

# 吹就想吐

〔緊張的歐帝斯第一次看診，病人奧莉薇雅坐在廁所隔間〕

**Otis** Hello, I'm your therapist today. How...might I serve you?

**Olivia** This is [11]**weird**. Can't we just talk face to face?

**Otis** No, we shouldn't see each other. How can...how can I help you?

**Olivia** Didn't Maeve tell you? I just...I don't wanna say it again.

**Otis** Yes! Yes, you, uh.... *[clears throat]* You [12]**encountered** some problems during *fellatio*, which resulted in you experiencing a [13]**bout** of *emesis*, correct?

**Olivia** Emesis?

**Otis** Uh, [14]**vomiting**.

**Olivia** Yeah, I **puked** on his dick, all right? He says I shouldn't ⓣ give BJs anymore. But if I don't ⓣ go down on him, then he won't go down on me. So what do I do?

歐帝斯　妳好，我是妳的治療師。妳⋯怎麼了嗎？

奧利維亞　這太詭異了，我們不可以直接面對面嗎？

歐帝斯　不行，我們不應該見面。妳⋯怎麼了嗎？

奧利維亞　梅芙沒說嗎？我⋯我不想再講一次。

歐帝斯　有，妳⋯呃〔清喉嚨〕妳在口交時遭遇一些困難，造成妳出現胃氣上逆作噁，對吧？

奧利維亞　胃氣上逆作噁？

歐帝斯　呃，嘔吐。

奧利維亞　對，我吐在他老二上了，可以嗎？他叫我不要再幫他吹了，但不那麼做他就不會幫我口交，我該怎麼辦？

11.**weird** [wɪrd] *(a.)* 詭異的，奇怪的

12.**encounter** [ɪn`kaʊntə] *(v./n.)* 遭遇，遇到

13.**bout** [baʊt] *(n.)* 一陣，發作

14.**vomit** [`vɑmɪt] *(v./n.)* 嘔吐

### 補充單字

**fellatio** [fə`leʃɪo] *(n.)* 口交（女對男）

**emesis** [`ɛməsɪs] *(n.)*（醫）嘔吐

**puke** [pjuk]（口）嘔吐

## 𝓣ongue-tied 𝓝o 𝓜ore

**flick the bean 女性自慰**
flick 是「手指輕彈、按壓」，bean「豆子」比喻為女性陰道

**give sb. a BJ 口交**
BJ 是 blow job 口交的縮寫

**go down on sb. 幫某人口交**
往某人的下體去，就是口交的意思

©IMDb.com

▲《性愛自修室》海報

全文朗讀 ♫ 025　單字 ♫ 026

©Shutterstock.com

## Vocabulary

1. **comprehensive** [ˌkɑmprɪˋhɛnsɪv]
   *(a.)* 綜合的，廣泛的
2. **concept** [ˋkɑnsɛpt] *(n.)* 概念
3. **contract** [kənˋtrækt] *(v.)* 感染，染上
4. **transmit** [trænsˋmɪt] *(v.)* 傳播
5. **outlook** [ˋaʊtˏlʊk] *(n.)* 觀點，看法
6. **equip** [ɪˋkwɪp] *(v.)* 使⋯具備
7. **curriculum** [kəˋrɪkjələm] *(n.)*
   學校課程

### 補充單字

**HIV** 人類免疫缺乏病毒（愛滋病毒）
全名為 human immunodeficiency virus，感染 HIV 為 HIV positive 陽性，目前使用藥物能控制病毒。當病毒發作時才會稱為後天免疫缺乏症候群（acquired immunodeficiency syndrome, AIDS）。
**reproductive** [ˌriprəˋdʌktɪv] *(a.)* 生殖的
**abstinence** [ˋæbstənəns] *(n.)* 節制，絕戒

# Let's Talk about Sex Ed 性教育上課囉

In the U.S., sex education (often called sex ed) varies from state to state. In general, it can include such important topics as **HIV** prevention, **reproductive** health, and healthy sexual relationships. This is known as "[1]**comprehensive** sex education," and it informs students how to make smart decisions when it comes to sex. In some states, however, this [2]**concept** is less popular. People there prefer to stress **abstinence** as the only way to avoid getting pregnant or [3]**contracting** an STD (sexually [4]**transmitted** disease). This [5]**outlook** is often based on people's religious beliefs, but the reality is that teens across the U.S. are exploring their sexuality. Therefore, comprehensive sex ed is more likely to [6]**equip** students with knowledge that an abstinence-only [7]**curriculum** cannot.

美國性教育（通常簡稱為 sex ed）教學內容因各州而異。一般來說，可能包括愛滋預防、生殖衛教與健康性關係等重要主題，稱為「綜合性教育」，提供學生資訊，遇到性方面問題，能做出明智決定。然而，在某些州，這種概念不太盛行。當地居民更偏向強調禁慾，認為是避免懷孕或感染傳播性病的唯一方法。這種觀點通常基於人們的宗教信仰，但現實中全美各地的青少年都在探索自己的性慾與性傾向。因此，綜合性教育更有可能為學生提供禁慾課程無法提供的知識。

# Bullying 拒絕校園與網路霸凌

全文朗讀 ♫ 027　　單字 ♫ 028

©Shutterstock.com

[1]**Despite** school [2]**administrators** and teachers working to stamp out bullying, it remains a problem [3]**plaguing** schools the world over. Today, bullying can take many forms. In episode two of the Netflix series *Sex Education*, for example, the audience watches as Adam bullies Eric by stealing his lunch and directing [a]**homophobic** [b]**slurs** at him. Bullies will often [4]**project** their own insecurities on others, as is the case with Adam.

儘管學校的行政與教師人員努力要消除霸凌行為，但它仍然是個困擾著世界各地的校園問題。現今霸凌存在著多種形式。例如，在 Netflix《性愛自修室》第二集中，觀眾看到亞當欺負艾瑞克，偷他的午餐，並以恐同的辱罵針對他。霸凌者通常會將自己的不安全感投射到他人身上，就像劇中的亞當一樣。

Another problem is that bullying has [5]**migrated** online, with [c]**perpetrators** posting mean and hurtful messages on social media, as we can see in the new HBO *Gossip Girl* series. [d]**Cyberbullying**, as it is called, can continue long after school lets out and cause as much [e]**anguish** as physical bullying. So, whether [6]**virtual** or physical, bullying is an issue that requires our attention.

另一個問題是霸凌已經轉移到網路上，加害者在社群媒體上發布刻薄傷人的訊息，正如同我們在 HBO 新版《花邊教主》。所謂的網路霸凌會持續到放學鐘響後，造成的傷害與肢體霸凌一樣痛苦。因此，無論網路霸凌還是校園霸凌，都應是我們更需要關注的問題。

## Vocabulary

1. **despite** [dɪˋspaɪt] *(prep.)* 儘管
2. **administrator** [ədˋmɪnəˏstretə] *(n.)* 行政人員
3. **plague** [pleg] *(v.)* 困擾，糾纏
4. **project** [prəˋdʒɛkt] *(v.)* 投射
5. **migrate** [ˋmaɪgret] *(v.)* 轉移，遷徙
6. **virtual** [ˋvɝtʃuəl] *(a.)* 虛擬的

### 補充單字

**homophobic** [ˏhoməˋfobɪk] *(a.)* 仇視同性戀的，恐同的

**slur** [slɝ] *(n.)* 辱罵，誹謗

**perpetrator** [ˋpɝpəˏtretə] *(n.)* 加害者，肇事者

**cyberbullying** [ˋsaɪbəˏbulɪɪŋ] *(n.)* 網路霸凌

# Rosy-hued Revenge

校園霸凌 性平教育《玫瑰少年》最美的盛開是反擊

聽新聞
學英文
with 賓狗

專欄撰稿／金曲譯者 Podcast 賓狗單字

---

「原來當時他們眼裡的我，是這樣的存在啊。」

數年前就讀台大外文系時，有一天在文學課上，教授提到了精神分析學家茱莉亞 克莉絲蒂娃（Julia Kristeva）提出的賤斥（abjection）一詞。「賤斥這個詞最經典的例子，就是在看見糞便、經血或屍體時，讓你感到噁心與反感，絲毫不想沾染到這類污穢之物的感覺…」當教授在台上講解時，我的眼前浮現的是五、六個身穿國中制服的男同學。他們的雙腳不斷後退，和我之間維持兩公尺的安全距離，臉上卻始終帶著不懷好意的笑容，用食指指著我不斷重複說：「娘娘腔，嘻嘻嘻，噁心，娘娘腔…」。

事到如今，我仍不知道當年他們到底害怕的是什麼。是害怕陰柔與男性之間的違和感，害怕自己體內陰柔的部分，還是害怕自己成為被霸凌的對象，所以先合力揪出一個顯眼的目標？我只知道，當年的自己已經算是非常幸運，因為世界上曾經發生過無數起像電影《為巴比祈禱》（Prayers for Bobby）或葉永鋕那樣的悲劇。葉永鋕因為氣質陰柔而長期遭到同學霸凌，結

果有一天被人發現在廁所倒臥血泊中，送醫後不治身亡。蔡依林在《玫瑰少年》這首歌中，除了再次講述葉永鋕的故事之外，也提醒大家莫忘性別教育的重要性。

我在翻譯《玫瑰少年》的歌詞時，把「多少無知罪愆／事過不境遷」這兩句歌詞翻譯成 "The banality of evil remains as ever."。我把「無知罪愆」翻譯成學者漢娜 鄂蘭（Hannah Arendt）提出的 the banality of evil，也就是邪惡的平庸性。banality 是名詞，意思是平庸、陳腐的意思，evil 可以是名詞「邪惡」，或是形容詞「邪惡的」。邪惡之所以平庸，是因為邪惡並非存在於一個遠在天邊的惡人體內，也不只是存在於人神共憤的滔天大罪中，而是存在於日常生活平凡的一言一行之中。當父母成天把「男生不可以哭」、「粉紅色是女生的顏色」、「本來就是這樣」掛在嘴邊的時候，一些心智尚未成熟的孩子，自然會認為「陰柔的男生」和「陽剛的女生」是值得被霸凌的對象。在這個世界上，有的人因為愛自己的家人，所以懂得如何愛陌生人，有的人則需要能夠憎恨的妖魔，才懂得如何敬愛自己的神。從古至今，這兩種人

都存在，未來也是如此，因此這類「無知罪愆」才會「事過不境遷」，依舊在日常生活中時有所聞。動詞 remain 是維持的意思，副詞 ever 則是自古至今的意思，因此 remain as ever 可以表示某事物一直以來都沒有出現改變。

然而，這首歌的目的並不是要大家沈浸在負面的情緒裡一蹶不振。既然罪惡無法根除，歷史不能改變，我們就要讓未來活得更美好，才能讓他人的惡意淪為無意義的雜訊。「最好的報復是美麗／最美的盛開是反擊」這兩句歌詞，我翻譯成 "A life in rosy hues shall be the cold dish of revenge we serve the haters."。這裡其實穿插了兩句俚語，分別是 a life in rosy hues 以及 revenge is a dish

Sony Music © WikiCommons

葉永鋕
Yeh Yung-Chih

©擷取蔡依林 YouTube

best served cold。rosy 是玫瑰花 rose 的形容詞，意思是「玫瑰的」，而名詞 hue 是顏色、色澤的意思，因此 a life in rosy hues 字面上的意思是「玫瑰色的人生」，用來比喻「美好的人生」。還有一個俚語也和玫瑰與人生相關，那就是 "Life is not a bed of roses."。a bed of roses 是滿床的玫瑰花瓣，而所謂的生活不像滿床玫瑰，意思就是指「人生不會總是一帆風順」。

在第二句俚語 revenge is a dish best served cold 中，revenge 是名詞，意思是復仇，而 serve 是動詞，指的是上菜的動作。這句話常被翻譯為「君子報仇，十年不晚」，而原文字面上的意思是「復仇這道菜最好是放冷了再上」，用端上菜餚來比喻進行復仇，表示復仇最好等對方已經放下戒心，或是先讓對方過幾年不得安寧的日子再進行，才會更有滿足感。因此，我把這兩句歌詞在英文中結合成一句，用 a life in rosy hues 表示「最美的盛開」，the cold dish of revenge 表示「最好的報復」，藉此避免直譯並增加詩意。

雖然萬分遺憾，但葉永鋕的事件後來催生出了性別平等教育法，

開始讓更多台灣的年輕人在面對各種性別氣質的人時不再如同蜀犬吠日，而葉永鋕當時就讀的國中也決定正視歷史，在男廁外牆裝上不鏽鋼的玫瑰圖案，女廁外裝上大樹圖案，藉此翻轉性別刻板印象，從生活中落實性別平等教育，試圖避免相同的憾事再次發生。

雖然經歷了漫長的時間，但世界上已經有越來越多國家懂得注重各種性別氣質與取向的人，台灣也在各界的努力之下通過了婚姻平權法案。或許還需要更多時間，但我相信隨著教育人員的努力、知識的普及與人口的更迭，我們的社會可以漸漸不再為某些特質而大驚小怪，也不再有人需要因為性格的剛毅或柔軟而成為被指指點點的污穢存在。願我們永誌不忘過去的教訓。

葉永鋕事件 21 週年 高樹國中廁所標誌男玫瑰女大樹 （圖片來源／高樹國中）

# EMILY IN PARIS

©Wikicommons

#EmilyinParis #LilyCollins
#fauxpas #Netflix

©Shutterstock.com

全文朗讀 ♪ 029　　單字 ♪ 030

## *Emily In Paris*《艾蜜莉在巴黎》
### 美國妞的浪漫異國巴黎夢

**NETFLIX**

### Vocabulary

1. **cuisine** [kwɪ`zin] (n.)
   料理，佳餚

2. **romance** [ro`mæns] (n.)
   浪漫，羅曼史

©Shutterstock.com

▲ Lily Collins 飾演 Emily

From Gene Kelly in *An American in Paris* to Audrey Hepburn in *Funny Face*, Hollywood has presented Paris as the perfect place for Americans to find culture, [1] **cuisine** and [2] **romance**. But Emily Cooper, [ ] **protagonist** of the Netflix comedy-drama *Emily in Paris*—created by Darren Star, producer of *Sex and the City*—is here to work. Don't worry, though. She still finds time in her busy schedule for food, fashion and, yes, romance. This is Paris, after all!

從金凱利的《花都舞影》到奧黛麗赫本的《甜姐兒》，好萊塢將巴黎呈現成美國人追尋文化、美食與浪漫的聖地。但《慾望城市》製片達倫斯塔打造的 Netflix 劇情喜劇《艾蜜莉在巴黎》主角艾蜜莉庫柏是來巴黎工作的。不過別擔心，她仍會在繁忙行程中抽空享受美食、時尚，當然還有浪漫，畢竟這是巴黎嘛！

Emily, played by Lily Collins, daughter of singer Phil Collins, is a 20-something [3] **marketing** [4] **assistant** at the Gilbert Group, a Chicago [ ] **pharmaceutical** marketing firm. The company has just [5] **acquired** Savior, a French [6] **luxury** marketing firm, and Emily is preparing to ❶ fill the shoes of her boss, Madeline, who is moving to Paris to help with the [7]**transition**. But when Madeline finds out she's pregnant, Emily gets the chance of a lifetime. When the company asks her to go to Paris instead, she ❶ jumps at the opportunity. Emily's boyfriend, Doug, doesn't like the idea of a long distance relationship, but she thinks they can make it work.

艾蜜莉由歌手菲爾柯林斯的女兒莉莉柯林斯飾演,是芝加哥製藥行銷公司吉爾伯集團的一名 20 多歲行銷助理。該公司剛收購法國奢侈品行銷公司薩維瓦。正當主管麥德琳即將調到巴黎幫忙,艾蜜莉準備接替她的職務時,麥德琳發現自己懷孕,而這畢生的機會轉向艾蜜莉。公司要求她代替去巴黎,她馬上欣然接受這個機會。艾蜜莉的男朋友道格不喜歡遠距戀愛,但她認為他們能克服辦到。

On arrival, Emily begins living the "American in Paris" dream. The handsome [8]**rental** [9]**agency** man ˚**flirts** with her as he shows her around her **chambre de bonne** in the 5th **arrondissement**. It may have been a servant's room once, but it has a beautiful view of the **Place de L'Estrapade**. "Oh, my God," she says, "I feel like Nicole Kidman in *Moulin Rouge*!" But when she starts her job, the dream ends and the culture [10]**clash** begins. Emily's first, and biggest, ˚**faux pas** is not speaking French. When she calls a meeting to talk about social media strategies, one woman flees in horror. [11]**Unfortunately**, Patricia, who speaks no English, is ❶ in charge of social media at the [12]**firm**.

抵達後,艾蜜莉開始實現「美國人在巴黎」的美夢。帥氣的租仲先生帶她參觀位於第五區的傭人房並與她調情。雖然曾經是一間傭人的房間,卻可以欣賞到

3. **marketing** [ˈmɑrkɪtɪŋ] (n.)
   市場行銷

4. **assistant** [əˈsɪstənt] (n.) 助理

5. **acquire** [əˈkwaɪr] (v.)
   收購,獲得

6. **luxury** [ˈlʌkʃərɪ] (n./a.)
   奢侈(品);奢華的

7. **transition** [trænˈzɪʃən] (n.)
   過渡期

8. **rental** [ˈrɛntəl] (n.) 租賃

9. **agency** [ˈedʒənsi] (n.)
   仲介公司

10. **clash** [klæʃ] (n./v.) 衝擊

11. **unfortunately** [ʌnˈfɔrtʃənɪtli]
    (adv.) 不幸地

12. **firm** [fɜm] (n.) 公司

---

### ❰ *Tongue-tied No More* ❱

**fill sb.'s shoes** 代替某人的職位
It will be hard for the newly elected German chancellor to fill Angela Merkel's shoes.
對新當選的德國總理來說,接任梅克爾的職位是件難事。

**jump at the opportunity** 立刻接受機會
Estella jumped at the opportunity to work as a fashion designer.
艾絲黛拉立刻欣然接受時尚設計師的工作機會。

**in charge of sth.** 負責
The new editor is in charge of coordinating the book project.
新任編輯負責統籌新書的製作計畫。

Noppasin Wongchum©Shutterstock.com

▲ 巴黎市景

13. **annoyed** [əˋnɔɪd] (a.)
被惹怒的

14. **colleague** [ˋkɑlig] (n.) 同事

15. **chef** [ʃɛf] (n.) 主廚

16. **perspective** [pɚˋspɛktɪv] (n.)
視角，觀點

17. **assign** [əˋsaɪn] (v.) 指派

補充單字

**protagonist** [proˋtægənɪst] (n.)
主角

**pharmaceutical** [ˌfɑrməˋsutɪkəl]
(n.) 製藥，藥物

**flirt** [flɝt] (v.) 調情，搭訕

**faux pas** [fo pɑ]【法語】失禮

**hick** [hɪk] (n.) 鄉巴佬

**Parisian** [pəˋrɪʒɪən] (n.) 巴黎人

©截圖 YouTube Magazine Technikart

▲ Lucas Bravo 飾演 Gabriel

吊刑廣場的美麗景色。「天哪」她說「我覺得自己就像《紅磨坊》裡的妮可基嫚！」但當她開始工作時，美夢就幻滅了，文化衝擊迎面而來。艾蜜莉首次也是最大的失禮是不會說法語。當她召集會議討論社群媒體策略時，一名女性驚恐地逃跑。不幸的是，這位不會說英語的柏翠珊卻是公司的社媒行銷主管。

[13] **Annoyed** at ⒢ having an American tell them how to do their jobs, Emily's new [14] **colleagues** do their best to make her feel unwelcome. They give her a nickname: *le plouc* (the ˈ**hick**), and leave her out of office lunches. "With me as her boss, we'll see how long she lasts," says marketing manager Sylvie. But not all ˈ**Parisians** ⓣ give Emily the cold shoulder. She soon makes friends with Gabriel, the hot [15] **chef** who lives below her, and also Mindy, a nanny from Shanghai she meets while eating lunch alone at a park.

艾蜜莉的新同事對一個美國人教他們如何工作感到惱火，他們竭盡所能讓她感到不受歡迎。他們為她取個綽號「鄉巴佬」，不跟她一起吃午餐。「有我當她的老闆，我們看她能稱多久」行銷經理希維爾說。但並非所有巴黎人都對艾蜜莉冷漠，她很快就認識住在樓下的性感主廚加百列，以及她在公園獨自吃午餐時，遇到來自上海的保母敏迪。

And Emily's American [16] **perspective** turns out to be valuable after all. After gaining thousands of new followers by posting photos of her life in Paris, she uses Instagram to promote Vaga-Jeune, the product she's been [17] **assigned**. When Brigitte Macron shares her post saying "The vagina is not male!" (the word is **masculine** in French) on Twitter, it goes viral, winning high praise from the client. Finally, Emily breaks up with Doug, opening up the possibility of romance in Paris. And that's just the first few episodes!

不過，艾蜜莉的美國視角卻很有價值。她在巴黎的生活照獲得了數千新粉絲追蹤，她利用 Instagram 宣傳她負責的產品 Vaga-Jeune。當法國第一夫人碧姬馬克宏在推特回覆並分享她的貼文：「陰道不是男性！」（這個字在法文是陽性字），造成網路瘋狂轉貼，結果艾蜜莉贏得客戶的高度讚揚。最後，艾蜜莉與道格分手，開啟了巴黎異國羅曼史尋覓之旅。這只是前幾集唷！

*Tongue-tied No More*

**give sb. the cold shoulder 對某人冷漠**
His wife has been giving him the cold shoulder ever since he forgot her birthday.
自從他忘記老婆生日後，老婆就對他非常冷漠。

### 使役動詞

"...have an American tell them how to do their jobs..." 的 have 為使役動詞，意思是「叫某人做某事」，後面的動詞不加 to，以下比較：

● **使役動詞 have/make + O + 原形動詞**

ex: My mom had/made me wash the dishes. 媽媽叫我去洗碗。

● **一般動詞 get/tell/want + O + to V**

ex: My mom got/told/wanted me to wash the dishes. 媽媽叫我去洗碗。

# E Z pedia

### chambre de bonne 法國傭人房

法國貴族時代的傭人房位於房屋最頂層，須爬上小樓梯才能到達。面積狹窄約只有 3 坪，共用衛浴且設備簡單，住起來擁擠。現在租傭人房的房客，通常是想省房租的學生或是單身族，在巴黎租金落在 500 歐元（約 1 萬 7 千台幣）。劇中艾蜜莉住的房間寬敞，單人獨立衛浴，並非真實的傭人房。

▲ 巴黎市區的傭人房。

### arrondissement 巴黎各行政分區

全巴黎市以數字編號，依順時針方向遞增，劃分為 20 個區。

### Place de L'Estrapade 吊刑廣場

法國巴黎第五區的一個三角形廣場。廣場因古代對逃兵處以吊刑得名，直到 18 世紀末才廢除。

### masculine（文法）陽性

在許多語言中，名詞會有陰（feminine）、陽（masculine）之分，如拉丁語系的法語、西班牙語…等。除了陰陽性，有些語言更有中性（neuter），如日耳曼語系的德語、斯拉夫語系

▲ Place de L'Estrapade 吊刑廣場

的俄語…等。古英文原有陰陽中性，11 世紀北歐諾曼人（Normans）攻下英格蘭後，這套系統很快瓦解。不同陰陽中性名詞，需要搭配對應的陰陽中性形容詞、冠詞，在動詞後面的受詞也會因為性別不同，做不同的變化。同樣的字在不同語言，陰陽中性不一定相同，劇中艾蜜莉不懂法語 le vagin 陰道為何是陽性，但在西班牙語 la vagina 即是陰性，主要以字尾作為分類依據。

〔艾蜜莉與麥德琳討論麥德琳即將搬到巴黎〕

Emily　This is going to be amazing for you.

Madeline　I have been dreaming of moving to Paris forever. I mean, French men, they love older women, you know? Look at their president. He's young. He's hot. He married his schoolteacher.

Emily　[laughs] Ooh, I just e-mailed you my thoughts on the ¹⁾**presentation** for the new **IBS** drug. It's a social ²⁾**initiative** to add ³⁾**meditation** to your ⁴⁾**medication**. If you like it, you can ⁵⁾**pitch** it later. Uh, you know, for your ❶ last hurrah.

Madeline　I want you to pitch it.

Emily　Seriously?

Madeline　Seriously. The client has to start getting comfortable with you.

Emily　I don't want to ❶ step on your toes.

Madeline　You're not. You're ❶ stepping into my shoes.

---

## Vocabulary

1. **presentation** [ˌprɛzənˈteʃən] (n.)
   呈現，行銷包裝
2. **initiative** [ɪˈnɪʃətɪv] (n.) 提倡行動
3. **meditation** [ˌmɛdəˈteʃən] (n.)
   沈思冥想
4. **medication** [ˌmɛdəˈkeʃən] (n.)
   藥物治療
5. **pitch** [pɪtʃ] (v./n.) 推銷宣傳
6. **facility** [fəˈsɪləti] (n.) 設備
7. **specialty** [ˈspɛʃəlti] (n.)
   招牌菜，專長
8. **disgusting** [dɪsˈɡʌstɪŋ] (a.) 令人作噁的
9. **cement** [sɪˈmɛnt] (n.) 水泥

### 補充單字

**IBS** 腸躁症 irritable bowel syndrome
**monsieur** [məˈsjɜ] (n.)【法語】先生
**geriatric** [ˌdʒɛriˈætrɪk] (a.) 老人的
**deep-dish** [ˈdepˌdɪʃ] (a.) 厚片的，深盤的
**quiche** [kiʃ] (n.) 法式鹹派

艾蜜莉　這對妳實在是太讚了！

麥德琳　我一直夢想要搬到巴黎生活，法國的男人都愛老女人，妳知道嗎？看他們的總統，帥氣小鮮肉，結果娶了自己學校老師。

艾蜜莉　〔笑〕我把自己有關新腸躁症藥簡報點子發給妳了，是一個社會倡議在藥物治療中加入沉思冥想，喜歡的話，妳可以去推銷，讓你最後一次接受喝采。

麥德琳　我希望妳去推銷。

艾蜜莉　認真？

麥德琳　認真，客戶要開始習慣跟妳合作了。

艾蜜莉　我不想越職冒犯妳。

麥德琳　才不會，妳是要代替我。

▲ 法國總統馬克宏與大 25 歲高中老師結婚

### Tongue-tied No More

**step on sb.'s toes** 冒犯、逾越某人的職責
I'd like to help John with the project, but I'm afraid of stepping on his toes.
我想幫約翰籌備計畫，但我怕逾越職責冒犯到他。

## 噁心的鹹派

〔第一天上班，艾蜜莉與希維爾、薩維瓦創辦人保羅寶樂沙說話〕

Emily It is so nice to meet you, **Monsieur** Brossard.

Paul It's a pleasure. Welcome to Paris. So, you've come to teach the French some American tricks?

Emily I'm sure we have a lot to learn from each other.

Paul But your experience is not with fashion and luxury brands.

Emily True. Most of my experience has been in promoting pharmaceuticals and **geriatric** care **facilities**.

Paul In Chicago.

Emily Yes. I mean, *oui*.

Paul I was in Chicago once, and I ate the **deep-dish** pizza.

Emily Ah. That is our **specialty**. We 🔊 take a lot of pride.

Paul It was, uh, *dégueulasse*. How you say?

Sylvie **Disgusting**.

Paul Like a **quiche** made of **cement**.

©Shutterstock.com

---

艾蜜莉 真是幸會了，寶樂沙先生。

保羅 榮幸之至，歡迎來到巴黎。妳過來教我們法國人你們美國的技倆嗎？

艾蜜莉 我們肯定有很多東西能互相學習。

保羅 不過妳在時尚和奢華品牌毫無經驗。

艾蜜莉 是的，我大部分經驗在於推銷藥品以及療養院。

保羅 在芝加哥嘛。

艾蜜莉 對，應該說 oui。

保羅 我曾去過芝加哥，吃過那款芝加哥式厚底披薩。

艾蜜莉 那是我們的招牌菜，我們引以為傲的。

保羅 那實在 dégueulasse，英文怎麼說？

希維爾 噁心。

保羅 像是用水泥做的法式鹹派。

### Tongue-tied No More

**step into sb.'s shoes**
代替某人的職責
Japanese prime minister Yoshihide Suga stepped into Shinzo Abe's shoes.
日本首相菅義偉接替安倍晉三的職位。

**last hurrah**（生涯）最後一次的表現
The quarterback said that this season will be his last hurrah as a player.
四分衛表示這季將是他運動生涯中最後一次參賽。

**take pride in sth./sb.** 引以為傲
Mary takes pride in her children's success. 瑪麗以她小孩的成就為傲。

## 法式奢華

〔艾蜜莉與希維爾討論新款香水達勞倫的發表〕

**Emily** Look, I know that you all aren't that happy to have me here and my French could use some work.

**Sylvie** A little bit.

**Emily** OK, it's basically *merde*, but I have some ideas about marketing De L'Heure that I'd like to share with you.

**Sylvie** I don't think that's your concern.

**Emily** I studied the marketing plan before I got to Paris. It's weak. You're *piggybacking* off the ad [10]*campaign*. Very little *social engagement*. I know you're about to launch, and you're ❶ <u>keeping me out of the loop</u>.

**Sylvie** Listen, I...don't agree with your [11]*approach*. You want everything to be everywhere, [12]*accessible* to everyone. You want to open doors. I want to close doors. We work with very [13]*exclusive* brands. And they require mystery, and...you have no mystery.

©Shutterstock.com

---

### Vocabulary

10. **campaign** [kæm`pen] 宣傳活動
11. **approach** [ə`protʃ] (n.) 方法，途徑
12. **accessible** [æk`sɛsəbəl] (a.) 易親近的；可獲得的
13. **exclusive** [ɪk`sklusɪv] (a.) 高檔的，獨家的
14. **vending machine** 自動販賣機
15. **preserves** [prɪ`zɜvz] (n.) 果醬，蜜餞

#### 補充單字

**merde** [merd] (n.)【法語】大便，爛東西
**piggyback** [`pɪgɪ.bæk] (v.) 豬馱式行銷，在其他大公司通路刊登廣告，沾光吸引買氣。
**social engagement** 社群參與
**croissant** [krwɑ`sɑn] (n.) 可頌
**condom** [`kɑndəm] (n.) 保險套
**bareback** [`bɛr.bæk] (v./adv.) 無戴保險套
**faux amis**【法語】假朋友

| | |
|---|---|
| 艾蜜莉 | 我知道大家都不太喜歡我，我的法文也有待改善。 |
| 希維爾 | 有一點。 |
| 艾蜜莉 | 好吧，我法文就是爛。但我有些達勞倫香水的行銷想法，想跟妳分享。 |
| 希維爾 | 這事不用妳費心吧。 |
| 艾蜜莉 | 我來巴黎之前有研究過你們的行銷方案，太弱了。 |
| 希維爾 | 怎麼說？ |
| 艾蜜莉 | 你們只是廣告活動宣傳，社交互動少得可憐。我知道你們馬上要發佈，而妳刻意不讓我參與。 |
| 希維爾 | 我告訴妳……我不喜歡妳的方式，妳想大肆宣傳讓品牌觸及所有人，妳想敞開大門，而我想緊緊關閉。我們與非常奢華的品牌合作，他們想要神秘感，而妳……並無神秘感可言。 |

# 無套早餐

〔艾蜜莉與敏迪在露天咖啡店點咖啡〕

Emily    Um, *j'aime le café, les fruits et un croissant avec le préservatif.*

Waiter    OK, there's a [14] **vending machine** for that in the men's room.

Emily    What did I just say?

Mindy    *Préservatif* doesn't mean [15] **preserves**. You just ordered a **croissant** ⓣ with a side of **condoms**.

Emily    *[to waiter]* Oh, my God! No, I don't want that!

Mindy    She's gonna **bareback** her breakfast!

Emily    See, I can't get anything right.

Mindy    It's a common mistake. They're called **faux amis.** So, *un crayon* isn't "crayon." It's "pencil." *Un médecin* isn't "medicine." It's "doctor."

Emily    *Faux amis*, is that, like, fake friends?

Mindy    Yep. Like you and Camille. You're gonna be friends with her, but just so you can stay close to her hot, hot boyfriend.

*Kathy Hutchins@Shutterstock.com*

▲ Ashley Park 飾演 Mindy

---

艾蜜莉    【法語】我想要咖啡、水果、可頌加保險套。

服務生    好，妳要的東西，男廁的販賣機有賣。

艾蜜莉    我說了甚麼？

敏迪    Préservatifs 不是果醬。妳剛才點的是可頌配安全套。

艾蜜莉    〔對服務生〕天啊！我不要啊！

敏迪    她的早餐要無套！

艾蜜莉    妳看，我連說句話都說不好。

敏迪    這些錯誤很常有，叫 faux amis。所以 un crayon 不是一支蠟筆，而是一支鉛筆。Un médecin 不是一粒藥，而是一位醫生。

艾蜜莉    faux amis 是假朋友嗎？

敏迪    對，像妳和卡蜜兒。妳會和她當朋友，但只是為了接近她超性感的男友。

## Tongue-tied No More

**keep sb. out of the loop 不讓某人了解參與**

loop 是「圓圈」，in the loop 在圈子內，就是了解參與動態，out of the loop 就是不了解狀況，無法參與的意思

I can't do my job properly if you keep me out of the loop.
如果你都不讓我參與，我沒辦法好好工作。

**with a side of sth. 搭某種配菜**

在盤子旁邊就是配菜的意思。

I ordered a burger with a side of fries. 我點了漢堡搭薯條配餐。

# False Friends!

## 假朋友

### 果醬、保險套傻傻分不清楚

《艾蜜莉在巴黎》第一季第四集中，艾蜜莉與閨蜜敏迪正優雅地坐在巴黎露天咖啡，享受法式慢活悠閒時光。然而點餐時，艾蜜莉怎麼語出驚人，莫名其妙用法語點了保險套？原來英文的果醬 preserve，直接翻成法文 préservatif 是保險套。其實這種錯誤很常見，很多學外語的人多多少少都有犯過這種錯（編輯自己的親身經驗！），直接把母語或熟悉的語言翻成另一種外語，雖然在外語中有相同的字，意思卻不同。拿我們熟悉的中文來說，「先生」在中文是男子；日文是老師、「大丈夫」在中文是男子漢；日文是不要緊、沒關係。

### 常見的中日假朋友

| 中日假朋友 | 中文意思 | 日文意思 |
| --- | --- | --- |
| 大丈夫 | 男子漢 | 沒關係、不要緊 |
| 先生 | 男子稱呼 | 老師 |
| 勉強 | 勉強 | 讀書 |
| 約束 | 束縛 | 承諾 |
| 新聞 | 新聞 | 報紙 |

那麼該如何避免這種超級尷尬的錯？最簡單的方式，就是以你學習的語言本身來思考，而非不斷在腦海中把自己的母語直接翻過來。大部分的台灣學生在學習其他歐洲第二外語時，很常會受熟悉的英文干擾。以下例子雖然看似好笑，卻是現實生活中很多學生會犯的常見錯誤，請一定要避免！

## 尷尬的英法假朋友

| 你其實想說 | English 🇬🇧 | French 🇫🇷 |
|---|---|---|
| 果醬 | perserves | ✕ préservatif 保險套<br>○ confiture |
| 介紹 | introduce | ✕ introduire 插入<br>○ présenter |
| 我很興奮 | I'm excited. | ✕ Je suis excité. 我很「性」奮。<br>○ Je suis enthousiaste. |
| 一點點 | a little bit | ✕ une petite bite 一個男性小生殖器<br>○ un petit peu |
| 我是個實習生 | I'm a trainee. | ✕ Je suis une traînée. 我是個婊子。<br>○ Je suis stagiaire. |

## 尷尬的英西假朋友

| 你其實想說 | English 🇬🇧 | Spanish 🇪🇸 |
|---|---|---|
| 防腐劑 | preservative | ✕ preservativo 保險套<br>○ coservante |
| 我覺得尷尬 | I'm embarrassed. | ✕ Estoy embarazada. 我懷孕了。<br>○ Me da vergüenza. |
| 我吃一個派 | I eat a pie. | ✕ Yo como un pie. 我吃一隻腳<br>○ Yo como un pastel. |
| 我很興奮 | I'm excited | ✕ Estoy excitado. 我很「性」奮。<br>○ Estoy emoncionado/enthusiamado. |
| 她很明智 | She is sensible. | ✕ Ella es sensible. 她很敏感。=（英文 sensitive）<br>○ Ella es sensata. |

# 有趣多元的外來語－「Loanwords」

《艾蜜莉在巴黎》影集中，我們可以聽到艾蜜莉在英文對話中，參雜使用許多法語字，如 merde（法文的shit），仔細聽這些字，其實在英文中也很常使用唷，他們就是所謂的「外來字」（loanword）。

回溯語源歷史，英文雖然屬於日耳曼語系（Germanic languages），但卻接受了許多拉丁字、法語字與古希臘字，經過時間演變而成現代的英文字。根據統計，60% 以上的英文字彙源自拉丁與古希臘字根。有趣的是，英文中有一句慣用語"all Greek to me"，表示完全聽不懂的語言，但其實英文本身就有許多古希臘字。雖然我們介紹「假朋友」，提醒大家學習語言時不要受熟悉語言干擾，但若能學好英文，在學其他歐語時，通常能夠更快在腦海中產生連結。同樣地，學了其他歐語再回來看英文，你可能覺得背英文單字怎麼變簡單了。

時間來到現代，隨著科技與交通的進步，全球化下移民、旅遊，各國文化交流頻繁，各種語言間彼此的影響也越來越深，英文雖然是強勢的國際語言，但也接受了許多外來字，讓英文字彙量更加豐富有趣。尤其外來語常給人一種異國的想像，若能在英文中適時地使用，能讓你的表達更佳令人印象深刻。

## 浪漫高雅的法語

單字 ♫ 033

| 法語外來語 | 意思 | 例句 |
|---|---|---|
| chic | 時尚的，高雅的 | She looks chic. 她看起來很時尚高雅。 |
| faux pas | 犯了失禮的禁忌 | Talking on cellphones during the performance is a huge faux pas. 在演出時講電話是一大失禮的禁忌。 |
| avant-garde | 前衛的 | an avant-garde artist 一位前衛的藝術家 |
| à la mode | 很潮、正流行 | Her dress is à la mode. 她的洋裝很流行。 |
| déjà vu | 似曾相似的感覺 | a feeling of déjà vu 一種似曾相似的感覺 |
| hors d'oeuvre | 開胃前菜 | The hors d'oeuvre is seasonal vegetables. 開胃菜是季節時蔬 |
| rendezvous | 浪漫的約會 | Edward turned up late for their rendezvous. 愛德華約會遲到。 |
| Je ne sais quoi. | 我不知道 | 用法 = I don't know.（有種無法形容，說不出來的特殊感覺） |

## 熱情奔放的西班牙語

西班牙語對美國有深度地影響，從歷史角度看來，美國西部有遼闊的土地原屬西班牙殖民地，在 1898 年美西戰爭後才割讓給美國，因此沿用許多西班牙語地名，如：加州 California、洛杉磯 Los Ángeles。

現今的美國擁有龐大的拉丁裔移民（Latinos），西班牙語影響英文之深，許多美國常見的墨西哥料理，直接使用西班牙文名稱，如：burrito 墨西哥捲餅、nacho 玉米脆片、salsa 莎莎醬、jalapeño 墨西哥辣椒等。此外，居住美國的拉丁裔年輕人，更喜歡使用英西交雜的 Spanglish（Spanish + English）。

| 西語外來語 | 意思 | 例句 |
|---|---|---|
| macho | 很 man，男子氣概 | Dwayne Johnson is very macho. 巨石強森很 man。 |
| siesta | 午覺 | take a siesta 睡午覺 |
| amigo/amiga | 朋友（男）/（女） | José is my amigo. 荷西是我的好朋友。 |
| Adiós. | 再見 | I'm off, adiós! 我要走了，掰！ |

哥倫比亞舉重選手在奧運上大喊的「馬英九」，其實就是西班牙文的「macho 男子氣概」，為自己精神喊話。／擷取 YouTube

馬英九！

## 你想不到的中文外來語

十九世紀許多中國移民前往美國從事鐵路建設、採礦挖金的工作，因此也帶入中華文化與語言。以下有些常見的英文字，你可能沒發現其實就是來自中文。

| 中文外來語 | 意思 | 例句 |
|---|---|---|
| ketchup | 番茄醬，來自福建話的「茄汁」。 | French fries dipped in ketchup 沾番茄醬的薯條 |
| chop-chop | 快一點，來自廣東話。 | Chop-chop! Hurry up. 快快，快一點。 |
| yen | 想要，來自中文的「願」。 | I've always had a yen to visit Dubai. 我一直很想去杜拜。 |
| kowtow | 卑躬屈膝，來自廣東話的「磕頭」。 | I have to kowtow to my boss. 我必須對老闆卑躬屈膝。 |

## 穩重內斂的日語外來語

日語在英文中除了常見的 sushi 壽司、anime 動漫、manga 漫畫，以下的字還給人一種高深內斂的感覺。

| 日文外來語 | 意思 | 例句 |
|---|---|---|
| zen | 平靜的、安定的。來自漢字「禪」 | Yoga helps us become more zen. 瑜伽幫助我們變得更安定。 |
| umami | 鮮味。來自日文「うま味」 | The tomato adds a rich umami taste to the soup. 番茄為湯增添豐富鮮味。 |
| origami | 摺紙藝術 | an expert in origami 摺紙達人 |
| bonsai | 盆栽造景 | a bonsai garden 日式造景庭園 |

# 浪漫巴黎魔幻寫實樣貌
## 外語新視界　知識是偷不走的寶物

專欄撰稿／泰山高中法語教師　曹芸瑄 Laëtitia

相信不少人看過 *Emily in Paris* 後，對劇中的場景充滿幻想。但我想一定會有人有疑問，現實中的巴黎真的如戲劇呈現的浪漫優雅嗎？根據我曾經在法國唸書以及工作的經驗，我認為劇情與現實虛實並存。接下來幾點文化差異都是令我頗有感觸的地方。

首先，法國同事跟 Emily 說我們 10 點才上班？不過根據我當時在法國的上班情況是 9 點上班，中午有一個半小時的午餐時間，晚上 5 點準時下班。注意哦，是準時！就算你手上還有一些東西要忙，他們也會叫你放下手邊工作！另外一天有兩次 break time，分別是早上 10 點跟下午 3 點。大家在這個時候就會享用點心，配上一杯咖啡，有的人還會在這個時候小睡片刻或抽根煙。對於在台灣生活的我們，真的是很大的文化衝擊。試想在台灣的工作環境，能準時下班就不錯了，遑論兩次 break time？

此外，同事對於這位美國小妞還帶有偏見，吃飯時間搞小圈圈，工作也不會給她好臉色。再加上前陣子在法國發生的恐怖攻擊（Samuel Paty 事件），你可能會產生一種「法國人是否歧視其他民族」的疑問？關於這一點，我認為「歧視」不管在任何國家都是一直存在的。難道你相信每位台灣人都友善地對待東南亞國家或是來自對岸的人民嗎？法國是一個種族多元的國家，有來自歐洲各國、非洲（特別是說法語的國家）、中東北非移民，以及難民問題。我認為我們不能以膚色或人種斷定一個人。我在法國的那段時間就曾被白人偷過手機，但也有被非裔熱情款待的經驗。我覺得要避免歧視，首先要懂得尊重多元文化，至少我敢保證，學一點法文一定有幫助。

最後，我們看到法國的露天咖啡，伴隨著咖啡香氣坐在室外曬太陽、看風景或跟朋友閒聊，好不愜意。為何台灣人沒這種閒情逸致？巴黎屬於溫帶海洋性氣候，夏季乾爽。台灣氣候濕熱，若在外面坐個幾分鐘一定滿頭大汗。當然是坐在室內吹冷氣，偶爾看看窗外的風景更舒服些吧！

▲ 在法國讀書時，Laëtitia（中）與同學出遊。

▲ Laëtitia 在課堂上導讀法語童書，提升學生的學習動機。

## 學習法語的歷程　打開全新視野

我在 13 歲時參加學校的法語課程，啟發了對法語的興趣。高中升學時，我想挑戰英文之外的其他外語。在仔細思考後，選擇歐語系（法語組），正式開啟了我的法語學習之路。

在我學習法語過程中基本上是滿快樂的。當你能夠享受學習的樂趣，你就會更有學習的成就感。在課餘時間，我也積極參與法語相關活動，像是聽寫比賽、戲劇表演、語言交換、法國在台協會舉辦的文化交流等。

不過，我在法語學習的路上並非一帆風順，也有遇到過挫折的時候。我在大學時期考了兩次 B2 法語檢定才通過。兩次考試的費用對當時還是學生的我，算是滿大的一筆開銷。但因為挫折讓自己下定決心，夜以繼日地讀書，拿到證書的那一刻，一切的努力都值得了。

然而再多的書本學習，都比不上實際體驗當地文化來得深刻。在法國交換與工作的經驗帶給我不同的觀點和視野，像是亞洲人可能受儒家思想「沉默是金」、「以和為貴」等教育影響，總在課堂上「默默地」耕耘。但在法國，不論課堂或工作，一定要踴躍發表己見，為自己爭取該有的權益，不然別人才沒有時間理你呢（我想這一點可以從他們引以為傲的罷工文化看出一點端倪吧）！

## 踏入法語教學　自主學習動機

在法語圈跑跳了幾年，某次機緣下很榮幸能到高中教授法語。這段意想不到的插曲，埋下了我的教學種子。教學過程中，遇到形形色色的學生，不見得每位學生都有學習外語的熱忱，隨著上課次數增加，學生間也產生進度落差。作為老師的心情一定會挫折，這時候發揮小宇宙，想辦法抓住學生的眼球，像是在課堂上品嘗法國點心、玩遊戲、看法語影片、導讀繪本等。也讓他們發揮團隊合作精神做一份法語區國家的相關報告，以自主學習方式認識文化。希望報告的成果能作為學生學習的見證。我鼓勵學生把這份報告放在他們的學習歷程檔案，作為未來升學甄試的作品。所幸，最後學生的表現都大於我的期待。我想這就是教學路上最大的成就感吧！

## 學習外語的初衷目標

最後，給想要學習外語以及正在閱讀這篇文章的你。學習外語是一條終身漫長道路，日積月累的練習與訓練。途中一定會遇到困難或想要放棄的時候，請想一想當初的你，為了什麼原因而學習這門外語？我想一定是為了某個目標或夢想吧。所以，請喚醒你想學這門外語的動機與熱忱，朝著這個目標努力！知識是誰也偷不走的寶物，好好投資自己吧！

#OLD #obsessivelove #stalker

Kathy Hutchins©Shutterstock.com

▲ John Stamos（左）飾演 Dr. Nicky、Elizabeth Lail（中）飾演 Beck、Penn Badgley（右）飾演 Joe

全文朗讀 ♫ 034　　單字 ♫ 035

# *You*《安眠書店》
## 跟蹤謀殺 恐怖情人令人窒息的愛

**NETFLIX**

## Vocabulary

1. **aspiring** [əˈspaɪrɪŋ] *(a.)*
   渴望成為的，有抱負的

2. **comedy** [ˈkɑmədi] *(n.)* 喜劇

3. **thriller** [ˈθrɪlə] *(n.)*
   驚悚片，驚悚小說

4. **serial killer** 連續殺人狂

5. **release** [rɪˈlis] *(v./n.)*
   發表，發行

Based on the novel of the same name by Caroline Kepnes, *You* tells the story of Joe Goldberg, a New York bookstore manager who falls in love with an NYU graduate student and ¹⁾**aspiring** writer named Guinevere Beck. Sounds like a romantic ²⁾**comedy**, right? But it's not. It's a psychological ³⁾**thriller**, and Joe is a ⁴⁾**serial killer**! When the show ˙**premiered** on the Lifetime cable channel in 2018, it attracted a limited audience, despite strong reviews. But things changed after Netflix acquired the rights and launched *You* on its streaming platform later that year. Within a month, 43 million viewers had watched the entire season. The second season, based on *Hidden Bodies*, Kepnes' ˙**sequel** to *You*, was ⁵⁾**released** as a Netflix Original in 2019.

《安眠書店》根據卡羅琳凱普尼斯的同名小說改編，故事描述紐約一家書店經理喬伊戈德伯格愛上一心想成為作家的紐約大學研究生格尼薇爾貝可。聽起來像是一部浪漫喜劇，對吧？ 但事實並非如此，這是一部心理驚悚片，喬伊可是一個連環殺手！ 2018 年該節目在 Lifetime 有線頻道首播時，儘管評價很高，吸引的觀眾卻有限。在 Netflix 獲得版權並同年稍後在串流平台推出後， 《安眠書店》煥然一新。短短一個月內，四千三百萬觀眾看完整季影集。第二季則改編自凱普尼斯的續作《隱藏之身》，2019 年 Netflix 原創發行。

©Wikipedia

▲ 《安眠書店》同名小說

As soon as Joe—played by Penn Badgley, who **T** <u>rose to fame</u> as Dan Humphrey on *Gossip Girl*—sees Beck enter his bookstore, he becomes **infatuated** with her. She's [6]**blond**, pretty, and has great taste in books. Beck pays for the book he [7]**recommends** with her credit card, which Joe takes to mean that she wants him to know her full name. "You smiled, laughed at my jokes, told me your name, asked for mine," he thinks to himself. Could she be "the one"? Returning to his apartment, Joe runs into Paco, a young boy who lives across the hall. His mother and [8]**abusive** boyfriend are arguing, so Paco is sitting outside reading a book Joe lent him. Knowing Paco hasn't eaten, Joe gives him his meatball [9]**sub**. Maybe Joe is a nice guy after all?

6. **blond** [blɑnd] *(a.)* 金髮的

7. **recommend** [͵rɛkəˋmɛnd] *(v.)* 推薦

8. **abusive** [əˋbjusɪv] *(a.)* 虐待的，濫用的

9. **sub** [sʌb] *(n.)* 潛艇堡三明治 = submarine sandwich

10. **random** [ˋrændəm] *(a.)* 隨機的

11. **stalk** [stɔk] *(v.)* 跟蹤

12. **yoga** [ˋjogə] *(n.)* 瑜珈

13. **professor** [prəˋfɛsɚ] *(n.)* 大學教授

當喬伊（飾演《花邊教主》丹漢弗瑞而聲名大噪的潘巴奇利 飾）一看到貝克走進他的書店，他就對她著迷了。她金髮碧眼、漂亮，對書還很有品味。貝克用信用卡支付了他推薦的書，喬伊認為這意味著她想讓他知道她的全名。他心裡想：「你帶著微笑，懂我的幽默，告訴我你的名字，又問我的名字。」她會是「真命天女」嗎？喬伊回到公寓，遇到住在走廊對面的小男孩帕克。他的母親和會虐待她的男友正在吵架，所以帕克坐在外面閱讀喬伊借給他的書。知道帕克沒有吃東西，喬伊把手上的肉丸三明治給了他。也許喬伊畢竟是個好人？

But remember, this isn't a romantic comedy. Instead of waiting for another [10]**random** encounter with Beck, Joe learns all about her life on social media—including her address—and begins [11]**stalking** her. Starting at the early morning [12]**yoga** class Beck teaches, he follows her to school, where she meets with her [13]**professor**, who obviously wants to **T** <u>get in her pants</u>. In the

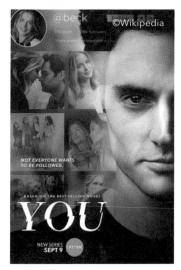
©Wikipedia

▲ 《安眠書店》第一季海報

14. **instantly** [ˋɪnstəntli] (a.)
立刻地，立即地

15. **indifferent** [ɪnˋdɪfərənt] (a.)
冷漠的

16. **miserable** [ˋmɪzərəbəl] (a.)
痛苦的，悲慘的

17. **rescue** [ˋrɛskju] (v./n.)
拯救，救援

18. **obstacle** [ˋɑbstəkəl] (n.)
障礙，阻礙

19. **lure** [lʊr] (v./n.)
引誘，誘惑

### 補充單字

**premiere** [prɪˋmjɛr] (v./n.)
首映，首播

**sequel** [ˋsikwəl] (n.) 續集

**infatuated** [ɪnˋfætʃʊˏetɪd] (a.)
對…著迷的、熱戀的

**philandering** [fɪˋlændərɪŋ] (a.)
玩弄女性的

**make-up sex** (phr.) 吵架復合炮

**artisanal** [ɑrˋtɪsənəl] (a.) 傳統手工的

**mallet** [ˋmælɪt] (n.) 木槌，球棍

**vault** [vɔlt] (n.) 保險庫，地窖

**love interest** (phr.) 感情對象

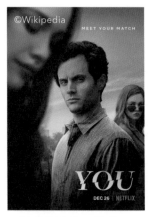

▲ 《安眠書店》第二季海報

evening, Joe follows her to a bar, where she has drinks with her rich college friends, who he [14]**instantly** dislikes. But he likes the next person in Beck's life that he sees even less. Standing outside Beck's apartment late that night, he sees her rich, `philandering` boyfriend, Benji, arrive for `make-up` sex.

但別忘了這可不是一部浪漫喜劇。喬伊沒有等待與貝克再一次巧遇邂逅，而是在社群媒體上搜刮她的一切生活，包括她的住址，並開始跟蹤她。從清晨貝克教授的瑜伽課開始，然後跟著她去學校與教授會面，教授顯然覬覦美色想染指她。晚上喬伊跟著她去一家酒吧，和她有錢的大學朋友喝酒，喬伊立刻對她同學反感。但他看到下一個貝克生命中的人就更不喜歡。那天深夜，他站在貝克的公寓外面，看到她有錢的玩咖男朋友班傑到來，準備來場和好炮。

The next day, ⒼJoe follows Beck to a bar in **Greenpoint**, where she reads one of her poems to an [15]**indifferent** crowd. What's worse, Benji doesn't show up. Drunk and [16]**miserable**, Beck falls onto the tracks at the subway station, ❶ only to be [17]**rescued** by Joe. It's clear that Benji isn't good for Beck, but more importantly, he's an [18]**obstacle** to Joe's relationship with her, which already exists in his mind. So Joe pretends to be someone from *New York* magazine interested in reviewing the `artisanal` sodas made by Benji's company. He then [19]**lures** Benji back to the bookstore, knocks him out with a `mallet` and locks him in the basement book `vault`. You can probably guess how he ends up. But will Joe and Beck live happily ever after? And will Beck even live? Here's a hint: in Season 2, Joe has a new `love interest`.

第二天，喬伊跟隨貝克來到綠點區的一家酒吧，她向冷漠的人群朗讀一首她的詩。更糟糕的是，班傑沒有出現。酒醉而悲慘的貝克倒在地鐵站跌落鐵軌，卻被喬伊救了上來。很明顯，班傑對貝克並不好，但更重要的是，他是喬伊與她感情的障礙，而這份感情已經存在他心中。所以喬伊假裝是《紐約》雜誌的人，對班傑公司生產的汽水感興趣，之後把班傑引回書店，用木槌打昏他並鎖在地下室的書庫裡。你大概能猜到他的下場。但是喬伊和貝克會從此過著幸福生活嗎？貝克甚至會活著嗎？這裡有一個提示：在第二季中，喬伊有了新的戀人。

**rise to fame 聲名大噪，成名**

Taiwanese judoka Yang Yung-wei rose to fame after winning silver at the Tokyo Olympics. 台灣柔道選手楊勇緯在東京奧運拿下銀牌後聲名大噪。

© 體育署

**get in(to) sb.'s pants 與某人上床**

Does Steve really like you, or is he just trying to get into your pants? 史蒂夫真的喜歡妳，還是他只想跟妳上床。

**only to v. 不料卻，沒想到卻**

I arrived at the museum only to find that it was closed due to the pandemic. 我抵達博物館，沒想到卻因為疫情閉館。

---

**Grammar** Master

## 非限定關係代名詞

Joe follows Beck to a bar in Greenpoint, <u>where</u> she reads one of her poems...

● **句中的關係代名詞 where = in which，which 代替 Greenpoint 原句為：**

Joe follows Beck to a bar in Greenpoint. <u>In Greenpoint</u> she reads one of her poems⋯

= Joe follows Beck to a bar in Greenpoint, <u>in which</u> she reads one of her poems⋯

● **Greenpoint 為獨一無二的專有名詞如（Taipei、New York）接關係代名詞，應加上「逗號」補充說明，為「非限定關係代名詞」以下比較：**

He's back from London, <u>which</u> he likes so much. 他從他超愛的倫敦回來。
（倫敦只有一個，加逗號補充非限定）

He's back from the city <u>which</u> (that) he likes so much. 他從他超愛的城市回來。
（城市有很多個，不加逗號限定）

---

**EZpedia**

**Greenpoint 綠點區**

位於紐約市布魯克林區（Brooklyn）最北部。該地區為波蘭裔移民聚集地，因此又有「小波蘭」之稱。原本為勞工和移民居住的社區，但自 2000 年代後，成為紐約夜生活的中心。

Leonard Zhukovsky©Shutterstock.com

〔貝克第一次來到喬伊工作的書店〕

Beck　Hello. Do you work here?

Joe　❶ Guilty. Can I help you find something?

Beck　Paula Fox.

Joe　It's a good choice.

Beck　Hmm, I feel ¹weirdly ²validated.

Joe　Follow me. She's gonna be in here.

Beck　Celebrity Authors? I thought Fox was pretty ³⁾obscure.

Joe　She is Courtney Love's ⁵maternal grandmother. You're not expected to know that. Mr. Mooney wants anyone in here who's even ⁶tangentially famous. He thinks it sells more books.

Beck　That's sad. People buying books because of what's popular, and not because they wanna be moved or changed in some way.

Joe　Yeah. It's an ⁴⁾epidemic.

---

## Vocabulary

1. **weirdly** [`wɪrdlɪ] (adv.) 詭異地
2. **validate** [`vælə‚det] (v.) 認可，確認
3. **obscure** [əb`skjur] (a.) 鮮為人知的
4. **epidemic** [‚ɛprˋdɛmɪk] (n.) 流行氾濫，流行病
6. **keep** [kip] (v.) 保持新鮮
7. **toss** [tɔs] (v.) 扔掉

### 補充單字

**maternal** [məˋtɝnəl] (a.)
母親的，母親那方的

**tangentially** [tænˋdʒɛnʃəlɪ] (adv.)
非直接相關地

**'sup** [sʌp] （口）你好嗎？
= What's up? 的縮寫

貝克　你好，請問你是這裡的店員嗎？

喬伊　沒錯。我能幫妳找什麼書嗎？

貝克　寶拉福克斯。

喬伊　選得好。

貝克　有種詭異的認可感。

喬伊　跟我來，她的書在這裡。

貝克　「知名作家」？ 我以為福克斯鮮為人知。

喬伊　她是寇特妮洛芙的外婆，妳應該是不會知道的。只要跟名人沾上一點邊的作家，穆尼先生都想歸在這區，他覺得這樣比較好賣。

貝克　真悲哀，大家買書就只是因為名氣，而不是因為想被感動或改變什麼。

喬伊　是啊，趕流行嘛。

## 我為人人

〔喬伊回到公寓看見帕克坐在走廊〕

Joe　Hey, Paco.

Paco　**'Sup**, Joe?

Joe　*[hears yelling inside Paco's apartment]*
Is everything cool in there?

Paco　Yeah, Mom and Ron are just talking.

Joe　Wow. You are ⊤ <u>burning through</u> that book, aren't you? Let me know when you finish. I'll get you another one. Are you hungry? 'Cause, you know, I just got this meatball sub, but I remembered I have Thai from last night.

Paco　Nah. My mom will just make me something later.

Joe　That's a shame. This won't [6]**keep**. It's getting [7]**tossed**.

Paco　You sure, Joe?

Joe　⊤ <u>All for one and one for all.</u>

---

喬伊　嗨，帕克。

帕克　喬伊，還好嗎？

喬伊　〔聽見帕克的家有人在大吼〕裡面還好吧？

帕克　對，媽媽和倫在談話。

喬伊　哇你那本書看得很快嘛。看完後告訴我，我再借你一本。你餓了嗎？我剛剛買了肉丸三明治，但我想起來我昨晚有剩泰國菜。

帕克　不用了，我媽媽等一下會做飯。

喬伊　可惜了，這會壞掉，最後也是要扔掉。

帕克　你確定嗎，喬伊？

喬伊　「我為人人，人人為我。」

© Shutterstock.com

# 偷吃鬼扯

〔當班傑出現在貝克的公寓，兩人便開始吵架〕

**Beck**　My best friend **❶ walked in on** you getting your dick sucked by some random woman in a bathroom at a party that I took you to!

**Benji**　I was [8]**wasted**. I didn't even finish.

**Beck**　That's your [9]**apology**? "I didn't **cum**." That's the one you're going with?

**Benji**　I [10]**obviously** shouldn't have gone in the bathroom with any girl that wasn't you. But she said she had good **coke**, and I'd been seriously stressed. I thought, when Johno and I started our line, it was gonna be like picking out flavors **❶ and shit.** It turns out it's 16-hour lectures on **microbial** management. And that's why no one starts their own artisanal soda company, and why America has to keep drinking **crap** that's giving them cancer.

**Beck**　You actually managed to connect your **illicit** blowjob to curing cancer. I'm [11]**genuinely** impressed.

---

## Vocabulary

8. **wasted** [ˋwestɪd] *(a.)*（口）喝醉的，嗑藥的

9. **apology** [əˋpɑlədʒɪ] *(n.)* 道歉

10. **obviously** [ˋɑbvɪəslɪ] *(adv.)* 明顯地

11. **genuinely** [ˋdʒɛnjuɪnlɪ] *(adv.)* 真正地

12. **transit** [ˋtrænsɪt] *(n./v.)* 運輸，運送

### 補充單字

**cum** *(v./n.)*（口）高潮

**coke** *(n.)* 古柯鹼 =cocaine

**crap** [kræp] *(n.)*（口）爛東西

**illicit** [ɪˋlɪsɪt] *(a.)* 非法的，不當的

**microbial** [maɪˋkrobɪəl] *(a.)* 微生物的

貝克　我最好的朋友在派對上撞見你，在廁所跟陌生女子口交，那個派對還是我帶你去的！

班傑　我當時嗑了藥，我根本沒到高潮。

貝克　這就是你的道歉？「我沒到高潮」，你就想這樣蒙混過關？

班傑　我當然不該跟妳之外的其他女人進廁所，但她說她有不錯的古柯鹼，我最近壓力真的超大。我以為姜諾和我只要挑選口味之類的就好，結果要花 16 小時上微生物管理課。難怪沒人要自己創辦手工汽水公司，所以美國人只好一直喝會讓人得癌症的垃圾飲料。

貝克　你還真會把不當口交的事扯到癌症治療，我真是大開眼界了。

©Shutterstock.com

## 救命恩人

〔貝克第二次來到書店拜訪喬伊〕

**Beck** Hey. Remember me? From almost dying on the train tracks?

**Joe** Uh, 🎧 it rings a bell. 🎧 Hang on, hang on.

**Beck** I wanted to say thank you.

**Joe** No. You already did that.

**Beck** Well, uh, thanks again. And I'm sorry for running off the other night. So, I got you a present.

**Joe** No, please. You don't have to get me anything.

**Beck** Shut up and just look at it. *[hands him copy of* The Da Vinci Code*]*

**Joe** *[reading her note to him in the book]* Engine engine number nine on the New York [12] **transit** line, if your girl falls on the track, pick her up pick her up pick her up.

**Beck** So...anyway, that. And I better....

**Joe** Maybe if you're not too busy, we could get a drink sometime?

**Beck** Sure. Ugh. But I still can't find my phone.

**Joe** I know, e-mail.

**Beck** That's right. See ya, Joe.

---

| | |
|---|---|
| 貝克 | 嗨,還記得我嗎?差點死在鐵軌上的那位? |
| 喬伊 | 好像有印象,等一下 |
| 貝克 | 我想跟你道謝。 |
| 喬伊 | 不用,妳已經謝過了。 |
| 貝克 | 呃,再次跟你道謝,抱歉那晚就這樣走掉。所以我帶禮物來給你。 |
| 喬伊 | 不用這麼客氣,妳不用送我禮物 |
| 貝克 | 閉嘴,就看一下〔遞給他一本《達文西密碼》〕 |
| 喬伊 | 〔閱讀書中她的紙條〕「九號火車,開在紐約地鐵線上你女友若跌落鐵軌上,快救她」 |
| 貝克 | 所以…總之,我最好… |
| 喬伊 | 妳若不會太忙的話,我們可以約時間喝一杯? |
| 貝克 | 好啊 但我還是找不到我的手機 |
| 喬伊 | 我知道,用 email |
| 貝克 | 沒錯!再見,喬伊。 |

### *Tongue-tied No More*

**walk in on sb. 撞見某人**
She walked in on me when I was getting undressed.
她正好撞見我在脫衣服。

**...and shit 等等,之類的**
= and whatnot 的粗俗口語用法
I keep tools and shit in the trunk of my car. 我後車箱放工具之類的東西。

**ring a bell 聽起來有點印象**
The name "Kamala Harris" rings a bell but I'm not sure who she is.
賀錦麗這個名字聽起來有點熟悉,但我不確定她是誰。

**hang on 稍等一下**
Hang on a minute, I'm almost ready to go. 稍等一下,我差不多準備出門了。

©Wikipedia

▲《不存在房間》海報

## Vocabulary

1. **authority** [əˋθɔrətɪ] (n.)
當局，權威

2. **captive** [ˋkæptɪv] (a.)
囚禁的，狹持的

3. **chamber** [ˋtʃembə] (n.) 室，房間

4. **repeatedly** [rɪˋpitɪdlɪ] (adv.)
重複不斷地

5. **terrifying** [ˋtɛrəˏfaɪɪŋ] (a.)
駭人的，恐怖的

6. **ordeal** [ɔrˋdil] (n.) 磨難

7. **engineer** [ˏɛndʒəˋnɪr] (v.)
策劃，謀策

8. **sentence** [ˋsɛntəns] (v.) 宣判，判刑

9. **inspire** [ɪnˋspaɪr] (v.) 給予靈感

### 補充單字

**cult** [kʌlt] (n.) 邪教組織

## The Fritzl Case
## 《不存在的房間》奧地利魔父囚禁女兒 24 年

In a story that ⭐ <u>sent shockwaves</u> across Europe in 2008, Elizabeth Fritzl reappeared in her Austrian hometown after being missing for 24 years. Her father, Josef Fritzl, first told the [1]**authorities** in 1984 that Elizabeth had run away to join a ˈ**cult**. In reality, however, he was holding his daughter [2]**captive** in a hidden [3]**chamber** in his basement. Throughout Elizabeth's captivity, Josef [4]**repeatedly** sexually assaulted and raped her, resulting in the birth of seven children. One baby died after childbirth, Josef and his wife raised three children as their own, and the others remained in captivity with Elizabeth. After this [5]**terrifying** [6]**ordeal**, Elizabeth managed to [7]**engineer** her escape, and following his trial, Fritzl was [8]**sentenced** to life in prison in 2009. Several films were [9]**inspired** by the case, including Oscar-winning *Room* (2015) and *Girl in the Basement* (2021).

2008 年震驚全歐洲的事件，伊麗莎白弗里茨失蹤 24 年後重新出現在奧地利家鄉。1984 年她的父親約瑟夫弗里茨通報當局，伊麗莎白逃跑加入一個邪教組織。然而，實際上，他把女兒囚禁在地下室一個隱蔽的房間。伊麗莎白囚禁期間，約瑟夫多次性侵強暴她，最終生下了七個小孩。一名嬰兒出生後夭折，約瑟夫和妻子撫養三名小孩作為自己的子嗣，其他人仍與伊麗莎白囚禁在一起。經歷這場可怕磨難後，伊麗莎白成功策劃逃脫。約瑟夫接受審判，2009 年判處終身監禁。許多電影根據該案改編，包含獲奧斯卡獎的 2015 年《不存在的房間》、2021 年的《地下室女孩》。

### 〔 Tongue-tied No More 〕

**send shockwaves** 席捲、震驚全（地區）
The assassination of Haiti president sent shock waves across the world. 海地總統刺殺案震驚全球。

# What is Obsessive Love Disorder (OLD)?
## 《安眠書店》恐怖情人戀愛強迫症

全文朗讀 ♫ 040　單字 ♫ 041

❶ <u>Being head over heels in love</u> with someone can be a wonderful feeling, but what if this love °**morphs** into something else entirely? °**Obsessive** Love Disorder (OLD) is a rare 1)**condition** in which one person is 2)**consumed** by their feelings for another. They want to protect the other person at all costs and control them as if they owned them. Often, they will become extremely jealous if the other person has any kind of relationship with someone. Needless to say, OLD is not healthy and if someone thinks they may be 3)**suffering** from it, they should seek °**psychiatric** help immediately. If someone is 4)**diagnosed** with OLD, a 5)**combination** of medication and therapy will be used to treat and hopefully cure it.

墜入愛河可能是一種美好的感覺，但如果這種愛整個演變成其他東西呢？ 戀愛強迫症是一種罕見的症狀，一個人被感情所吞噬，瘋狂愛著對方。他們不惜一切代價想保護對方並控制他們，就好像擁有他們一般。往往對方與他人產生任何關係，他們會變得非常嫉妒。毋庸置疑地，戀愛強迫症並不健康，如果覺得自己可能患有此症，應立即尋求精神救助。若被診斷出患有戀愛強迫症，將使用藥物與心理諮商的混合治療，並有望治癒。

## Vocabulary

1. **condition** [kənˋdɪʃən] (n.)
   疾病，條件
2. **consume** [kənˋsum] (v.) 被情感吞噬
3. **suffer (from)** [ˋsʌfɚ] (v.)
   遭受，罹患
4. **diagnose** [ˋdaɪəg͵nos] (v.) 診斷
5. **combination** [͵kɑmbəˋneʃən] (n.)
   組合，結合

### 補充單字

**morph** [mɔrf] (v.) 逐漸演變
**obsessive** [əbˋsɛsɪv] (a.)
癡迷狂愛的，強迫症的
**psychiatric** [͵saɪkɪˋætrɪk] (a.) 精神病的

### *Tongue-tied No More*

**be head over heels (in love)**
墜入愛河、熱戀期
My parents are still head over heels in love after 20 years of marriage. 我的父母結婚二十年後依然深愛著對方。

**at all costs 不惜一切代價**
You should avoid changing money on the street at all costs. 不管怎麼樣你都應該避免在街上換錢。

#dufferbrothers #upsidedown
#alternatedimension #hawkins

全文朗讀 🎵 042　　單字 🎵 043

# *Stranger Things*《怪奇物語》

**NETFLIX**

致敬經典恐怖電影 顛倒世界異次元維度空間

## Vocabulary

1. **dash** [dæʃ] *(n.)*
   稍微，少量

▲《E.T. 外星人》海報

In the world of Netflix **megahit** *Stranger Things*, nothing is ever what it seems. The lady from child protective services might shoot you dead; a high school **jerk** may help save the day; and there may be *way* 🚇 more to a young girl found in the woods 🚇 than meets the eye. Created by the Duffer brothers, this sci-fi horror series is a **throwback** to the 1980's movies the twins watched growing up, such as E.T., *Stand By Me* and *The Goonies,* with a ¹⁾**dash** of Stephen King horror 🚇 for good measure.

在 Netflix 強檔影集《怪奇物語》中，外表看似的一切都是假象。兒童保護機構的女士可能一槍把你斃命；高中混蛋可能出手相救；森林中發現的一個年輕女孩可能並非我們看到得這麼單純。這部科幻恐怖影集由杜夫兄弟創作，充滿 1980 年代懷舊電影風格，像雙胞胎兄弟從小看的電影，如《E.T. 外星人》、《站在我這邊》與《七寶奇謀》，另外還帶有一點史蒂芬金的恐怖。

Season one starts out in 1983 in the fictional town of Hawkins, Indiana, with a group of middle school friends— ²⁾**conscientious** Mike, ³**goofy** Dustin, ³⁾**cautious** Lucas and sensitive Will— playing ⁴**Dungeons** & Dragons. Just as Will rolls the ⁵**dice** and is about to be eaten by the **fearsome** Demogorgon, Mike's mom ends their 10-hour ⁴⁾**session** and sends the boys home. Riding through the woods, Will sees something that ⁵⁾**horrifies** him and crashes his bike. He runs home and hides in the ⁶⁾**shed** behind his house, but then a ⁷⁾**growl** is heard, the light ⁸⁾**flickers**, and Will vanishes.

©Wikipedia

第一季始於 1983 年虛構的印第安納州霍金斯鎮，一群中學朋友——努力認真的麥克、滑稽可愛的達斯汀、謹慎的路卡斯和敏感的威爾——正在玩龍與地下城角色扮演遊戲。 正當威爾甩骰子，即將被可怕的魔神吃掉時，麥克的媽媽結束了他們 10 小時的遊戲，並叫男孩們回家。 威爾騎腳踏車穿過森林時，看到了令他恐懼的東西，並從腳踏車摔了下來。 他跑回家躲在房子後方的儲藏棚裡，但之後聽到一聲咆哮，燈光閃爍，接著威爾就消失了。

As people try to find the missing Will, things just get stranger and stranger. **G** While searching the woods, his buddies run into Eleven, a young girl with her head shaved ⁹**practically** ¹⁰**bald**. Will's mom and brother look everywhere for him, but he's **T** nowhere to be found. A ⁵**sinister** group of scientists from the government ¹¹**laboratory** on the ¹²**outskirts** of town show up looking for Eleven and find strange goop in the shed where

2. **conscientious** [ˌkɑnʃɪˈɛnʃəs]
   (a.) 勤勉認真的

3. **cautious** [ˈkɔʃəs] (a.)
   小心謹慎的

4. **session** [ˈsɛʃən] (n.)
   一段時間

5. **horrify** [ˈhɔrəˌfaɪ] (v.)
   使震驚，使恐懼

6. **shed** [ʃɛd] (n.)
   儲藏棚

7. **growl** [ɡraʊl] (n./v.)
   咆哮，嗥叫

8. **flicker** [ˈflɪkə] (v./n.)
   閃爍，閃光

9. **practically** [ˈpræktɪklɪ] (adv.)
   幾乎地

10. **bald** [bɔld] (a.)
    禿頭的，光禿的

11. **laboratory** [ˈlæbrəˌtorɪ] (n.)
    實驗室

12. **outskirts** [ˈaʊtˌskɜts] (n.)
    郊區，外圍區域

©DFree / Shutterstock.com

▲《怪奇物語》童星演員

## Vocabulary

13. **mysterious** [mɪsˋtɪrɪəs] (a.)
神秘的

14. **slam** [slæm] (v.)
用力關上，抨擊

15. **alternate** [ˋɔltənɪt] (a.)
替代的，交替的

16. **dimension** [dɪˋmɛnʃən] (n.)
次元，維度空間

17. **desperate** [ˋdɛspərɪt] (a.)
極度渴望的

18. **emerge** [ɪˋmɝdʒ] (v.)
浮現，浮出

19. **corpse** [kɔrps] (n.)
屍體

### 補充單字

**megahit** [ˋmɛgə͵hɪt] (n.)
非常成功的作品

**jerk** [dʒɝk] (n.) 混蛋

**throwback** [ˋθro͵bæk] (n.)
懷舊復古的事物

**goofy** [ˋgufɪ] (a.) 傻傻的，滑稽的

**dungeon** [ˋdʌndʒən] (n.) 地牢

**dice** [daɪs] (n.) 骰子

**fearsome** [ˋfɪrsəm] (a.)
駭人的，怵目驚心的

**sinister** [ˋsɪnɪstə] (a.)
險惡的，陰險的

**psychokinetic** [͵saɪkokəˋnɛtɪk]
(a.) 念力的

**slug** [slʌg] (n.) 蛞蝓

**momentarily** [͵momənˋtɛrəlɪ]
(adv.) 瞬間地，短暫地

Will disappeared. The [13] **mysterious** Eleven indicates she knows what happened to Will and then shocks the boys with her *psychokinetic* powers when she uses her mind to [14] **slam** a door. She tells the boys about an [15] **alternate** [16] **dimension** called the Upside Down, and says Will is there hiding from a monster.

當大夥試圖找到失蹤的威爾時，事情發展得越來越詭異。 正當他的夥伴們在搜索森林時，他們遇見了伊萊雯，一個幾乎剃光頭髮的女孩。 威爾的母親和哥哥到處找他，卻完全沒有他的下落。 一群來自鎮郊政府實驗室的險惡科學家現身尋找伊萊雯，並在威爾失蹤的棚子裡找到了奇怪的黏液。 神秘的伊萊雯表示她知道威爾發生了什麼事，然後她使用念力將門大力關上，把男孩們嚇傻了。 她告訴男孩們一個叫做顛倒世界的異次元維度空間，並說威爾在那裡躲避怪物。

As the season goes on, the [17] **desperate** search for Will continues. Will's mom, Joyce, sees the Demogorgon (that's right, the Demogorgon is real, and it's in Hawkins!) [18] **emerging** from the wall of her house. Will's [19] **corpse** is found, but Hopper, the Hawkins police chief, investigates and discovers that it isn't real. Eleven uses her powers to find where Will is hiding, and a trip into the Upside Down by Joyce and Hopper results in Will's rescue. As the season comes to a close with Will's mom and brother happily preparing for Christmas dinner, Will throws up a *slug*-like creature in the bathroom and is *momentarily* back in the Upside Down. More strange things are sure to be ahead!

隨著本季的演進，搜尋威爾的迫切行動持續進行。 威爾的母親喬伊斯看到了魔神（沒錯，是真的魔神，而且它就在霍金斯鎮！）從她家的牆上浮現。 威爾的屍體被發現，但霍金斯警長哈普調查發現屍體是假的。 伊萊雯使用她的念力找到威爾的藏身之處，喬伊斯和哈普前往顛倒世界，解救出威爾。 隨著威爾的母親和哥哥高興地準備聖誕晚餐，本季來到尾身，威爾在浴室裡吐出了一個像蛞蝓般的生物，並且臨時又回到了顛倒世界。 更怪奇的事物肯定還在後面！

©Wikicommons

### 「while/when 當⋯時候」的比較用法

"<u>While</u> his buddies are searching the woods, they run into Eleven…" while 表達「正當⋯的過程中」，因此接進行式；when 表達「當⋯的時刻」接簡單式。此句用 when 改寫為 "<u>When</u> the buddies run into Eleven, they are searching the woods." 連接詞 while/when 可放置句首或句中。

- 例：**I was watching TV <u>when</u> my phone rang.**
  當手機響的那個時刻，我正在看電視。

- 例：**My phone rang <u>while</u> I was watching TV.**
  當我在看電視的過程中，手機響了。

─────────── *Tongue-tied No More* ───────────

**be more to sth./sb. than meets the eye 非表象那般單純**
I have a feeling there's more to this story than meets the eye.
我有種感覺故事沒有那單純。

**nowhere to be found 無跡可尋，找不到**
I looked everywhere, but my keys are nowhere to be found.
我到處都找了，就是找不到我的鑰匙。

©Shutterstock.com

〔大夥打完龍與地下城後準備回家〕

Dustin　There's something wrong with your sister.

Mike　What are you talking about?

Dustin　She's ❶ got a stick up her [1]butt.

Lucas　Yeah. It's because she's been dating that [*]douchebag, Steve Harrington.

Dustin　Yeah, she's turning into a real jerk.

Mike　She's always been a real jerk.

Dustin　[2]Nuh-uh, she used to be cool. Like that time she dressed up as an [*]elf for our Elder Tree campaign.

Mike　Four years ago!

Dustin　❶ Just saying.

[Dustin and Lucas ride off and Will turns to Mike]

Will　It was a seven. The roll. It was a seven. The Demogorgon, it got me.

## Vocabulary

1. **butt** [bʌt] (n.) 屁股 = buttocks
2. **nuh-uh** [ˋnʌŋʌŋ] (int.)（口）才不
3. **freak** [frik] (n.) 怪人

### 補充單字

**douchebag** [ˋduʃ͵bæg]（粗）混蛋
**elf** [ɛlf] (n.) 小精靈
**loony bin**（口）瘋人院

### Tongue-tied No More

**have a stick up one's butt/ass**
**死板的，嚴苛的**
I hope I don't get Mr. Simpson for math—he really has a stick up his butt. 我希望不會上到辛普森老師的數學課，他真的很嚴格。

達斯汀　你姊姊怪怪的。

麥克　什麼意思？

達斯汀　她好機車哦。

路卡斯　對，因為她和那個混蛋史帝夫哈林頓約會。

達斯汀　對，她變得很討人厭。

麥克　她一直都很討人厭。

達斯汀　才不，她以前挺酷的。例如有一次她打扮成小精靈，幫我們打長老樹戰役。

麥克　那是四年前了！

達斯汀　只是說說。

〔達斯汀與麥克騎腳踏車離開，威爾向麥可說〕

威爾　是七點，擲出七點。魔神抓到我了。

# 麥克遲到

〔麥克把伊萊雯藏在家裡的隔天早上，達斯汀與路卡斯在課堂上聊天〕

| | |
|---|---|
| Dustin | Oh, this is weird. He's never this late. |
| Lucas | I'm telling you, his stupid plan failed. |
| Dustin | I thought you liked his plan. |
| Lucas | Yeah, but obviously it was stupid, or he'd be here. |
| Dustin | If his mom found out a girl spent the night.... |
| Lucas | He's ⓣ in deep shit right about now. |
| Dustin | Hey, what if she slept naked? |
| Lucas | Oh, my God, she didn't. |
| Dustin | Oh, if Mrs. Wheeler tells my parents.... |
| Lucas | No way. Mike would never ⓣ rat us out. |
| Dustin | I don't know. |
| Lucas | All that matters is, after school, the ³**freak** will be back in the ⁴**loony bin**, and we can focus on what really matters, finding Will. |

| | |
|---|---|
| 達斯汀 | 這真怪。他不曾遲到這麼久。 |
| 路卡斯 | 告訴你，他的蠢計畫失敗了。 |
| 達斯汀 | 我以為你喜歡他的計畫。 |
| 路卡斯 | 對，但顯然很蠢，不然他早該到了。 |
| 達斯汀 | 如果他媽媽發現有個女孩在家過夜… |
| 路卡斯 | 他現在麻煩大了。 |
| 達斯汀 | 如果她裸睡呢？ |
| 路卡斯 | 天啊，她才沒有。 |
| 達斯汀 | 如果惠勒太太告訴我爸媽。 |
| 路卡斯 | 才不會，麥克絕不會當廖北啊打小報告。 |
| 達斯汀 | 我不知道。 |
| 路卡斯 | 重點是，放學之後那個怪人就回到瘋人院了，我們就可以專注在真正要緊的事，尋找威爾。 |

**(I'm) just saying 我只是說說意見**
If you don't like it, you shouldn't have bought it. Just saying.
如果你不喜歡，當初就不應該買，只是說說意見。

**be in deep shit 倒大楣，完蛋了**
You'll be in deep shit if you're not home by 11:00.
如果你沒在 11 點前回到家，你就倒大楣了。

**rat sb. out 出賣某人，打小報告**
I can't believe you ratted me out to Mom and Dad.
我不敢相信你竟然出賣我，跟爸媽打小報告。

## 失蹤報案

〔喬伊斯來到警局報案威爾失蹤〕

Joyce　　I have been waiting here over an hour, Hopper.

Hopper　And I [4]**apologize** again.

Joyce　　I'm ❶ going out of my mind!

Hopper　Look, boy his age, he's probably just ❶ playing hooky, OK?

Joyce　　No, not my Will. He's not like that. He wouldn't do that.

Hopper　Well, you never know. My mom thought I was on the debate team, when really I was just [5]**screwing** Chrissy Carpenter in my dad's Oldsmobile.

Joyce　　Look, he's not like you, Hopper. He's not like me. He's not like...most. He has a couple of friends, but, you know, the kids, they're mean. They ❶ make fun of him. They ❶ call him names. They laugh at him, his clothes....

Hopper　His clothes? What's wrong with his clothes?

Joyce　　I don't know. Does that matter? Look, he's...he's a sensitive kid. Lonnie...Lonnie used to say he was [6]**queer**. Called him a [7]**fag**.

Hopper　Is he?

Joyce　　He's *missing* is what he is.

---

## Vocabulary

4. **apologize** [əˋpɑləˏdʒaɪz] *(v.)* 道歉
5. **screw** [skru] *(v.)* （口）性交
6. **queer** [kwɪr] *(a./n.)* 同性戀，酷兒，原為「古怪的」，19 世紀帶有貶義，現今已成為多元性向的總稱
7. **mental** [ˋmɛntəl] *(a.)* （口）瘋狂的
8. **wizard** [ˋwɪzəd] *(n.)* 巫師

### 補充單字

**fag** [fæg] *(n.)* （粗）男同性戀
**superpower** [ˋsupəˏpauə] *(n.)* 超能力

---

喬伊斯　哈普，我在這裡等了一個多小時。

哈普　　我再度向妳道歉。

喬伊斯　我快瘋了！

哈普　　聽著，像他這年紀的男孩很可能只是翹課了，好嗎？

喬伊斯　不，我的威爾不會，他不是那種孩子，他不會那樣做。

哈普　　難說哦。以前我媽以為我參加辯論社，其實我只是在我爸的汽車和克莉絲卡本特亂搞。

喬伊斯　哈普，他不像你，他不像我，他不像…大部分的人。他有幾個朋友，但你也知道有些孩子很壞，他們取笑他、罵他，他們嘲笑他和他的衣服…

哈普　　他的衣服？他的衣服怎麼了？

喬伊斯　我不知道。那重要嗎？聽著，他是…很敏感的小孩。隆尼…以前說他是娘砲，罵他同性戀。

哈普　　他是嗎？

喬伊斯　他失蹤了，就是這樣。

# 回到維度

〔麥可、路卡斯、達斯汀到醫院探訪威爾〕

Lucas    You won't believe what happened when you were gone, man.

Dustin    It was [7]**mental**.

Lucas    You had a funeral.

Dustin    Jennifer Hayes was crying.

Lucas    And Troy ☎ peed himself.

Dustin    In front of the whole school!

Mike    *[to Will, who is coughing]* You OK?

Will    It got me. The Demogorgon.

Mike    We know. It's OK. It's dead. We made a new friend. She stopped it. She saved us. But she's gone now. Her name's Eleven.

Will    Like the number?

Lucas    Well, we call her "El" ☎ for short.

Dustin    She's basically a [8]**wizard**.

Lucas    *[whispering]* She has **superpowers.**

路卡斯    你絕對不相信你不在時發生了什麼事，老兄。

達斯汀    超瘋狂的 。

路卡斯    你有一場喪禮。

達斯汀    珍妮佛海茲還哭了。

路卡斯    特洛伊尿褲子。

達斯汀    當著全校的面！

麥可    [ 向咳嗽的威爾 ] 你還好嗎？

威爾    魔神，牠抓住我了。

麥可    我們知道。沒關係，牠死了。我們認識一個新朋友。她阻止了牠，救了我們，但現在她走了。 她叫伊萊雯。

威爾    數字的伊萊雯？

路卡斯    我們簡稱她「小伊」。

達斯汀    基本上她就是巫師。

路卡斯    [ 輕聲細語 ] 她有超能力。

## Tongue-tied No More

**go out of one's mind**
某人發瘋了
I'm gonna go out of my mind if I have to keep working from home.
如果繼續在家上班，我真的會發瘋。

**play hooky** 翹課，逃學
Me and my friends played hooky and went fishing. 我和朋友翹課去釣魚。

**make fun of** 嘲笑
It's not nice to make fun of other people. 嘲笑別人是不對的。

**call sb. names** 咒罵、辱罵某人
John got in trouble for calling another student names.
約翰因為辱罵另一位學生惹上麻煩。

**pee oneself**
笑到或嚇到「屁滾尿流」
Greg sometimes pees himself when he laughs too hard.
格雷有時候笑到「屁滾尿流」。

**for short** 簡稱，暱稱為
My name is Katherine, but you can call me Kate for short.
我的名字叫凱薩琳，但你可以簡稱我為凱特。

©Wikipedia

▲ 擁有念力的伊萊雯

# BLACK MIRROR

© Wikicommons

THE FUTURE IS BRIGHT

**#blackmirror #dystopia**
**#darktechnology**

Lindsay Silveira©Flickr

全文朗讀 ♪ **046**　單字 ♪ **047**

## *Black Mirror*《黑鏡》
反烏托邦幻想 科技未來的冰冷暗黑面

**NETFLIX**

### Vocabulary

1. **setting** [ˋsɛtɪŋ] *(n.)*
   場景，背景

2. **clumsy** [ˋklʌmzɪ] *(a.)*
   笨拙的

3. **refer (to)** [rɪˋfɝ] *(v.)*
   指的是，提及

4. **monitor** [ˋmɑnətɚ] *(n./v.)*
   顯示器，監視

Inspired by classic TV shows like **The Twilight Zone**, *Black Mirror* is a sci-fi ˚**anthology** series that explores the (mostly) dark side of people's relationship with technology. "Each episode has a different cast, a different ¹⁾**setting**, even a different reality," says the show's creator, Charlie Brooker. "But they're all about the way we live now—and the way we might be living in 10 minutes' time if we're ²⁾**clumsy**." According to Brooker, the show's title ³⁾**refers** to the thing found in every office, home and palm: "the cold, shiny screen of a TV, a ⁴⁾**monitor**, a smartphone." *Black Mirror* first aired on the UK's Channel 4 in 2011, and after two seasons moved to Netflix, which has released another three seasons, the latest in 2019.

受《迷離境界》等經典電視節目的靈感啟發，《黑鏡》是一部科幻集選影集，探討人們與科技之間關係的（往往是）黑暗面。影集製作查理布魯克說：「每一集都有不同的演員、不同的場景，甚至不同的現實，但都涉及我們當前的生

活方式——以及如果我們一時糊塗，十分鐘內可能出現的生活方式。」根據布魯克，劇名「黑鏡」指的是每個辦公室、家庭和手掌上隨處可見的物品：電視、顯示器、智慧手機的冰冷閃耀螢幕。2011 年《黑鏡》首次在英國第 4 頻道播出兩季後，移至 Netflix 推出三季，最新一季於 2019 年上架。

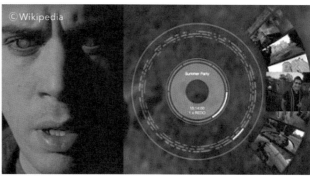

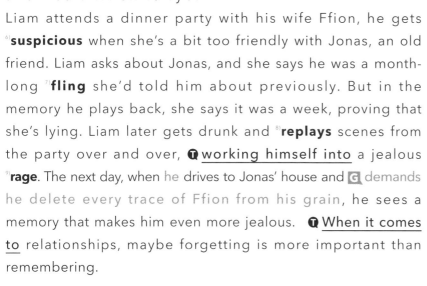

The Season 1 episode "The Entire History of You" is set in a future where "grain" [5]**devices** **implanted** behind the ear allow people to record everything they see and hear. When lawyer Liam attends a dinner party with his wife Ffion, he gets [6]**suspicious** when she's a bit too friendly with Jonas, an old friend. Liam asks about Jonas, and she says he was a month-long [7]**fling** she'd told him about previously. But in the memory he plays back, she says it was a week, proving that she's lying. Liam later gets drunk and [8]**replays** scenes from the party over and over, 🅣<u>working himself into</u> a jealous [9]**rage**. The next day, when he drives to Jonas' house and 🅖 demands he delete every trace of Ffion from his grain, he sees a memory that makes him even more jealous. 🅣<u>When it comes to</u> relationships, maybe forgetting is more important than remembering.

5. **device** [dɪˋvaɪs] (n.) 裝置

6. **suspicious (of/about)** [səˋspɪʃəs] (a.) 懷疑的

7. **fling** [flɪŋ] (n.) 短暫熱戀

8. **replay** [riˋple] (v.) 重播

9. **rage** [redʒ] (n.) 憤怒

### Tongue-tied No More

**work oneself into sth.**
**讓自己陷入某狀態**
He worked himself into a lather thinking about his former wife and her new boyfriend. 他想到前妻與她新男友，讓自己陷入焦躁不安。

**when it comes to sth.**
**說到某事**
When it comes to sci-fi series, *Black Mirror* is one of my favorites. 說到科幻影集，《黑鏡》是我最愛的之一。

### Grammar Master

**帶有「要求、命令」強制性的「意志動詞」**
文中 "He <u>demands</u> he <u>delete</u> every trace of Ffion from his grain." demand 為意志動詞，後面子句省略 should，第三人稱單數動詞 delete 使用原形動詞不加 s。

● **demand/order/command/suggest + (that) + sb. (should) + VR** 要求／命令／建議某人（應）做某事
例：People demand that the government (should) <u>ban</u> U.S. pork imports. 人民要求政府禁止美豬進口。

## Vocabulary

10. **nightmare** [ˋnaɪt.mɛr] (n.)
惡夢

11. **interaction** [ˌɪntɚˋrækʃən] (n.)
互動、交流

12. **scale** [skel] (n.)
等級；規模

13. **status** [ˋstætəs] (n.)
地位，身分

14. **crash** [kræʃ] (v.)
擅自闖入

15. **outgoing** [ˋaʊt.goɪŋ] (a.)
外向的

16. **regular** [ˋrɛgjələ] (n.)
常客

第一季的〈你的全部人生經歷〉場景設定在未來，人們在耳後植入「微粒」裝置，讓他們記錄一切的所見所聞。當律師連恩與妻子菲恩參加晚宴時，他開始懷疑她與老朋友喬納斯有點過於親密。連恩問起關於喬納斯的事，她說之前就提過他們曾經短暫交往一個月。但連恩回播記憶，她說這是一星期，證明她在撒謊。連恩後來喝醉了，一遍又一遍地重播派對上的場景，讓自己陷入嫉妒與憤怒。第二天，當他開車到喬納斯家，要求他從微粒中刪除所有關於菲恩的紀錄，他看到讓他更加嫉妒的記憶。說到感情關係，也許忘記比記住更重要。

In the Season 3 episode "Nosedive," people live in a social media [10]**nightmare** world where every [11]**interaction** is rated on a five-star [12]**scale**, and each person's rating affects their **socioeconomic** [13]**status**. Lacie, a 4.2, is working hard to reach 4.5 so she can afford a nicer apartment. When her childhood friend Naomi, a 4.8, invites her to be **maid of honor** at her wedding, she knows this is her chance to get high ratings from high 4's. But when her flight is cancelled, Lacie <u>loses her temper</u> and gets a whole point subtracted from her rating. Things go from bad to worse, and by the time she arrives in town the next day, her rating is so low that Naomi uninvites her. **Enraged**, Lacie decides to [14]**crash** the wedding, and as you can imagine, it doesn't turn out well. Sounds a little like **China's Social Credit System**, doesn't it?

## EZpedia

**The Twilight Zone** 《迷離境界》
1959-1964 由編劇洛德瑟林（Rod Serling）創作的美國電視影集。每集均為不同的獨立故事，類型包括心理恐怖、幻想、科幻、懸疑和心理驚悚，劇情常以一個可怕的大逆轉作為結局，同時帶出警世寓意。儘管洛德瑟林在 1975 年去世，《迷離境界》受歡迎程度讓他由不同編劇接手，一共推出三次重拍影集，第一次重拍（1985-89）、第二次（2002-03）、第三次（2019-2020）。

© Wikicommons

**Social Credit System 社會信用體系**
2014 年中國為了提高人民水準啟用此獎懲機制。全國設有 2 億台臉部偵測攝影機，闖紅燈、亂丟垃圾、訂餐廳 no show、地鐵進食喧嘩等，社會信用就扣分；捐血、捐款、當志工則加分。信用分數高，享有生活、教育、買房等優惠補助，工作招募優先錄取；若信用過低被列入「黑名單」，除了影響銀行信貸，機票、高鐵票都不能買。

© Wikicommons

▲《迷離境界》編劇 Rod Serling

第 3 季的〈急轉直下〉中，人們生活在社群媒體嘔夢般的世界中，每一次互動會被五星評比，每個人的評價都會影響他們的社經地位。4.2 星的蕾西正在努力達到 4.5 星，這樣她才能負擔更好的公寓。當她 4.8 星的兒時好友娜歐蜜邀請她在婚禮上擔任伴娘時，她知道這是她獲得 4 星以上的高評好機會。但是當她的航

▲ Lacie 為達到高評分，總是笑臉迎人

班被取消時，蕾西發脾氣並從評分中被減去整整一星。於是事情變得越來越糟，當她第二天到達鎮上時，她的評價過低，以至於娜歐蜜取消邀請她。被激怒的蕾西決定闖入婚禮，正如你想像的那樣，結果很糟。聽起來有點像中國的社會信用體系，對吧？

But not every story is **dystopian**. In "San Junipero," also from Season 3, two young women—shy Yorkie and [15]**outgoing** Kelly—meet at a nightclub called Tucker's in the beach town of San Junipero in 1987. The two meet again at Tucker's the following week, and Kelly takes Yorkie home for a one-night stand. But when Yorkie can't find Kelly on her next visit, a club [16]**regular** tells her to "try a different time." So she tries different decades till she finally finds Kelly in 2002. Wait, what's going on here? San Junipero, it turns out, is a **simulated** reality where the dead can live and the elderly can visit. Are Yorkie and Kelly dead or alive? And will they end up together in San Junipero? In this episode, for a change, technology helps create a happy ending.

▲ Gugu Mbatha-Raw 飾演 Kelly

▲ Mackenzie Davis 飾演 Yorkie

但並非每個故事都是暗黑社會的。同樣第 3 季的〈聖朱尼佩洛〉中，1987 年，兩個年輕女性——害羞的約克和外向的凱莉——在海灘小鎮聖朱尼佩洛的一家名為圖克酒吧的夜店見面。接下來的一周，兩人再次在圖克酒吧見面，凱莉帶約克回家發生一夜情。但是當約克在下次到鎮上找不到凱莉時，一位夜店常客告訴她「嘗試不同的時間」。所以她嘗試了不同的幾十年，直到 2002 年她終於找到了凱莉。等等，這是怎麼回事？原來聖朱尼佩羅是一個模擬現實，死者可以在此生活，老人可以參觀。約克和凱莉是死是活？他們最終會在聖朱尼佩羅在一起嗎？在這一集中，來點不一樣的科技幫助創造一個美好結局。

## 你的全部人生經歷

〔連恩與菲恩因為喬納斯而吵架〕

**Ffion** We've all **got our skeletons**. How about you and Gemma?

**Liam** What? I told you about Gemma. Gemma was a **nutcase**. But you never mentioned Jonas.

**Ffion** I did. I told you I **hooked up with** someone in Marrakesh.

**Liam** Jonas is Mr. Marrakesh?

**Ffion** It was a stupid thing....

**Liam** I thought Mr. Marrakesh was some sort of super cool.... Well, not him. Are you [1]**embarrassed** by that? 'Cause it's embarrassing. I'm sorry, [2]**Christ**, are you not embarrassed?

**Ffion** It was years ago.

**Liam** But you dated him for a month?

**Ffion** That's what I said.

**Liam** 'Cause when you told me about Mr. Marrakesh, it was a week.

©Wikipedia

©Shutterstock.com

---

## Vocabulary

1. **embarrassed** [ɪmˋbærəst] *(a.)*
   感到尷尬的
2. **Christ** [kraɪst] *(int./n.)* 天啊；基督

### 𝒯ongue-tied 𝒩o 𝑀ore

**have skeletons (in the closet)**
**家醜不得外揚**
Most people have a few skeletons in the closet. 每個人都有一些不為人知的秘密。

**hook up (with sb.) 與某人有染（交往，上床），與某人見面**
Did you hook up with that girl you met at the club last night? 昨晚你有跟在夜店認識的女生上床嗎？

菲恩　誰沒有過去啊，你跟潔瑪怎麼說？

連恩　什麼？我跟妳說過潔瑪的事，潔瑪是個蕭查某。但妳從來沒提過喬納斯。

菲恩　我有，我跟你說過在馬拉喀什跟人交往過。

連恩　喬納斯是馬拉喀什先生？

菲恩　當年不懂事嘛……

連恩　我以為馬拉喀什先生是個超酷的人，怎會是他。妳會覺得尷尬嗎？我覺得很丟臉。抱歉……天啊，妳不覺得尷尬嗎？

菲恩　那是多年前的事了。

連恩　但妳跟他交往過一個月？

菲恩　我說過啦。

連恩　但妳告訴我馬拉喀什先生的事，說的是一星期。

## 急轉直下 I

〔蕾西在機場劃位，地勤告訴她機位已滿〕

**³⁾Agent**　There's just nothing I can do.

Lacie　Christ, I mean, **⁴⁾surely**.

Agent　I'm gonna have to ask you to <u>moderate your language</u> there.

Lacie　Sorry. I'm maid of honor. I cannot miss this wedding.

Agent　And I am so sorry about that.

Lacie　Can you just call the **⁵⁾supervisor**?

Agent　I cannot do that.

Lacie　Call the fucking supervisor!

Agent　OK, that's **⁷⁾profanity**. We're <u>zero tolerance</u> on profanity. I have to serve the next customer. Can you step away, **⁰⁾ma'am**?

Lacie　No, no, no, no. God, just fucking help me!

地勤　我也沒辦法幫忙。

蕾西　天啊，一定有辦法吧？

地勤　請妳說話尊重點。

蕾西　對不起，我是伴娘，我不能錯過婚禮。

地勤　而我對此深感抱歉。

蕾西　妳能請主管來嗎？

地勤　我不能。

蕾西　立刻叫混蛋主管過來。

地勤　這樣很不敬，我們不容忍客人說粗口。我必須為下一位客人服務。能請妳讓位嗎，女士？

蕾西　不行，不行，這樣不行！天啊，快點幫我！

---

3. **agent** [ˋedʒənt] *(n.)* 地勤，代理人
4. **surely** [ˋʃʊrli] *(adv.)* 當然地，肯定地
5. **supervisor** [ˋsupə͵vaɪzə] *(n.)* 主管，監督者
6. **ma'am** [mæm] *(n.)* 女士尊稱 = madam

### 補充單字

**nutcase** [ˋnʌt͵kes] *(n.)*（口）瘋子
**profanity** [prəˋfænəti] *(n.)* 褻瀆語言

### *Tongue-tied No More*

**moderate one's language**
說話尊重點
Could you please moderate your language?
可以請你說話放尊重點嗎？

**zero tolerance**
絕不容許、毫不寬恕
Our school has a zero tolerance policy for bullying.
我們學校秉持絕不容許霸凌的政策。

## 急轉直下 II

〔蕾西的車子拋錨後，搭一位卡車司機的便車〕

Susan    Checking my ⁷**feed** for danger signs? I get it a lot. 1.4 gotta be an ˈ**antisocial** ˈ**maniac**, right?

Lacie    You seem….normal.

Susan    Thank you. It took some effort. What happened to you? I mean, you're a 2.8, but you don't look 2.8.

Lacie    That's not…this is temporary. I'm gonna ❶<u>turn it around</u>. I'm going to a wedding. Maid of honor. Wanna hear my speech?

Susan    No. So how come you're a 2.8?

Lacie    Well, I got ❶<u>marked down</u> at the airport for yelling, and they put me on double damage.

Susan    How did it feel?

Lacie    Awful. I was mad. Look at where it got me. But as long as I get to the wedding, do the speech, they'll overlook the 2.8. I'm with the bride.

## Vocabulary

7. **feed** [fid] *(n.)* 貼文動態

### Tongue-tied No More

**turn sth. around 扭轉局勢**
With the pandemic under control, the government hopes to turn the economy around.
隨著疫情受到控制，政府希望經濟可以復甦。

**mark down 減分，降價**
The teacher liked my essay, but she marked me down for poor spelling.
老師喜歡我的作文，但因為我拼字錯誤被她扣分。

蘇珊　在看我的貼文，怕我是危險人物？常有人這麼做，1.4 星一定是反社會瘋子，對吧？

蕾西　妳看起來很⋯正常。

蘇珊　謝謝。這需要一點努力。妳是怎麼了？我是說 2.8 星，但妳看起來不像會是 2.8 星。

蕾西　不，這只是暫時的。我會補回分數，我要去參加婚禮，我是伴娘。要聽我的致詞嗎？

蘇珊　不想。那妳怎麼會變成 2.8 星？

蕾西　呃，我在機場大叫，所以被降級，而且他們還加乘扣分。

蘇珊　感覺如何？

蕾西　很難過。當時我氣壞了，妳看現在我的下場。不過只要我在婚禮致詞，大家會忽視我只有 2.8 星。我是新娘的朋友。

# 聖朱尼佩洛

〔第一次跳完舞後，約克與凱莉正在聊天〕

**Yorkie** I've never been on a dance floor.

**Kelly** Never? As in the whole time you've been alive never?

**Yorkie** Never.

**Kelly** What are you, like, **Amish**? That's one [8]**sheltered** [9]**existence** you got there.

**Yorkie** Yeah, well. ⓣ As far as my family's concerned, I can't do anything.

**Kelly** Well, no one knows about even half the shit I ⓣ get up to. With your [10]**folks**, though, it's from a place of love, though, right? They worry.

**Yorkie** They don't worry. Just the concept of me enjoying myself would ⓣ blow their minds.

**Kelly** What would you like to do? That you've never done?

**Yorkie** Oh...so many things.

---

約克 我從沒站在舞池上。

凱莉 從來沒有？妳從小到大都沒有過？

約克 從來沒有。

凱莉 難不成妳是艾米許人嗎？妳的生活方式還真受到保護。

約克 是的…對我家人來說，我什麼都不能做。

凱莉 我是根本沒人知道我做什麼鳥事。不過妳父母是出於愛意吧？他們擔心妳。

約克 他們才不擔心。他們光想到我享受人生，一定會大吃一驚。

凱莉 妳想做什麼從沒做過的事情？

約克 哦…有好多想做的事。

---

8. **sheltered** [ˋʃɛltəd] *(a.)* 被保護的

9. **existence** [ɪgˋzɪstəns] *(n.)* 生活方式，存在

10. **folks** [foks] *(n.)* 父母，親屬

## *Tongue-tied No More*

### as far as sb./sth. is concerned 就某人、事而言

As far as I'm concerned, it's better to wait till the pandemic is over before going back to the gym. 就就我個人而言，最好等疫情結束再回健身房運動。

### get up to sth. 在做某事

I wonder what those two got up to last night. 我好奇那兩個人昨天晚上做了什麼事。

### blow one's mind 讓某人大吃一驚，使感到極度興奮

The movie *Black Widow* really blew my mind. 電影《黑寡婦》真的讓我超震撼的。

©Wikipedia

CRIME SCENE DO NOT CROSS

#cecilhotel #elisalam #joeberlinger

Felons Hub©Flicr

全文朗讀 ♫ 050　　單字 ♫ 051

# Crime Scene: Vanishing at the Cecil Hotel
## 《犯罪現場：賽西爾酒店失蹤事件》

NETFLIX

藍可兒恐怖飯店的死亡真相究竟為何

## Vocabulary

1. **documentary** [ˌdɑkjəˈmɛntəri]
   (n.) 紀錄片

2. **largely** [ˈlɑrdʒli] *(adv.)*
   大致上地

3. **miniseries** [ˈmɪniˌsɪriz] *(n.)*
   迷你影集

©pt.wikipedia

▲ 藍可兒照

Starting with the award-winning *Brother's Keeper*, a 1992 [1]**documentary** about a murder in a small New York town, Joe Berlinger has ❶ made a career out of directing true crime films and series. The director is most famous for *Paradise Lost: The Child Murders at Robin Hood Hills*, about the murder trial of three teenagers, who were released from prison after 18 years, [2]**largely** because of the film and its two sequels. After creating *Conversations with A Killer: The Ted Bundy Tapes* for Netflix in 2019, Berlinger returned to the streaming platform in 2021 with a second four-part [3]**miniseries**, *Crime Scene: The Vanishing at the Cecil Hotel*, about the mysterious disappearance and death of Canadian college student Elisa Lam.

喬貝林傑從 1992 年獲獎紀錄片《兄弟守護人》講述一起紐約小鎮謀殺案，就開始拍攝真實犯罪電影、影集作為職業導演生涯。這位導演最著名的作品是《失樂園：湖泊謀殺》，講述了三名青少年的謀殺案審判。他們在 18 年後釋放出獄，很大的原因就是因為這部電影及兩部續作。2019 年貝林傑為 Netflix 創作《與殺人魔對話：泰德邦迪訪談錄》之後，2021 年以第二部共四集的迷你影集《犯罪現場：塞西爾酒店的消失》重返串流平台，講述加拿大女大生藍可兒神秘的失蹤死亡案。

▲ 犯罪紀錄片導演
Joe Berlinger

▲《失樂園：湖泊謀殺》海報

In January 2013, 21-year-old Elisa Lam, the daughter of [1]**Cantonese** [4]**immigrants**, leaves Vancouver on a solo trip to California. In a blog post, she writes that she's [5]**stressed** about university and trying to figure out what she wants out of life. After spending a few days in San Diego, she arrives in L.A. and [6]**checks into** the Cecil Hotel on January 28. Over the next few days, Lam does typical tourist things, like going to the [7]**taping** of a TV show, and visiting a bookstore to buy gifts for friends and family. But then, she just vanishes. Lam has the habit of calling her parents every day, and when they don't [8]**hear from** her on February 1, they call the Los Angeles Police Department, LAPD and report her missing.

4. **immigrant** [ˋɪməɡrənt] *(n.)*
移民

5. **stressed** [strɛst] *(a.)*
感到緊張壓力的

6. **check into/in** *(phr.)*
入住（飯店）

7. **taping** [ˋtepɪŋ] *(n.)*
節目錄影

8. **hear from** *(phr.)*
得知某人的消息

9. **depression** [dɪˋprɛʃən] *(n.)*
蕭條，不景氣

10. **decline** [dɪˋklaɪn] *(n./v.)*
衰退，下降

2013 年 1 月 21 歲的廣東裔移民第二代女子藍可兒離開溫哥華，獨自前往加州旅行。在一篇部落格貼文中，她寫道對大學感到壓力，並試圖要想清楚她人生到底要的是什麼。在聖地亞哥待了幾天後，她於 1 月 28 日抵達洛杉磯，入住塞西爾酒店。在接下來的幾天裡，藍可兒就像典型觀光客，參觀電視節目錄影現場，去書店買禮物給家人、朋友。但隨後，她就突然消失了。藍可兒有每天打電話給父母的習慣，但 2 月 1 日他們沒有接到她的消息時，因此打電話聯絡洛杉磯警方並報失蹤。

But before the investigation begins, we learn more about the show's other main character: the Cecil Hotel. Built in 1924 as a business hotel for $1 million—a large sum back then—the 700-room Cecil was a success in its early years. But when the Great [9]**Depression** hit in 1929, the hotel, and the area around it, known as **Skid Row**, went into a long period of [10]**decline**. Skid Row turned into one of the country's most dangerous neighborhoods, but the Cecil seemed to attract more than its

▲ 賽西爾酒店已改名 Stay on Main Hotel

11. **resident** [ˋrɛzədənt] (n.)
　　居民，住戶

12. **stalker** [ˋstɔkɚ] (n.)
　　潛行跟蹤者

13. **detective** [dɪˋtɛktɪv] (n.)
　　偵探

14. **eventually** [ɪˋvɛntʃuəli] (adv.)
　　最終地，最後地

15. **fascinate** [ˋfæsən͵et] (v.)
　　迷住，吸引

16. **bizarre** [bɪˋzɑr] (a.)
　　奇異古怪的

### 補充單字

**Cantonese** [͵kæntəˋniz] (a./n.)
　　廣東的；廣東話
**sleuth** [sluθ] (n.) 偵探

© Shutterstock.com

share of violence and death. So many suicides happened there over the years that [11]**residents** began calling it "The Suicide, and it was even home to serial killers like **Richard Ramirez** better known as the Night [12]**Stalker**.

但在調查開始之前，我們更了解該影集的另一個主角：塞西爾酒店。建於 192_ 年，耗資 100 萬美元（當年是一筆巨款）建造為商務酒店，擁有 700 間客房 的塞西爾酒店初期生意興隆。然而 1929 年美國經濟大蕭條衝擊，酒店及其周 邊地區，也就是現在洛杉磯著名的貧民窟 Skid Row，陷入了長期的衰退。Skid Row 成為全美國最危險的街區之一，但塞西爾酒店似乎吸引更多暴力與死亡。 多年來，這裡發生過無數自殺事件，住戶開始稱它為「自殺酒店」，甚至人稱「夜 行者」的連環殺人魔理察拉米雷茲等，也居住在這裡。

As soon as Lam goes missing, the LAPD sends a team o_ [13]**detectives** to search the Cecil, but no trace of the girl is found [14]**Eventually**, after viewing hundreds of hours of security camera footage, police spot Lam in one of the hotel elevators on the day of her disappearance. But then ❼the trail grows cold, so the LAPD releases the video to the public, hoping for new leads Because of Lam's strange behavior, it instantly goes viral. In the video, she enters the elevator, pushes random buttons, steps in and out of the elevator, waves her arms, hides in the corner, and finally leaves. [15]**Fascinated** by the video, Internet `sleuths` come up with dozens of theories to explain her [16]**bizarre** behavior and disappearance, from drugs to mental illness to ghosts. But in the end, it's not the Internet sleuths, or the police, who solve the mystery. To find out what happened to Lam, you'll have to watch *Crime Scene*!

藍可兒失蹤後，洛杉磯警方立刻派出偵探大隊搜索塞西爾酒店，但完全沒發現 她的蹤跡。最終，觀看數百小時監視影片後，警方在她失蹤當天酒店的一處電 梯中，發現了藍可兒的畫面，但後來這條線索沒有結果了。洛杉磯警方因此向 大眾發布了這段影片，希望能有新的線索。由於藍可兒的怪異行為，影片立刻 在網路上瘋狂轉發。影片中，她進入電梯，隨意按按鈕，進出電梯，揮舞手臂， 躲在角落，最後離開。網友鄉民偵探被這段影片所吸引，紛紛提出許多種理論 來解釋她的怪異行為與消失，從吸毒到精神疾病再到鬼魂纏身。但最終，解開 謎團的不是網友鄉民偵探，也不是警察。要了解藍可兒事件真相，你必須親自 收看《犯罪現場》！

**make a career out of sth. 以…作為職業**
Taiwanese Olympic athlete Kuo Hsing-chun has made a career out of weightlifting.
台灣奧運選手郭婞淳以舉重運動作為職業。

**the trail grows cold 隨時間線索證據消失匿跡**
The police now fear the criminal's trail has gone cold. 警方擔心現在已無法追蹤罪犯的線索。

## Grammar Master

### 被動分詞構句

"Fascinated by the video, Internet sleuths come up with theories…"
原句為 Internet sleuths are fascinated by the video, and Internet sleuths come up with theories… 主詞都是 Internet sleuths 網友偵探，省略重複主詞，are fascinated 被吸引著迷為被動，省略 be 動詞留下 Vpp. 過去分詞，最後省略連接詞 and。分詞構句可讓句子閱讀起來更精簡，更多例子：
例：The family was shocked by the train derailment, and the family burst into tears.
→ Shocked by the train derailment, the family burst into tears. 家屬因火車出軌意外，潸然落淚。
例：Harvey Weinstein was found guilty of sex abuse, and he was sentenced to 23 years in prison.
→ Found guilty of sex abuse, Harvey Weinstein was sentenced to 23 years in prison.
哈維溫斯坦被判性侵罪，判刑行 23 年監禁。

## EZpedia

**Great Depression 經濟大蕭條**
1929 年～ 1933 年間最嚴重的全球經濟大衰退。第一次世界大戰後，美國經濟快速成長。大量資金湧入股市，許多人舉債高風險投資，造成經濟泡沫化。1929 年 10 月 24 日華爾街股市崩盤，到 10 月 29 日已成為全球股災。大量公司破產，國際貿易銳減 50%，美國失業率飆升到 25%，經濟大蕭條也釀成自殺潮。

**Skid Row 貧民窟**
skid 是「打滑」，慣用語 on the skids 形容不斷衰退、每下愈況。skid row 在英文中指經濟條件落後的街區，也就是「貧民窟」的意思。許多美國大城市都有 skid row，節目中的 Skid Row 位於洛杉磯市中心，正式行政名稱為 Central City East 中央東區，佔地 56 個街區，有全美國最多的街友人口，約 6,000 ～ 10,000 名露宿街頭。該區充斥暴力、犯罪、毒品、情色交易等問題。

Juan Llauro©Shutterstock.com

**Richard Ramirez 理察拉米雷茲**
美國連環殺手、強姦犯，媒體稱為「夜間狙擊者」及「夜行者」（Night Stalker）。1984 年 4 月到 1985 年 8 月，在大洛杉磯、舊金山犯下多起女性謀殺案。2021 年 Netflix 也推出紀錄影集《夜行者：極惡連環殺手 Night Stalker: The Hunt For a Serial Killer》。

〔藍可兒在 Tumblr 發貼文〕

Stressed about university.

Somehow we're supposed to jump to some kind of [1]**maturity** right after leaving high school. You enter a ❶ <u>crash course</u> into the *shithole* that is figuring out what the hell you want out of life. Damn it, people. We're trying to figure things out.

I want to get away. Travel. Must travel this summer for *sanity*.

Must find job to get monies for traveling.

Must [2]**convince** parents to allow me to travel on my own.

I'm *freaking* 21 now. Going to be OK.

Planning, planning, planning.

San Diego, Los Angeles, Santa Cruz, and San Francisco. The West Coast tour.

[3]**Suggestions** and [4]**recommendations** highly, highly appreciated and needed.

---

## Vocabulary

1. **maturity** [məˋtjʊrəti] (n.) 成熟期
2. **convince** [kənˋvɪns] (v.) 成熟，說服
3. **suggestion** [səgˋdʒɛstʃən] (n.) 建議
4. **recommendation** [͵rɛkəmɛnˋdeʃən] (n.) 推薦
5. **urgency** [ˋɝdʒənsi] (n.) 緊急，迫切
6. **investigator** [ɪnˋvɛstə͵getə] (n.) 調查員

### 補充單字

**shithole** [ˋʃɪt͵hol] (n.) 骯髒不堪的地方
**sanity** [ˋsænəti] (n.) 神智清楚，精神健康
**freaking** [ˋfrikɪŋ] (a./adv.) 用以加強語氣或表示憤怒
**homicide** [ˋhɑmə͵saɪd] (n.) 他殺，謀殺
**disoriented** [dɪsˋɔriɛntɪd] (a.) 失去方向的

上大學壓力很大。

怎麼我們才一離開高中，就要馬上跳到成熟階段。進入屎坑速成課，釐清自己想要怎麼樣的人生。天殺的！大家，我們還在努力摸索。

我想要逃得遠遠，去旅行。這個夏天必須旅行，否則會瘋掉。

必須找工作，才有錢旅行。

必須說服父母讓我自己一個人去旅行。

拜託，我都已經 21 歲好嗎！一定沒問題的。

計畫⋯計畫⋯計畫。

聖地牙哥、洛杉磯、聖塔克魯茲到舊金山，西岸之旅。

亟需也感激任何的旅行建議和推薦。

## 警探調查

〔前洛杉磯刑警偵探提姆馬希亞與格雷卡丁討論藍可兒失蹤案〕

Marcia　We were told that we had picked up a missing persons case. She was a young female from Canada, traveling throughout California by herself, and there was a sense of panic. There was probably about 18 detectives from Robbery-**Homicide** Division that responded.

Kading　Elisa Lam's family told the police department that she would typically call every day. It was just routine for her to check in, and she hadn't called, and that concerned them. So there was a true sense of [5]**urgency**.

Marcia　We sat there and we discussed, "What are the possibilities?" One, that she doesn't want to be found. She's 🄣 <u>off the radar</u> by choice. Maybe she was **disoriented**, not being familiar with Los Angeles, and she's lost. Or could it be something worse than that…where she was a victim of some type of accident or some type of crime?

Kading　The [6]**investigators** begin to exchange information with Elisa Lam's family to figure out where she was last seen, last known to have been, and they had learned that it was the hotel where she was staying.

---

馬希亞　我們得知已接下一起人口失蹤案，一名加拿大年輕女子獨自來加州旅行。這起案件不禁讓人恐慌，大概有 18 位重案組警探到現場處理。

卡丁　藍可兒的家人告訴警方，她每天都會打電話照例報平安。但那天她都沒打電話回家，讓他們很擔憂，感覺真的很緊急。

馬希亞　我們坐下討論會有哪些可能性　第一，她不想被找到，她選擇失去音訊；又或許因為她不熟悉洛杉磯，分不清方向迷路；也可能是更糟糕的狀況，她遭到某種意外，或成為某種犯罪下的受害者？

卡丁　調查人員開始和藍可兒的家人交換資訊，釐清最後她被看見的地方。他們所知的最後去處是她住的酒店。

### Tongue-tied No More

**crash course 速成課程**
I took a crash course in French before my trip to Paris.
我去巴黎前參加了一個法語速成班。

**off the radar**
**消失不知去向，不為所知的**
radar 雷達，在雷達範圍外就是「消失的，不為所知的」。
The Instagram celeb suddenly went off the radar.
IG 網紅突然隱身匿跡。

## 電梯畫面

### Tongue-tied No More

**back to square one 回到原點**

The idea didn't work, so we had to go back to square one.

原本的想法無效，所以我們只好重新開始。

**no-brainer 不用思考的決定**

Accepting such a good position was a no-brainer for Michael.

對麥可而言，如此優渥的職位不需思考就接受了。

**an eye-opener
令人大開眼界的事物**

My trip to India was an eye-opener.

去印度旅行讓我大開眼界。

▲《犯罪現場》海報

〔警探決定公布電梯監視畫面〕

| | |
|---|---|
| Marcia | And since there was no information that was developed out of the hotel, now we're **back to square one**. |
| Kading | They really don't have any other answers. So now you're hoping that the public can assist you. |
| Marcia | We need the public's help to put more eyes out on the street. The last **footage** that we had of Elisa before her disappearance was the footage we found of her inside the elevator. So it was decided that we would release the video. We owe it to the family to find her. We don't have the resources. It was a **no-brainer**. So we put it out. That's where the case starts to go **askew**. |

馬希亞　因為在酒店內的搜索毫無斬獲，我們回到了原點。

卡丁　他們真的沒有其他答案，所以現在是希望大眾可以協助。

馬希亞　我們需要大眾幫忙，有更多的耳目能在街上注意。我們取得藍可兒失蹤前最後的畫面是發現她在電梯裡頭，所以我們決定公布那段監視器畫面。為了家屬我們必須找到她。我們資源不夠，所以不用想也知道，要公布出去。此時本案開始變調。

© 截圖 YouTube BuzzFeed Unsolved Network

# 死亡飯店

〔前賽西爾酒店飯店經理訪問中談到這裡發生許多死亡案〕

Unfortunately, a lot of them were thinking there's some crazy, [7]**creepy** person behind the scenes that just doesn't care and is running this hotel where all these bad things happen, and it's not true. That's one of the reasons I wanted to do the interview, because I want the world to see that who was actually running it really cared about the hotel and was running it properly. But I would say there are a lot of, like, [8]**unique** challenges when you are running a hotel like the Cecil. A lot came with the place. It wasn't even first couple days in the job where the [9]**maintenance** manager said that we had a problem. I said, "What do you mean?" One of the, um, guests died at the hotel. It was hard to [10]**process**. Before working at the hotel, I mean, I'd never had any experience with a dead body or **coroner**, you know, or even the police. That was, like, ❶ <u>a real eye-opener</u> for me. Come to find out, well, you know, this happens all the time. The maintenance manager, he walked me through the entire hotel. Along the way, he would just point and say, "Someone died here, someone died there." Suicides, **overdoses**, murders. At one point, I think I asked him, "Is there a room here that, like, maybe somebody hasn't died in?"

可惜很多人認為幕後有個毫不在乎的詭異瘋子，在經營這家發生這些壞事的酒店。這不是真的，那也是我要受訪的原因之一，因為我要全世界看到當初的經理很在意酒店，也有妥善經營。但我會說經營賽西爾這樣的酒店會遇到許多獨特的挑戰，和這地方本身很有關係。我當時來這裡工作才沒幾天，維護經理就說有問題了，我說：「什麼意思？」酒店有個住客死了，這很難消化。到這家酒店工作前，我從來沒有遇到過屍體或是驗屍官，甚至警察。那真的讓我大開眼界，後來發現這裡動不動就發生這種事。維護經理帶著我看整家酒店，沿途他會指出：「有人死在這裡，有人死在那裡。」自殺、吸毒過量、謀殺案。有一度我還問他「有哪間房是沒死過人的嗎？」

# NETFLIX

# NARCOS

CARCEL OTTO JUDICIAL
MEDELLIN

128482

**#pabloescobar #narco**
**#medellincartel #DEA**

©Wikicommons

## *Narcos*《毒梟》

### 一日賺進 **21** 億哥倫比亞巨富毒梟艾斯科巴

**NETFLIX**

### Vocabulary

1. **height** [haɪt] *(n.)* 鼎盛時期

2. **establish** [ɪˈstæblɪʃ] *(v.)*
   建立，創辦

3. **smuggle** [ˈsmʌɡəl] *(v.)*
   走私，smuggler *(n.)* 走私販

©Wikicommons

▲ 巴西演員 Wagner Moura 以流利西班牙語飾演艾斯科巴

During the ¹⁾**height** of his power in the 1980s, ˙**drug lord** Pablo Escobar controlled 80% of the world's ˙**cocaine** market. The Medellín **Cartel**, which he ²⁾**established** and ran, made $70 million a day ²⁾**smuggling** the drug, most of which ended up in the United States. **G** By the time of his death in 1993, he'd built a fortune of $30 billion, making him one of the world's richest men, and the wealthiest criminal in history. The first two seasons of Netflix crime drama *Narcos*, filmed on location in Colombia, tell Escobar's story, from his rise in the 1970s and reign as the "King of Cocaine" in the '80s, to his ˙**downfall** at the hands of Colombian police and U.S. **DEA agents** in the '90s. Season 3 of *Narcos* follows the story of the Cali Cartel, which rises to replace the Medellín Cartel after Escobar's death.

1980 年代鼎盛時期，毒梟大王帕布洛艾斯科巴掌控了全球 80% 的古柯鹼市場。他創立經營的麥德林販毒集團，透過走私古柯鹼一日可賺取 7000 萬美元，大

部分毒品最終流向美國。到 1993 年去世時，他已經積累了 300 億美元的財富，使他成為世界上最富有的富豪之一，也是歷史上最有錢的罪犯。Netflix 警匪劇《毒梟》前兩季場景攝於哥倫比亞，講述艾斯科巴的故事，從 1970 年代崛起，80 年代榮升「古柯鹼之王」，到 90 年代在哥倫比亞警察和美國緝毒局探員手中衰弱。《毒梟》第 3 季敘述在艾斯科巴死後，卡利集團如何取代麥德林集團。

We first meet DEA agent Steve Murphy and his "**asshole**" partner Javier Peña in 1989 in Bogotá, Colombia, where they're working to ❶ take down Escobar and his cartel. Using a plane to listen to [4]**satellite** phone conversations, they learn that Poison, one of the drug lord's top **hitmen**, is meeting with friends at a bar that night. So they inform a special Colombian police unit, which arrives at the bar and [5]**sprays** it with bullets, killing Poison and two other hitmen. Next, we jump back to 1973 to learn about the cartel's origins—in Chile. **Augusto Pinochet** has just ❷ come to power, and he's busy shutting down cocaine [6]**labs** and killing dealers. When the firing [7]**squad** bullets miss drug [8]**chemist** Mateo "Cockroach" Moreno, he flees to Colombia and partners with Pablo Escobar, a smuggler of TVs and cigarettes who has larger ambitions—the U.S. illegal drug market.

Kathy Hutchins©S

▲ Boyd Holbrook 飾演墨菲

4. **satellite** [ˋsætə͵laɪt] (n.) 衛星

5. **spray** [spre] (v.) 掃射

6. **lab** [læb] (n.)
實驗室 = laboratory

7. **squad** [skwɑd] (n.) 小隊

8. **chemist** [ˋkɛmɪst] (n.)
製藥家，化學家

1989 年緝毒局探員史蒂夫墨菲和他的「混蛋」搭檔哈維爾潘納，在哥倫比亞首都波哥大籌劃打敗艾斯科巴販毒集團。他們利用偵察機監聽衛星電話，得知毒梟大王手下其中一名頭號殺手毒藥當晚將在酒吧與朋友會面，於是通報哥倫比亞特殊警察部隊。當晚特殊部隊抵達酒吧掃射子彈，殺死了毒藥與另外兩名殺手。接下來，我們回溯到 1973 年認識販毒集團的起源——智利。奧古斯托皮諾切特剛上台，正著手關閉古柯實驗室與斬除毒販。行刑隊子彈未擊中製藥化學家「蟑螂」馬泰歐莫雷諾，他逃往哥倫比亞並與帕布洛艾斯科合作。帕布洛艾斯科原是電視與香煙走私販，但他有更大的野心——美國非法毒品市場。

### 補充單字

**drug lord** 毒梟 = drug baron
**cocaine** [koˋken] (n.) 古柯鹼
**downfall** [ˋdaʊn͵fɔl] (n.)
沒落，毀滅
**asshole** [ˋæs͵hol] (n.)（粗）混蛋
**hitman** [ˋhɪt͵mæn] (n.) 職業殺手
**bust** [bʌst] (v./n.) 逮捕，突襲緝查

Which brings us to Miami. The year is 1979, and Steve Murphy is a young DEA agent [9]**busting** hippies for small amounts of [10]**marijuana**. By the early '80s, thanks to the Medellin Cartel's

─────────────────────────

**⟨ Tongue-tied No More ⟩**

**take sb. down 擊敗、打垮某人**
The Indiana Pacers took down Cleveland, 80-74. 印第安納溜馬隊以 80 比 74 擊敗克里夫蘭騎士隊。

**come to power 上台，奪得政權**
The Nazis came to power in Germany in 1933. 德國納粹於 1933 年上台取得政權。

9. **seize** [siz] (v.)
扣押，沒收

10. **demand** [dɪˋmænd] (n./v.)
需求

11. **supply** [səˋplaɪ] (n./v.)
供應

12. **bail** [bel] (n./v.)
保釋金；保釋

13. **betray** [bɪˋtre] (v.)
背叛，出賣

14. **vow** [vaʊ] (v./n.)
發誓，誓言

15. **revenge** [rɪˋvɛndʒ] (n./v.)
復仇，報復

### 補充單字

**marijuana** [ˌmɛrəˋwɑnə] (n.) 大麻
**pellet** [ˋpɛlɪt] (n.) 顆粒，彈丸
**undercover** [ˌʌndəˋkʌvɚ] (a.)
臥底的，秘密的
**bounty** [ˋbaʊntɪ] (n.) 懸賞金

### Tongue-tied No More

**take sb. out**
殺害、除掉某人
Foreign killers took Haiti's president out. 外國殺手槍殺海地總統。

**on one's home turf**
在某人的地盤、勢力範圍
England lost the Euro2020 championship on their home turf.
2020 歐洲盃冠軍賽英格蘭足球隊在自己的主場上挫敗。

growing business, Murphy and his fellow agents go from [9]**seizing** grams of marijuana to kilos of cocaine. Escobar hires Lion, who flies to Miami with the drug hidden in his clothes, and then hires women to make the same trip after swallowing cocaine **pellets**. As [10]**demand** and [11]**supply** increase, they bring in a crazy German-Colombian named Carlos Lehder to fly coke to Miami in their own small planes—over 1,000 kilos a flight.

現在來到邁阿密。1979 這一年，史蒂夫墨菲是一名年輕的緝毒局探員，負責取締逮補持有少量大麻的嬉皮。到了 80 年代初期，由於麥德林販毒集團日益壯大，墨菲和他的同事從原本取締幾克大麻，變成數公斤的古柯鹼。埃斯科巴雇用萊昂，讓他將毒品藏在衣內攜帶飛往邁阿密，並雇用女性吞下古柯鹼藥丸一同加入旅行。隨著供需的增加，他們請來了一個名叫卡洛斯萊德的瘋狂德裔哥倫比亞人，用他們的私人小飛機將古柯鹼空運到邁阿密——每次飛行超過 1,000 公斤。

Murphy gets a taste of this violence during an **undercover** drug buy from a Colombian dealer named Germán Zapata. During the deal, a hitman named La Quica shows up and kills Zapata and Murphy's partner, then escapes back to Colombia after Escobar pays his $2 million [12]**bail**. Zapata, it turns out, was selling coke for Cockroach, who was not only stealing from Escobar, but also [13]**betrayed** him to the police. After sending La Quica to ⓣ **take out** Zapata, Escobar shoots Cockroach himself. [14]**Vowing** [15]**revenge** for the murder of his partner, Murphy moves to Colombia to fight Escobar ⓣ **on his home turf**, which brings us back to where we started in 1989. When one of Escobar's men sees Murphy counting bodies at the bar where Poison was taken out, the drug lord puts a $500,000 **bounty** on the agent's head. Now the fight is personal.

墨菲與一位名叫赫曼薩帕塔的哥倫比亞毒販進行臥底毒品交易時，嚐到了這種暴力的滋味。在交易期間，一名叫做拉奎卡的殺手現身擊斃薩帕塔和墨菲的搭檔。在艾斯科巴支付了 200 萬美元的保釋金後，拉奎卡逃回哥倫比亞。原來薩帕塔為蟑螂效命賣古柯鹼，蟑螂不僅從艾斯科巴那竊取，而且還背叛他，把他出賣給警方。在派拉奎卡去除掉薩帕塔後，艾斯科巴親手擊斃蟑螂。墨菲發誓要為殺死的搭檔報仇，為了打擊艾斯科巴，他搬到毒梟大王的地盤哥倫比亞，故事就這樣回到 1989 年。當艾斯科巴的一名手下看到墨菲正在毒藥陣亡的酒吧檢視死亡數時，毒梟大王祭出 50 萬美元懸賞金，要獵探員墨菲。這場鬥爭現在演變成私人恩怨。

## 過去完成式

"By the time of his death in 1993, he'd built a fortune of $30 billion." 在 1993 年去世前,他已累積 300 億美元的財富。句中 he'd built = he had built(過去完成式)

● **By 是「在⋯之前」的意思,1993 年是過去,搭配「過去完成式 had + vpp」,表達「在過去某件事前就已經發生了」,例如:**

例:By the time I arrived at the theater, the movie <u>had</u> already <u>started</u>.
　　早在我抵達電影院前(過去簡單式),電影就已經開始了(過去完成式)。

例:By the time my father came home, we <u>had gone</u> to bed.
　　在爸爸回家之前(過去簡單式),我們早已睡了(過去完成式)。

# E Z pedia

### narco 毒販,毒品的
字根 narco- 來自古希臘字 nárkē,代表「麻木的,幻覺的」,如 narcosis「昏迷狀態」、narcotic「麻醉藥,幻覺迷藥、毒品」。narco 這個字泛指「毒品」相關的事物,如:緝毒警員(narc);毒品的。劇名 Narcos 源自於西班牙語 narcotraficante(drug dealer)指的就是毒販的意思。

### cartel 販毒集團
來自德語 *kartell*,原指同類型產業組成集團控制價格與數量,避免過度競爭導致的整體利益下跌。例如,石油出口國組織(OPEC)成員國達成統一國際油價與產量。
然而,現今用法則是西班牙文的 *cártel*,指墨西哥、哥倫比亞等國的「販毒集團」。早期集團達成共同的毒品價格,但因為權力、利益鬥爭分裂,這個詞彙卻沿用下來,指從事毒品走私等暴力犯罪組織。

### Drug Enforcement Administration, DEA 美國緝毒局
美國司法部下屬的執法機構,負責打擊非法毒品交易與使用,並且承擔國外毒品進口之調查。DEA agent 為「美國緝毒局特探員」。

### Augusto Pinochet 奧古斯多皮諾契特
(1915 年 11 月 25 日- 2006 年 12 月 10 日)前智利總統、軍事獨裁者,統治智利長達 16 年,為任職時間最長的總統。1973 年,皮諾契特在美國支持下發動流血政變,推翻蘇聯支持的民選左翼總統阿葉德(Salvador Allende),建立右翼軍政府。任內進行自由經濟改革,使智利經濟快速發展,並致力打擊毒品犯罪。但另一方面,迫害屠殺反對人士、社會主義者,智利陷入軍事獨裁統治,民主與人權倒退,直到 1980 年下台,智利才得以民主化。

### hippy 嬉皮
1960 至 1970 年代反抗傳統習俗與政治的年輕人,批判社會不公、企業貪婪、傳統道德約束,以及美國參與越戰的殘酷。嬉皮常使用藥物逃脫現實以改變心境。

〔帕布洛的堂弟古斯托沃在一間餐廳將他介紹給蟑螂〕

Cockroach　Well, I get the 1)**paste** in Peru. I will handle the chemical part of production, and all the other details in producing this 2)**exquisite** white powder. What I need from you is to help me get it into Colombia.

Gustavo　Now tell him how much it costs.

Cockroach　In Chile, this little thing costs ten 3)**bucks** a gram.

Pablo　They sell it by grams?

Cockroach　Yes, it's very good. Look, you do a little bit, and in 20 minutes, you want to do some more. Also, it's a 4)**digestive** aid. It makes you want to ☞take a shit. It's very clean, this stuff. Want some?

Pablo　If this is really that good and we can make some money, we can find room on our trucks.

Cockroach　We can sell it in Bogotá, Barranquilla, Cali, Cartagena. We're going to be rich.

Pablo　Well, look, Cockroach. You don't have any 5)**vision**, my friend. If it costs ten dollars a gram here, imagine how much it will sell for in Miami.

---

## Vocabulary

1. **paste** [pest] (n.) 膏狀
2. **exquisite** [ɪk`skwɪzɪt] (a.) 精緻的
3. **buck** [bʌk]（口）美元，錢
4. **digestive** [dɪ`dʒɛstɪv] (a.) 消化的
5. **vision** [`vɪʒən] (n.) 遠見，眼光

### Tongue-tied No More

**take a shit 拉屎**
The neighbor's dog is taking a shit in our front yard again! 鄰居的狗又在我們家前面庭院拉屎。

蟑螂　好，我在秘魯有古柯膏，我會處理化學製程與所有其他製造頂級白粉的細節。我只需要你幫我弄進哥倫比亞。

古斯托沃　告訴他這值多少錢。

蟑螂　在智利，這個小東西 一公克值十塊美金。

帕布洛　他們用公克賣嗎？

蟑螂　對，這非常好，你看，你吸一點，20分鐘內你就想吸更多。還有這幫助消化，讓你想上廁所。這東西非常純，想來一點嗎？

帕布洛　如果這真的那麼好，有錢可賺，可以在我們的卡車裡，挪點空間出來。

蟑螂　我們可以在波哥大、巴蘭幾亞、卡利、卡塔赫納大賺一筆。

帕布洛　好聽著， 蟑螂，你真沒有遠見，如果在這裡一公克值十美金，想像一下，在邁阿密會賣多少錢？

# 重新談判

〔警察上校埃雷拉想從艾斯科巴分到更大餅〕

Herrera　Sit down, Mr. Pablo. We counted more than 300 kilos in those trucks. That's a [1]**street value** of over four million dollars, Mr. Escobar. And you only gave us $150,000.

Robert Avgustin©shutterstock.com

Pablo　Well, that's what we agreed upon.

Herrera　You know something? I make deals for a living. Now you can either accept my deal or accept the consequences. You decide.

Pablo　Or we can [6]**renegotiate**, ❶ come to an agreement, and everyone goes home happy. I'll give you one million dollars...under one [7]**condition**.

Herrera　What is it?

Pablo　Someone in my organization gave you the street value of my cocaine. [8]**Otherwise**, how would you know? Give me a name...and you won't have to split the cash with him.

---

埃雷拉　請坐，帕布洛先生。我們數過那些卡車裡，有超過三百公斤的貨，黑市價超過四百萬美金，艾斯科巴先生，而你只給我們 15 萬美金。

帕布洛　呃，那是我們原本都同意的。

埃雷拉　你知道嗎？我做交易維生。你不是接受我交易，就是接受結果，你來決定。

帕布洛　或者我們可以重新談判，達成共識，大家都快樂回家。我願意給你一百萬美金……只有一個條件。

埃雷拉　什麼條件？

帕布洛　我的組織內有人告訴你，我古柯鹼的市價。否則你怎麼會知道呢？告訴我名字，你就不必跟他分錢。

6. **renegotiate** [ˌrinɪˈgoʃiˌet] (v.)
   重新協商
7. **condition** [kənˈdɪʃən] (n.) 條件
8. **otherwise** [ˈʌðəˌwaɪz] (adv.)
   否則，不然

### 補充單字

street value 黑市價格

### Tongue-tied No More

**come to an agreement**
**達成協議、共識**
Israel and Palestine came to an agreement after days of bombing.
在多日轟炸後，以色列與巴勒斯坦達成協議。

# 埋藏現金

[ 古斯塔沃與帕布洛正討論該如何處理堆積如山賺來的現金 ]

Gustavo　You're spending too much cash, Pablo. You have Picassos, Dalís, farms, houses, apartments, boats, planes, cars. I told you we have to ❶ <u>fly low</u>. If you keep spending like that, you're going to end up in *Forbes* magazine. And if that happens, the government is going to ❶ <u>have our asses</u>.

Pablo　Enough, Gustavo, enough. What do you want me to say? Bury it.

Gustavo　How's that?

Pablo　Bury the cash. And ❶ <u>cut the bullshit</u>. Go on, **pussy**.

---

### ⟨ Tongue-tied No More ⟩

**fly low 低調謹慎行事**

I was late for work, but I managed to fly low and slip into the office unnoticed. 我上班遲到，但成功低調潛入辦公室，沒被發現。

**have sb.'s ass (in a sling)**
**嚴刑處罰**

My boss is gonna have my ass in a sling if I don't finish this project on time. 如果我不準時完成企劃案，老闆會嚴重處罰我。

**cut the bullshit/crap 廢話少說**

Cut the bullshit——I know you're lying to me. 廢話少說，我知道你是在騙我。

**Eat me! 不爽咬我啊！**

Oh, eat me, will you? I won't do anything you say! 不爽咬我啊！敢嗎？我才不會照你說的做！

古斯塔沃　你花太多錢了，帕布洛。畢卡索和米羅的畫作、農場、房子、公寓、船、飛機、車子。我告訴過你我們必須低調。如果一直這樣花錢，你最後會上《富比士》雜誌。如果發生那種事，政府就會抓到我們。

帕布洛　夠了，古斯塔沃，夠了。你要我說什麼？就埋起來啊。

古斯塔沃　你說什麼？

帕布洛　把現金埋起來。然後別再胡扯了。去做啊，死娘炮。

# 毒梟開趴

〔哈維爾潘納將墨菲介紹給美國駐波哥大大使館緝毒局小組〕

Peña      Murphy, this is Weaver and Wisnicki. These guys are **R.I.P.** "**Retired** in place."

Wisnicki    ❶ Eat me, Peña.

Peña      Paid vacation's over, **fellas**. *[in the Military Group office]* **Jarheads**, this is Murphy. Murphy, this is Mil Group. They advise Colombian military on **communist** threats in the countryside. *[picks up files]*

Officer    Hey, those are **classified**.

Peña      Now they're declassified. *[throws files back on desk]*

*[Peña and Murphy enter the ambassador's office]*

Ambassador    Why do you need this **intel**?

Peña      There's an unusual number of **prostitutes** headed to Medellín this weekend. Every **high-end** girl in Bogotá. First class **airfare**, five-star hotels. The narcos are having a meeting and then a party.

---

潘納      墨菲，這是韋佛和威士尼奇。這些人就是所謂的混吃等退休。

威士尼奇    不爽咬我啊，潘納。

潘納      給薪假結束了，同學，墨菲和我要去麥德林。〔進入軍隊辦公室〕各位，這位是墨菲。墨菲，這是軍團。他們會告知哥倫比亞軍方共產黨在鄉間的威脅。〔拿起檔案〕

官員      嘿，那些是機密

潘納      現在銷密了。〔將檔案丟回桌上〕

〔潘納與墨菲進入大使辦公室〕

大使      你為什麼需要這個情報？

潘納      有不尋常數量的妓女，波哥大所有高價女子要在這週末前往麥德林，購買頭等艙機票，訂五星級飯店。很顯然毒販要開會，然後開派對。

## Vocabulary

9. **retired** [rɪˋtaɪrd] *(a.)* 退休的
10. **fella** [ˋfɛlə] *(n.)* 夥計，朋友 = fellow
11. **communist** [ˋkɑmjənɪst] *(a./n.)* 共產的；共產主義者
12. **classified** [ˋklæsəˏfaɪd] *(a.)* 機密的，declassified 解密的
13. **intel** [ˋɪntɛl] *(n.)* （軍事、政治）情報 = intelligence

### 補充單字

**pussy** [ˋpusɪ] *(n.)* （粗）軟弱的男子

**R.I.P.** 安息此地
拉丁文 requiescat in pace、英文 rest in peace，台詞用雙關語（pun），retired in place 指「坐在崗位等退休」

**jarhead** [ˋdʒɑrˏhɛd] *(n.)* （口）美國海軍陸戰隊隊員

**prostitute** [ˋprɑstəˏtut] *(n.)* 娼妓

**high-end** [ˋhaɪˏɛnd] *(a.)* 高檔的，頂尖的

**airfare** [ˋɛrˏfɛr] *(n.)* 機票價格

全文朗讀 ♫ 058  單字 ♫ 059

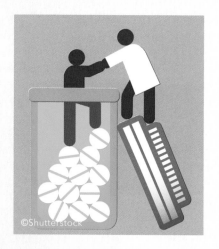
©Shutterstock

## Vocabulary

1. **substance** [ˈsʌbstəns] (n.)
   藥物，物質
2. **statistic** [stəˈtɪstɪk] (n./a.)
   統計數據，統計的
3. **alcohol** [ˈælkəˌhɔl] (n.) 酒精
4. **fatal** [ˈfetəl] (a.) 致命的
5. **strained** [ˈstrend] (a.)
   緊張的，緊繃的
6. **financial** [faɪˈnænʃəl] (a.)
   財務的，金融的

# Drug Abuse in the U.S.
## 美國藥物濫用問題

Today, [1]**substance** abuse is one of the biggest *scourges* on public health in the U.S. Substance abuse refers to the use of a drug in an amount that is harmful to an individual or others. According to the Centers for Disease Control (CDC), 31.9 million Americans over the age of 12, or 11.7% of the population, used an illicit drug in 2018. This [2]**statistic** does not include [3]**alcohol**, the abuse of which leads to health problems like liver disease and can also result in [4]**fatal** automobile accidents. Substance abuse commonly causes [5]**strained** family relations, [6]**financial** problems, failure at work and school, domestic violence, child abuse and more. While drug education and treatment programs can help, more still needs to be done to address the problem of substance abuse.

現今美國公共衛生的最大禍害之一可以說是藥物濫用。藥物濫用是指使用對個人或他人有害的藥物劑量。根據美國疾病管制中心的數據，2018 年有 3190 萬 12 歲以上的美國人，即全美 11.7% 總人口使用了非法藥物。這一統計數據不包括酗酒，酒精的濫用會導致肝臟疾病等健康問題，也可能釀成致命車禍。濫用藥物通常會導致家庭關係緊張、財務問題、工作與學業挫敗、家庭暴力、虐待兒童及更多的問題。雖然毒品教育與戒癮治療可提供協助，但仍需要採取更多行動來解決藥物濫用問題。

# Marijuana Legalization in the U.S.
## 美國大麻合法化

全文朗讀 ♫ 060　單字 ♫ 061

©Shutterstock

Who wants to ❶ get high? The question of marijuana `legalization` continues to be a hot topic in the U.S. [1]**Advocates** for legalization `tout` its benefits as a pain and stress [2]**reliever**, and claim that marijuana is no more dangerous than alcohol. [3]**Opponents**, on the other hand, point to its [4]**potential** risks to public health and safety or object on moral `grounds`. Currently, [5]**recreational** marijuana is legal in 18 U.S. states as well as Washington D.C., with more votes expected in the future. For his part, President Biden supports `decriminalization` of marijuana, but ❶ stops short of proposing legalization at the `federal` level. So if you want to get high, make sure it's legal where you are.

誰想玩嗨？大麻合法化一直是美國熱門的話題。 合法化的提倡者宣揚大麻可用來紓解疼痛和壓力的好處，並聲稱大麻的危險性並不高於酒精。反對者則指出其對公共健康與安全的潛在風險，或以道德為由反對。 目前，娛樂性大麻在美國 18 個州和華府特區是合法的，預計未來會有更多州進行公投。 就拜登總統而言，他支持大麻除罪化，但他也未提出任何全國聯邦性的合法案。因此，如果你想嗨，請確保你所在地區大麻是合法的。

## Vocabulary

1. **advocate** [ˋædvəkɪt] (n./v.)
   提倡者；提倡
2. **reliever** [rɪˋlivə] (n.) 舒緩劑，
   relieve (v.) 舒緩
3. **opponent** [əˋponənt] (n.)
   反對者，對手
4. **potential** [pəˋtɛnʃəl] (a.)
   潛在的，可能的
5. **recreational** [͵rɛkrɪˋeʃənəl] (a.)
   娛樂的
6. **federal** [ˋfɛdərəl] (a.) 聯邦的

### 補充單字

**scourge** [skɜdʒ] (n.) 禍害，鞭子
**legalization** [͵ligələˋzeʃən] (n.) 合法化
**tout** [taut] (v.) 宣傳好處，兜售
**ground** [graund] (n.) 理由，原因
**decriminalization** [di͵krɪmɪnələˋzeʃən] (n.) 除罪化

---

### 🎙 *Tongue-tied No More*

**get high 玩藥嗨**

If you spent more time studying and less time getting high, you'd have better grades.
如果你多花點時間唸書，少花點時間玩藥，你的成績就會進步。

**stop short of sth. 儘管幾乎很接近，卻未達到某事**

The boss criticized Dan's work, but stopped short of firing him.
老闆批評丹的工作，但也沒有解雇他。

# 全球娛樂性大麻
# 合法化國家與地區

## 加拿大 Canada

2018 年合法。全國個省合法使用年齡為 18 歲，除了艾伯塔省（Alberta）18 歲、魁北克省（Quebec）21 歲。

▲ 加拿大大麻國旗

## 墨西哥 Mexico

2021 年合法。只能持有、使用，種植須取得核可，禁止販售。

大麻（cannabis, marijuana）在英文俚語中可稱為 weed、pot、bud、grass、Mary Jane、herb、pot、ganja 等等。大麻是將其「花」風乾搗碎捲成香煙，或加入食物中攝取。

大麻使用分為「醫療性 medical」與「娛樂性 recreational」，各國合法性皆不同。台灣將大麻列為二級毒品，無論醫療、娛樂性大麻都是非法。多數人以為歐洲國家（如：荷蘭）娛樂性大麻已合法化，其實並不然，這些國家只是將大麻除罪化（decriminalize），並授權合法證照給販售商店。

娛樂性大麻合法化的國家只有如烏拉圭、加拿大、喬治亞、南非（2018）以及墨西哥。地區性合法，包含美國 18 州與華盛頓特區、澳洲首都坎培拉（Canberra）。

▲ 烏拉圭街頭大麻販售店

## 烏拉圭 Uruguay

2013 年合法。個人種植最多 6 株。禁止外國人購買。

# MARIJUANA

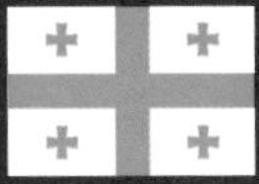

## 喬治亞 Georgia

2018 年合法。只能個人持有、種植、使用,禁止大規模種植與販售。

## 南非 South Africa

2018 年合法。只能個人持有、種植、使用,禁止販售。

- ● 娛樂性大麻合法
- ● 娛樂性大麻非法,但已除罪化
- ● 娛樂性大麻非法,但未執法
- ● 娛樂性大麻非法

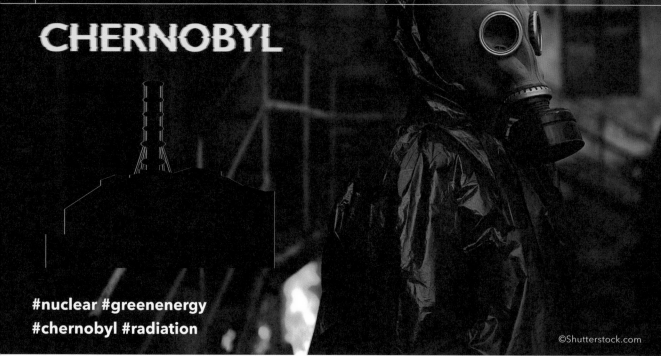

# CHERNOBYL

#nuclear #greenenergy
#chernobyl #radiation

©Shutterstock.com

全文朗讀 ♫ 062　　單字 ♫ 063

# *Chernobyl* 《核爆家園》

**蘇聯隱瞞的悲慘車諾比核災**

## Vocabulary

1. **horrifying** [ˋhɔrəˏfaɪɪŋ] (a.)
   怵目驚心的

2. **disaster** [dɪˋzæstə] (n.)
   災難

3. **nuclear** [ˋnukliə] (a.)
   核能的

4. **nomination** [ˏnɑməˋneʃən] (n.)
   提名

5. **category** [ˋkætəˏgori] (n.)
   種類，範疇

6. **subsequent** [ˋsʌbsɪkwənt] (a.)
   隨後的

*Chernobyl*, a five-part miniseries that first aired in May 2019, tells the [1]**horrifying** story of the 1986 Chernobyl [2]**disaster**—the worst [3]**nuclear** accident in history—and its immediate **aftermath**. **Co-produced** by HBO in the U.S. and Sky in the U.K., the historical drama was well received by viewers and critics alike, **garnering** 19 Emmy [4]**nominations** and wins in the directing and writing [5]**categories**. *Chernobyl* also features **standout** performances from big name actors like Stellan Skarsgard, Emily Watson and Jared Harris, as their characters ⊤ **come to grips with** the scale of the disaster and participate in the [6]**subsequent** **containment** efforts.

《核爆家園》是一部於 2019 年 5 月首播的五集迷你影集，講述 1986 年車諾比核災的震驚事件（歷史上最嚴重的核電事故）以及隨之而來的後果餘波。這部由美國 HBO 和英國 Sky 聯合製作的歷史劇受到觀眾和評論家的好評，榮獲 19 項艾美獎提名，最終贏得最佳導演與劇本獎項。《核爆家園》還有史戴倫史柯斯嘉、艾蜜莉華森與傑瑞德哈里斯等大牌演員的精湛演技，他們理解到災難的規模，細膩處理角色性格，隨後並努力投入核能遏制。

As the series opens, we watch as [7]**Reactor** 4 of the Chernobyl Nuclear Power Plant in Pripyat, Ukraine explodes shortly after midnight on April 26, 1986. Initially, the explosion is [7]**dismissed** by Deputy Chief Engineer Anatoly Dyatlov (Paul Ritter), despite the [8]**objections** of his staff. Meanwhile, firefighter Vasily Ignatenko (Adam Nagaitis) must leave his pregnant wife Lyudmilla (Jessie Buckley) at home while he fights the fire at the plant. Like all of Pripyat, he is **oblivious** to the dangers posed by the [9]**radiation** now escaping from the disaster zone in a blue cloud and filling the night sky. While the town [10]**council** refuses to order an [11]**evacuation**, it does take steps to [12]**ensure** that news of the explosion doesn't leak out.

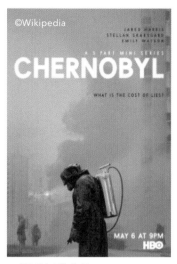

▲《核爆家園》海報

在影集的一開場，我們看到 1986 年 4 月 26 日午夜剛過不久，位於烏克蘭普里皮亞特的車諾比核電廠 4 號反應爐發生爆炸。最初，副總工程師阿納托利迪亞特洛夫（保羅里特 飾）駁斥爆炸事件，儘管其員工持反對意見。 與此同時，消防員瓦西里伊格納堅科（亞當納格提斯 飾）必須將懷孕的妻子柳德米拉（潔西伯克利 飾）留在家中，而自己在核電廠滅火。 他跟普里皮亞特的所有人一樣，並未察覺當前從災區散出並籠罩夜空、夾帶輻射的藍色煙霧所帶來的危險。鎮議會不但拒絕下令疏散，反而還採取措施以確保不會洩露爆炸消息。

Later that morning, Ulana Khomyuk (Watson), a nuclear [13]**physicist**, detects high levels of radiation in the air from her office in Minsk, but has trouble [14]**identifying** the source. Fellow scientist Valery Legasov (Harris) is tasked with advising on the [15]**incident** and sent to Chernobyl to investigate. Eventually, Legasov convinces Boris Shcherbina (Skarsgard), a communist official who reports directly to **Soviet** leader **Mikhail Gorbachev**, that the reactor is open and the radiation can no longer be contained. Khomyuk soon also arrives on the scene and warns that the worst is yet to come: a **meltdown** of the reactor [16]**core** is **imminent**.

稍後當日早晨，核物理學家烏拉娜霍繆克 （艾蜜莉華森 飾）在明斯克的辦公室檢測到空氣中的高輻射量，但無法確定來源。研究同事瓦列里列加索夫（傑瑞德哈里斯 飾）的任務就是該事件提供建議，並被派往車諾比進行調查。 最終，列加索夫說服了直接向蘇聯領導人戈巴契夫報告的共產黨官員鮑里斯謝爾比納（史戴倫史柯斯嘉 飾），反應爐已炸開，無法再控制輻射。 霍繆克隨後也趕到現場，並警告最壞的情形尚未到來：反應爐心熔毀迫在眉睫。

7. **dismiss** [dɪsˋmɪs] (v.)
   駁斥，不屑一提

8. **objection** [əbˋdʒɛkʃən] (n.)
   反對

9. **radiation** [ˏrediˋeʃən] (n.)
   輻射

10. **council** [ˋkaʊnsəl] (n.)
    議會

11. **evacuation** [ɪˏvækjuˋeʃən] (n.)
    撤離，疏散

12. **ensure** [ɪnˋʃʊr] (v.)
    確保

13. **physicist** [ˋfɪzɪsɪst] (n.)
    物理學家

14. **identify** [aɪˋdɛntəˏfaɪ] (v.)
    鑑定，識別

15. **incident** [ˋɪnsədənt] (n.)
    事件

16. **core** [kor] (n.)
    核心，爐心

17. **depict** [dɪˋpɪkt] *(v.)*
描繪，描述

18. **license** [ˋlaɪsəns] *(n.)*
打破格局

19. **volunteer** [ˌvɑlənˋtɪr] *(n./v.)*
志工，自願

20. **neglect** [nɪˋglɛkt] *(v.)*
忽視，忽略

21. **dedicate** [ˋdɛdəˌket] *(v.)*
奉獻

### 補充單字

**aftermath** [ˋæftəˌmæθ] *(n.)*
後果，餘波

**co-produce** [ˌkoprəˋdus] *(v.)*
聯合製作

**garner** [ˋgɑrnə] *(v.)*
獲得，得到

**standout** [ˋstændˌaut] *(a.)*
傑出的

**containment** [kənˋtenmənt] *(n.)*
控制，遏制

**reactor** [rɪˋæktə] *(n.)* 反應爐

**oblivious** [əˋblɪvɪəs] *(a.)*
未察覺的

**meltdown** [ˋmɛltˌdaun] *(n.)*
爐心熔毀

**imminent** [ˋɪmənənt] *(a.)*
（不好的事）迫近的，逼近的

**fateful** [ˋfetfəl] *(a.)*
重大的，決定命運的

While *Chernobyl* attempts to [17]**depict** the events of that `fateful April night and what followed accurately, the writers did take some dramatic [18]**license**. For example, Watson's character wasn't a real person, but rather a combination of several real-life scientists. The series also focuses on the emergency workers and [19]**volunteers** who cleaned up the toxic site following the disaster. They are often [20]**neglected** by history, so **G** it is to them that this powerful series is [21]**dedicated**.

雖然《核爆家園》試圖真實描繪那場四月夜晚的災難事件以及災後的情形，但劇作家確實為了戲劇效果加入了新元素，例如華森的角色並非真實存在，而是現實事件中幾位科學家的合體化身。該影集也將焦點放在警消人員與志工，災後他們清除有害物質現場，卻經常被歷史所忽略，因此這部精彩動人的影集就是要獻給他們以示致敬。

### ʃTongue-tied No More

**come to grips (with) 理解接受並著手處理**
It took Tom a long time to come to grips with his parents' accidental death. 湯姆花了很長的時間才能接受雙親的在意外中身亡。

▶ 車諾比廢棄遺址，牆上寫著俄語標示「對生命造成危害！」

## it is…that 的強調句型

當我們想強調句子裡某事件、某時、某人等的時候，可把欲強調事物前面加上虛主詞 it，並將剩餘句子置於句尾，如本句 "…it is to them that this powerful series is dedicated." 就是強調「獻給他們」。

● **強調主詞：**

例：It was Dr. White who/that made me fall in love with literature.
　　是懷特教授讓我愛上文學。

● **強調受詞：**

例：It was the antique vase that the boy broke accidentally.
　　男孩不小心打破的是古董花瓶。

● **強調地方：**

例：It was the restaurant where her boyfriend proposed to her.
　　就是在那餐廳她男友和她求婚的。

# E Z pedia

### meltdown 爐心熔毀

核能反應爐因無法及時冷卻而熔化造成的損毀。爐心熔毀後可能引發輻射物質外洩，影響人類及其他生物的健康。車諾比事件輻射造成當地居民罹患癌症死亡，嬰兒出生畸形。至今核電廠方圓 30 公里仍不適合居住。

### Soviet Union 蘇聯

正式名稱為「蘇維埃社會主義共和國聯邦」（Union of Soviet Socialist Republics, USSR）。蘇維埃（Soviet, Совет）俄語是「建議、意見」的意思，原是「人民代表議會」的名稱。1917 年列寧為首的布爾什維克黨（Bolsheviks）發動二月革命與十月革命，先後推翻沙皇與臨時政府，控制蘇維埃議會，建立世界上第一個共產政權「蘇維埃俄國」。1922 年蘇俄納入其他 14 個加盟共和國組成「蘇聯」，與美國並列兩大國際強權，直到 1991 年蘇聯瓦解 15 國獨立。

### Mikhail Gorbachev 米哈伊爾戈巴契夫

1985 年上任的最後一任蘇聯領導人。戈巴契夫任內推行開放重建改革（perestroika, reconstruction），1987 年和 1989 年兩度當選美國時代年度風雲人物，1990 年獲得諾貝爾和平獎，在西方世界中的受到讚賞。然而在俄國人民心中，他是蘇聯垮台的原因，任內蘇聯經濟民不聊生，車諾比事件與出兵阿富汗等爭議雪上加霜，至今在俄國民調中為歷史上最不受歡迎的領導人。

〔核電廠爆炸後，副工程長迪亞特洛夫在控制室處理警急狀況〕

Dyatlov　This is an emergency. Everyone ⊕ <u>stay calm</u>. Our first 1)**priority** is....

Perevozchenko　It exploded.

Dyatlov　We know. Akimov, are we cooling the reactor core?

Akimov　We shut it down. But the control 2)**rods** are still...they're not all the way in. I ˙**disengaged** the 3)**clutch**. I don't....

Dyatlov　All right. I'll 4)**disconnect** the servos from the ˙**standby** 5)**console**. You two! Get the ˙**backup** pumps running. We need water moving through the core. That's all that matters.

Perevozchenko　There is no core. It exploded. The core exploded.

Dyatlov　He's ⊕ <u>in shock</u>. Get him out of here.

Perevozchenko　The lid is off. The 6)**stack** is burning. I saw it.

Dyatlov　You're confused. RBMK reactor cores don't explode.

## Vocabulary

1. **priority** [praɪˋɔrətɪ] (n.) 優先
2. **rod** [rɑd] (n.) 竿，握柄
3. **clutch** [klʌtʃ] (n.) 離合器
4. **disconnect** [͵dɪskəˋnɛkt] (v.) 切斷，分開
5. **console** [ˋkɑn͵sol] (n.) 控制台
6. **stack** [stæk] (n.) 堆，疊

### 補充單字

**disengage** [͵dɪsɪnˋgedʒ] (v.) 使脫離
**standby** [ˋstænd͵baɪ] (n.) 待機，待命
**backup** [ˋbæk͵ʌp] (n.) 備用

迪亞特洛夫　這是緊急情況，大家保持冷靜。我們的首要任務是…

佩列佛茲程柯　它爆炸了。

迪亞特洛夫　我們知道。 阿基莫夫，我們有在冷卻反應爐心嗎？

阿基莫夫　我們關掉了，但是控制桿仍然……沒有完全插入。 我鬆開了離合器。 我不…。

迪亞特洛夫　好的。 我會斷開待機控制台的舵機連接。 你們倆！去啟動備用幫浦。 我們要讓水通過核心，這才是最重要的。

佩列佛茲程柯　沒有核心，它爆炸了， 核心爆炸了。

迪亞特洛夫　他嚇昏頭了， 把他帶走。

佩列佛茲程柯　蓋子是脫離的，反應爐堆正在燃燒。 我看到了。

迪亞特洛夫　你搞錯了。 壓力管式石墨慢化沸水反應爐心是不可能會爆炸的。

## 呈報中央

〔核電廠負責人布留哈諾夫詢問工程長福明、迪亞特洛夫反應爐心爆炸原因〕

Bryukhanov   🅣 **I take it** the safety test was a failure?

Dyatlov   We have the situation under control.

Fomin   Under control? It doesn't look like it's under control.

Bryukhanov   Shut up, Fomin. I have to tell the Central Committee about this. Do you realize that? I have to get on the phone and tell Maryin, or 🅣 <u>God forbid</u> Frolyshev, that my power plant is on fire.

Dyatlov   No one can blame you for this, Director Bryukanov.

Bryukhanov   Of course no one can blame me for this. How can I be responsible? I was sleeping.

---

布留哈諾夫   所以說安全測試失敗了？

迪亞特洛夫   我們已經控制住了局勢。

福明   控制住了？ 現在看起來不像控制住了。

布留哈諾夫   閉嘴，福明。 我必須把這件事呈報給中央委員會。 你有意識到嗎？ 我必須打電話給馬利安，上帝保佑啊，或是孚羅利雪夫，告訴他們我的發電廠著火了。

迪亞特洛夫   沒有人可以為此責怪你，布留哈諾夫長官。

布留哈諾夫   當然沒有人可以為此責怪我。 我怎麼能負責？ 我當時正在睡覺。

### Tongue-tied No More

**stay/remain calm 保持鎮定**
Please stay calm while our repair crew works to restore power.
請保持鎮定，我們的維修人員正在恢復電力中。

**in shock 震驚，嚇傻**
We were all in shock when we heard our teacher was murdered.
聽到老師被殺害，我們都很震驚。

**I take it 所以說**
I never heard from you, so I take it you didn't get my message.
我都沒有你的消息，所以你應該沒收到我的訊息。

**God/heaven forbid
上帝保佑，老天保佑**
If you were to have an accident, God forbid, the insurance would cover your medical costs. 如果你出什麼意外，老天保佑，保險會支付你的醫療費用。

## 輻射爆表

〔工程人員西特尼科夫檢查完爐心，呈報給布留哈諾夫與迪亞特洛夫〕

**Bryukhanov**  Well?

**Sitnikov**  I sent my [1]**dosimetrists** into the reactor building. The large [2]**dosimeter** from the safe, the one with the 1,000-[6]**roentgen** [7]**capacity**….

**Dyatlov**  What was the number?

**Sitnikov**  There was none. The meter [8]**burned out** the second it was turned on.

**Dyatlov**  *[to Bryukhanov]* It's [9]**typical**.

**Bryukhanov**  See, this is what Moscow does. Sends us [10]**shit** equipment, then wonders why things go wrong.

**Sitnikov**  We found another dosimeter, from the military fire department. It only goes to 200 roentgen, but it's better than the small ones.

**Fomin**  And?

**Sitnikov**  It ❶ <u>maxed out</u>. 200 roentgen.

---

### Vocabulary

7. **capacity** [kəˋpæsəti] *(n.)* 容量
8. **burn out** *(phr.)* 燒壞
9. **typical** [ˋtɪpɪkəl] *(a.)* （口）不意外的
10. **shit** [ʃɪt] *(a.)* （粗）爛的，低劣的

#### 補充單字

**dosimetrist** [doˋsɪmətrɪst] *(n.)*
輻射測量師 dosimeter 輻射測量儀
**roentgen** [ˋrɛntgən] *(n.)*
倫琴，輻射量單位
**vent** [vɛnt] *(n.)* 出風口
**medic** [ˋmɛdɪk] *(n.)* 軍醫，衛生員

布留哈諾夫　如何？

西特尼科夫　我派輻射測量師進入反應爐室。保險櫃中最大的輻射測量儀，容量為 1,000 倫琴…。

迪亞特洛夫　檢測值多少？

西特尼科夫　沒測出，測量儀一打開就燒壞了。

迪亞特洛夫　總是這樣。

布留哈諾夫　你們看，莫斯科都這樣。 寄給我們爛設備，然後想知道為什麼會出錯。

西特尼科夫　我們從軍事消防部門找到了另一個輻射測量儀。 它只到 200 倫琴，但比小的好。

福明　　　　然後呢？

西特尼科夫　它已經達到極限了， 200 倫琴。

## 嘔吐昏迷

〔西特尼科夫呈報布留哈諾夫與迪亞特洛夫爐心爆炸了〕

Fomin　　Sitnikov, you're a nuclear engineer. So am I. Now, please tell me how an RBMK reactor core explodes. Not a meltdown. An explosion. I'd love to know.

©Shutterstock.com

Sitnikov　　I can't.

Fomin　　Are you stupid?

Sitnikov　　No.

Fomin　　Then why can't you?

Sitnikov　　I...I don't see how it could explode. But it did.

Dyatlov　　Enough. I'll go up to the **vent** block roof. From there, you can look right down into Reactor Building 4. I'll ☏ <u>see it with my own eyes</u>. *[suddenly vomits]* I apologize. *[collapses]*

Bryukhanov　　Guards! Guards! Get him to the **medic**, or the, or the hospital, whatever he needs!

---

福明　　西特尼科夫，你是核能工程師，我也是。現在請告訴我 RBMK 反應爐心是怎麼爆炸的，不是熔毀，而是爆炸。我很想知道。

西特尼科夫　　我無法。

福明　　你無腦嗎？

西特尼科夫　　不是。

福明　　那你為什麼無法？

西特尼科夫　　我⋯⋯我不知道它怎麼爆炸，但它就是爆炸了。

迪亞特洛夫　　夠了，我要上去出風口屋頂。從那裡，你可以直接看到 4 號反應爐室。我自己親眼看。[ 突然嘔吐 ] 抱歉。[ 暈倒 ]

布留哈諾夫　　警衛！警衛！帶他去看軍醫或醫院，看他需要什麼！

### 𝒯ongue-tied 𝒩o 𝒨ore

**max out**
**達到頂標，刷爆（信用卡）**
I wanted to buy more at the mall, but I maxed out my credit card.
在購物中心我還想買更多，但我刷爆了我的信用卡。

**see sth. with one's own eyes**
**親眼見證**
I wouldn't have believed it if I hadn't seen it with my own eyes.
如果這件事我沒有親眼看到，我也不會相信。

## Vocabulary

1. **anniversary** [͵ænəˋvɜsəri] (n.) 週年
2. **deadly** [ˋdɛdli] (a.) 致命的
3. **magnitude** [ˋmægnə͵tud] (n.)
   強度，巨大
4. **evacuate** [ɪˋvækju͵et] (v.)
   撤離，疏散
5. **impact** [ˋɪmpækt] (n./v.) 衝擊

### 補充單字

**tsunami** [tsuˋnɑmi] (n.)
海嘯，來自日文「津波」
**adverse** [ˋæd͵vɜs] (a.) 有害的，不利的
**lead-up** [ˋlid͵ʌp] (n.) 到⋯之前的時間

▲ 2011 年 9.0 級強震重創日本東北地區

# Fukushima Nuclear Disaster Ten-Year Anniversary 311 日本福島核災十週年

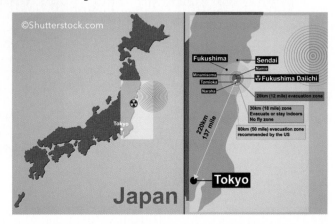

©Shutterstock.com

March 11, 2021 marked the tenth [1]**anniversary** of the [2]**deadly** 9.0 [3]**magnitude** Tohoku earthquake and resulting **tsunami** that struck the island of Honshu, Japan in 2011. These natural disasters caused explosions and the subsequent meltdowns of three reactors at the Fukushima Daiichi Nuclear Power Plant when the tsunami wave overwhelmed the cooling systems. In total, 154,000 people who lived within 20 km of the plant were [4]**evacuated** in what has been called the worst nuclear accident since the Chernobyl disaster of April 1986. While the U.N. reported no **adverse** health effects from the disaster in the **lead-up** to the anniversary, many residents are still unable to return to their homes. Thus, the [5]**impact** of the Fukushima nuclear disaster continues to be felt today.

2021 年 3 月 11 日為東日本大震災十週年。2011 年日本東北發生 9.0 級致命強震，隨之引發海嘯侵襲日本本州島。當海嘯波浪淹沒冷卻系統時，天然災害導致福島第一核電廠爆炸，隨後三座反應爐熔毀。這場被稱為 1986 年 4 月車諾比核災以來最嚴重的核能事故，共有 15.4 萬居住在核電廠 20 公里範圍內的居民被撤離。雖然聯合國在週年紀念日前報告此次災難並未造成有害的健康影響，至今許多居民仍然無法返回家園。 因此，時至今日我們仍能感受到福島核災的衝擊影響。

## 東京奧運「勝利花束」綻放福島經濟復甦

日本為了紀念 311 福島核災，本屆 2020 東京奧運頒發獲獎選手的「勝利花束」，特別選用震災東北地區所種植的花卉，分別為福島縣的洋桔梗、玉竹、宮城縣的向日葵、岩手縣的龍膽花以及東京的一葉蘭。該地區的農產品由於輻射值問題不利銷售，當地農民化危機為轉機，開始種植花卉作為高附加價值的經濟作物，豔麗盎然的花朵也為東北地區帶來嶄新的活力生機。勝利花束搭配裝飾本屆東京奧運吉祥物「未來永遠郎 Miraitowa」，寓意為期望永遠有美好的未來，向世界綻放日本復甦的元氣。

▲ 奧運羽球男雙冠軍李洋（左）、王齊麟（右）獲頒金色勝利花束

▲ 世界羽球天后戴資穎獲頒奧運銀色勝利花束

©Tokyo Olympics

▲頒發獲獎選手的勝利花束，吉祥物「未來永遠郎 Miraitowa」分別以金銀銅三色代表獲獎名次。

## 福島點燃奧運「復興之火」

2020 東京奧運聖火傳遞從福島起跑，「復興之火」照亮希望，象徵福島浴火而重生。儘管新冠肺炎疫情肆虐日本，國內發出許多反對奧運的聲浪，但主辦國細心籌劃這場世界體壇的盛宴，加上日本選手在各個運動項目的優秀表現，讓全球見證日本重生，點燃璀璨耀眼的復興之火。

© 截圖 YouTube CNA 頻道

Source: BP Statistical Review of World Energy & Ember

# Global Renewable Energy

# 全球
# 綠色替代能源

---

# Europe 歐洲

GREEN DEAL

歐盟提出《歐洲綠色協議 European Green Deal》，目標在 2050 年成為氣候中和大陸（climate-neutral continent），也就是使用再生能源取代化石燃料、植樹造林、節能減碳等方式，抵消所產生的二氧化碳排放量。以 歐洲 1990 年排放量為基準，2030 年減少 50-55%，在 2050 年實現「零排放」。因此歐盟各國逐年增加再生能源的發電比例，在 2050 年前達到 100%。

### — 冰島 Iceland —

冰島 99% 以上的電力來自可再生能源，73% 的電力來自水力發電，26.8% 來自地熱能。

### — 挪威 Norway —

挪威 99% 以上的電力生產來自水力發電。挪威雖然位處高緯度，不適合發展太陽能發電，卻是全球最大的太陽能級矽原料（solar grade silicon, SGS）生產國之一。

### — 德國 Germany —

Ilona Seipp © Shutterstock

德國的再生能源主要以風力、太陽能和生質能源為主。德國在 2014 年之前擁有全球最多的太陽能光電裝置量，現為全球第四（僅次中國、日本、美國），也是 2020 年風力發電裝置量全球第三的國家（僅次中國、美國），德國被稱為「世界首要再生能源經濟體」。

### — 阿爾巴尼亞 Albania —

阿爾巴尼亞 97% 以上電力來自水力發電資源，然而位處地中海氣候帶，夏季乾燥水位變低，必須以其他能源替代分散風險。阿爾巴尼亞地中海氣候夏季日照長，因此正致力發展太陽能。山脈地區適合發展風力發電。由於擁有天然井，極具地熱發電的潛力。

# The Americas 美洲

### 加拿大 Canada

加拿大 67% 的電力來自再生能源。加拿大是世界第三大水力發電生產國，約 8% 電力出口美國，目前有 34 條主要輸電線，把電力運往美國。

### 哥斯達黎加 Costa Rica

哥斯達黎加 99% 以上的電力來自可再生能源，其中大 67.5% 來自水電，風力發電佔 17%，地熱能佔 13.5%，生質能源與太陽能佔 0.84%。

### 巴拉圭 Paraguay

巴拉圭是全球最大的電力出口國之一。位於巴拉圭、巴西、阿根廷邊界，被譽為「新世界七大奇景」的伊瓜蘇瀑布（Iguazú Falls），提供巴拉圭豐富的水力發電，全國消耗電力只佔 10%，剩下 90% 出口到鄰國巴西、阿根廷，是巴拉圭重要的經濟命脈。

# Asia-Pacific 亞太

### 北韓 North Korea

北韓 76% 以上的電力來自水力發電，剩下 24% 倚賴燃煤與石油。由於供電不穩，有許多家庭從中國引進太陽能板作為備電。

### 不丹 Bhutan

不丹 99% 以上的電力生產來自水力發電。不丹致力於環境保育，更是世界上第一個，也是唯一的負碳排放量國家。由於嚴格的樹木砍伐限制，不丹國土超過 70% 的森林覆蓋率，吸收的二氧化碳遠大於排放量。

### 紐西蘭 New Zealand

紐西蘭超過 80% 的電力來自可再生能源，約 60% 來自水力發電，15% 地熱發電，5 % 風力發電。紐西蘭在地熱發電技術佔有領導地位，擁有世界上第二大地熱發電廠（僅次義大利）。

# Africa 非洲

部分非洲國家如尚比亞、安哥拉、剛果民主共和國、賴索托、莫三比克等，水力發電佔全國電力 90% 以上，然而因為乾旱水位下降，供電量也會受到影響。

國際組織也積極在偏遠地區建設小規模的太陽能、風力與地熱發電，因為從大型電廠運輸電力到偏遠地區成本過高，再生能源可改善供電不穩的問題。

#queensgambit #grandmaster
#prodigy #chess

Charis Tsevis©Flickr

全文朗讀 🎵 068　　單字 🎵 069

# *The Queen's Gambit* 《后翼棄兵》

## 西洋棋神童貝絲成長蛻變站上國際舞台

**NETFLIX**

### Vocabulary

1. **overcome** [ˌovɚˋkʌm] *(v.)*
   克服

2. **period** [ˋpɪrɪəd] *(a.)*
   某時代的，古裝的

3. **explosion** [ɪkˋsploʒən] *(n.)*
   突然爆發，爆炸

4. **dramatically** [drəˋmætɪklɪ]
   *(adv.)* 劇烈地，戲劇性地

**CHESS**

©Shutterstock.com

Based on the 1983 Walter Tevis novel of the same name, *The Queen's Gambit* is one of the most successful Netflix original series ❶ to date. The seven-part miniseries is a coming-of-age drama that tells the story of chess prodigy Beth Harmon, who [1]overcomes many obstacles on her rise to the top of the chess world. The title comes from a chess opening called the Queen's Gambit, which Beth learns as a young orphan and uses ❶ to great effect in the show's final episode. Considering *The Queen's Gambit* is a [2]period drama about chess, many were surprised just how popular the show became after its release in October 2020. Within a month, it was Netflix' top miniseries in 63 countries. The show has even caused an [3]explosion of new interest in the ancient game, with sales of chess sets and books increasing [4]dramatically.

《后翼棄兵》根據 1983 年沃爾特特維斯的同名小說改編，是 Netflix 史上最成功的原創影集之一。 這部七集組成的迷你影集是一部成年劇，講述西洋棋神童

貝絲哈蒙克服多重障礙，登上西洋棋世界巔峰的故事。 劇名源自西洋棋開局，稱為「女王的開局」，身為孤兒的貝絲小時候學習女王的開局，並在最後一集中，將它發揮得淋漓盡致。 考慮到《后翼棄兵》是一部西洋棋時代劇，許多人對這部劇在 2020 年 10 月播出後受歡迎程度感到驚訝。短短一個月內，它成為 Netflix 全球 63 個國家的排行榜當中，排名第一的迷你影集。 該影集甚至掀起了一股對這個古代遊戲的熱潮，西洋棋組和書籍的銷量急劇暴增。

▲ Anya Taylor-Joy 飾演 Beth

When we first meet Beth in 1967, she's just been awakened by a knock on her Paris hotel room door. After ⊤ <u>washing</u> a couple of pills ⊤ <u>down</u> with ˈvodka, she rushes downstairs for her match with Russian world chess champion Vasily Borgov. But first Ⓖ we need to understand how she got here. Jumping back to Lexington, Kentucky in the mid-'50s, we see Beth become an orphan at the age of nine when her mother dies in a car crash. At the ⁵⁾**orphanage** she's taken to, the girls are given daily "vitamins"—which are actually ⁶**tranquilizers**—to "even their ˈ**disposition**." On the advice of Jolene, an older girl with a dirty mouth who becomes her friend, Beth saves the pills to take at bedtime. While cleaning erasers in the basement one day, she sees the ⁷**janitor**, Mr. Shaibel, playing chess against himself— her first encounter with the game that will change her life.

1967 年我們第一次見到貝絲時，她在巴黎飯店剛被人敲門叫醒。 用伏特加吞下幾顆藥丸後，她趕緊衝下樓，參加與俄羅斯西洋棋世界冠軍瓦西里博戈夫的比賽。 但首先我們需了解她如何達到今日成就。回到 50 年代中期的肯塔基州列萊辛頓市，我們看到貝絲在 9 歲時，因為母親死於車禍變成孤兒。 在她被送進的孤兒院，女孩們每天都要吃「維他命」——實際上是鎮定劑——以「穩定她們的性格」。 滿嘴髒話的大女孩喬琳成為貝絲的朋友，在她的建議下，貝絲將藥丸留到睡前才服用。 有一天，她在地下室清理黑板擦時，看到工友薛波先生正在和自己下棋——這是她第一次接觸西洋棋，這也是將改變她一生的遊戲。

5. **orphanage** [ˋɔrfənɪdʒ] (n.)
孤兒院

6. **tranquilizer** [ˋtræŋkwɪˏlaɪzə]
(n.) 鎮定劑

7. **janitor** [ˋdʒænɪtɚ] (n.)
工友，清潔工

8. **visualize** [ˋvɪʒuəˏlaɪz] (v.)
視覺化，想象

9. **demonstrate** [ˋdɛmənˏstret]
(v.) 展現，示範

10. **resign** [rɪˋzaɪn] (v.)
西洋棋投子認輸

With the aid of her nightly tranquilizer, Beth finds that she can ⁸⁾**visualize** the board, the pieces and the way they move on the ceiling above her. Mr. Shaibel refuses to let her play at first, saying, "Girls do not play chess." But when she ⁹⁾**demonstrates** how much she's learned just by observing him, he changes his mind. Mr. Shaibel beats her easily the first time, forces her to ¹⁰⁾**resign** the second

11. **simultaneous** [ˌsaɪməlˈtenɪəs]
    *(a.)* 同時進行的

12. **foster** [ˈfɔstɚ] *(a./v.)*
    收養的，收養

13. **championship** [ˈtʃæmpɪənˌʃɪp]
    *(n.)* 冠軍賽

14. **short (on)** [ʃɔrt] *(a.)*
    缺少的，不足的

15. **tournament** [ˈtɝnəmənt] *(n.)*
    錦標賽

16. **take on** *(phr.)*
    與…較量

**gambit** [ˈgæmbɪt] *(n.)* 開局讓棋
法，西洋棋開局時犧牲一卒以取得
優勢

**coming-of-age** *(a.)*
青少年即將成年的

**prodigy** [ˈprɑdədʒi] *(n.)* 天才神童

**vodka** [ˈvɑdkə] *(n.)* 伏特加

**disposition** [ˌdɪspəˈzɪʃən] *(n.)*
性格，性情

**upcoming** [ˈʌpˌkʌmɪŋ] *(a.)*
即將到來的

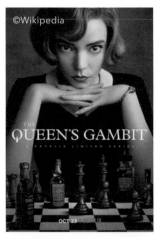

▲《后翼棄兵》海報

time, and then never wins again. Realizing he has nothing left to teach her, he lends Beth a thick chess book, which she quickly masters by playing games in her head. She gets the chance to show off her new skills when Mr. Ganz, who teaches chess at the local high school, invites her to a chess club meeting. Playing a [11]**simultaneous** game against 12 players, she beats them all easily.

晚上在鎮靜劑的幫助下，貝絲發現她可以在頭頂天花板上想像出棋盤、棋子以及它們的移動方式。 薛波先生一開始不讓她下棋，他說：「女孩不能下棋。」但是當她展現自己只是透過觀察薛波先生就學到如何下棋時，他改變了心意。薛波先生第一次輕鬆地打敗她，第二次強迫她退賽，然後就再也沒有贏過了。薛波先生意識到自己已經沒有什麼可以教她了，他借給貝絲一本厚重的西洋棋書，她藉由在腦海中下棋，很快掌握了書的內容。當地高中的西洋棋教師甘茲先生邀請她參加西洋棋社活動時，她有機會展現自己的新技能。 貝絲同時與 12 名棋手對決，並輕而易舉地擊敗他們。

After being adopted by Lexington couple Allston and Alma Wheatley in her teens, Beth continues playing chess in her head—with the aid of tranquilizers stolen from her [12]**foster** mother. She also steals a chess magazine, where she learns about the **upcoming** Kentucky state [13]**championship**. [14]**Short** on cash, she borrows $5 from Mr. Shaibel for the entrance fee and, you guessed it, wins the [15]**tournament**. This is just the first of many victories, but as her fame and bank account begin to grow, Beth begins mixing alcohol with her pills. As she moves up the ranks into international competition, will she be able to get her substance abuse under control and [16]**take on** world chess champion Vasily Borgov in Moscow? Yes! But will she win?

在十幾歲時，貝絲被萊辛頓市的奧斯頓和艾瑪惠特利夫婦收養後，繼續在她的腦海中下棋——借助從養母那裡偷來的鎮定劑。 她還偷了一本西洋棋雜誌，得知肯塔基州即將舉辦一場州級冠軍賽。 由於不夠錢，她向薛波先生借了 5 美元作為報名費，被你猜對了，她贏得了錦標賽。這只是眾多勝利中的第一場，但隨著貝絲的名氣與銀行存款增長，她也開始將烈酒配藥丸服用。 當她躋升國際比賽的排名時，她能否控制藥物濫用，並在莫斯科與世界西洋棋冠軍瓦西里博戈夫一較高下？ 是的！ 她可以，但她會贏嗎？

**to date 至今，到目前為止**
I think *Folklore* is Taylor Swift's best album to date. 我認為《美麗傳說》是泰勒絲至今最棒的專輯。

**to great/good/fine effect 達到最佳效果**
The company has used social media to great effect in promoting its products. 這間公司用社群媒體將產品行銷達到最佳效果。

**wash down 搭配（液體）吃下**
We washed our steaks down with an expensive red wine. 我們吃牛排搭配昂貴的紅酒。

**Grammar** Master

## 間接問句

"We need to know how she got here." 是由 "We need to know it." "How did she get here?" 兩個句子組成。「間接問句」句型：主要子句 + 疑問詞 + S + V，句末標點符號視主要子句而定。

間接問句可簡化為：疑問詞 + to + V。

例：I don't know. How old is Beth?

→　I don't know how old Beth is. 我不知道貝絲幾歲。

例：Please tell me. Why did you lie to me?

→　Please tell me why you lied to me. 請告訴我為什麼你要騙我。

例：Can you teach me? How do I play chess?

→　Can you teach me how I play chess?

→　Can you teach me how to play chess? 可以請你教我下棋嗎？

©Shutterstock.com

〔貝絲與薛波先生在孤兒院地下室下棋〕

Beth　I'm playing White?

Shaibel　From now on, we ❶ take turns. It's the way the game should be played.

Beth　Then, how come I couldn't go first before?

Shaibel　Play.

Beth　*[moves queen]* 1)**Check**. *[moves pawn]* 2)**Mate**. *[Mr. Shaibel gets up and takes drink from bottle]* Is that 3)**whiskey**?

Shaibel　Mm-hmm. Yes. And don't tell.

Beth　I won't. *[Mr. Shaibel hands her a book]* Modern Chess Openings.

Shaibel　It's the best book for you. It will tell you all you wanna know. You'll need to learn chess **notation** before you can read it. I'll teach you now.

Beth　Am I good enough now?

Shaibel　How old are you?

Beth　Nine. I'll be ten in November.

Shaibel　To tell you the truth of it, child…you're **astounding**.

## Vocabulary

1. **check** [tʃɛk] *(v./n.)* （西洋棋）將軍，下一步即可將對方的國王吃掉，提醒喊出「將軍」
2. **mate** [met] *(v./n.)* （西洋棋）將殺，對方的國王被將軍後，無法逃離解圍
3. **whiskey** [ˋwɪski] *(n.)* 威士忌
4. **gifted** [ˋgɪftɪd] *(a.)* 有天份的
5. **unusual** [ʌnˋjuʒʊəl] *(a.)* 不尋常的
6. **maintain** [menˋten] *(v.)* 主張，堅持
7. **wary** [ˋwɛri] *(a.)* 警惕的，唯恐的
8. **accompany** [əˋkʌmpəni] *(v.)* 陪同，伴隨
9. **assume** [əˋsum] *(v.)* 假定，以為
10. **abandon** [əˋbændən] *(v.)* 拋棄，離棄

貝絲　我下白棋？

薛波先生　從現在起，我們輪流，下棋就該這樣。

貝絲　那以前我為什麼不能先下？

薛波先生　趕快下。

貝絲　〔下皇后〕將軍。〔下兵〕將殺。〔薛波先生起身拿瓶子喝一口〕那是威士忌嗎？

薛波先生　嗯哼，不要告訴別人。

貝絲　我不會。〔薛波給她一本書〕《現代西洋棋開局》。

薛波先生　最適合妳的書，書上有妳想知道的一切。妳需要先學會西洋棋的棋譜，才看得懂這本書。我現在要教妳了。

貝絲　我現在夠資格了？

薛波先生　妳幾歲？

貝絲　九歲，11月我就十歲了。

薛波先生　告訴妳實話，孩子…妳太驚人了。

# 高中車輪戰

〔貝絲與甘茲先生在孤兒院院長迪爾朵女士的辦公室〕

**Deardorff**  Mr. Ganz tells me that you are a [4]**gifted** child. He has an [5]**unusual** request to make. He would like you to be taken to the high school on Thursday. He [6]**maintains** that you are a *phenomenal* chess player. He would like you to perform for the chess club.

**Ganz**  We have a dozen members, and I was suggesting to Mrs. Deardorff that you come along and play all of them in a simultaneous.

**Deardorff**  We like to give our girls a chance for experience outside whenever we can, but I'm a bit [7]**wary** of letting Elizabeth go off to the local high school.

**Ganz**  I would *chaperone*. I'd pick her up and take her to the school, then bring her straight back here.

**Deardorff**  I was thinking a young lady might also [8]**accompany** her.

**Ganz**  I [9]**assumed** that you would come, as my guest.

**Deardorff**  Oh. No, I...I couldn't possibly [10]**abandon** my duties here.

**Ganz**  Well, then what if Shirley Munson, club *treasurer* and one of my best students, comes along?

**Deardorff**  OK. ❶ It's settled then.

---

| 迪爾朵 | 甘茲先生告訴我，妳是很有天分的孩子。他有個不尋常的要求，星期四下午他想帶妳去高中。他說妳是非常傑出的棋手，他想找妳去棋社下棋。 |
|---|---|
| 甘茲先生 | 我們有 12 位成員，我向迪爾朵女士建議讓妳過來和他們同時下橫，進行車輪戰。 |
| 迪爾朵 | 我們樂於提供院童機會，盡可能讓她們體驗外界生活，但是我點害怕讓伊莉莎白去當地的高中。 |
| 甘茲先生 | 我會陪同，載她到學校，結束後直接載回來。 |
| 迪爾朵 | 我以為也會有年輕姊姊陪她。 |
| 甘茲先生 | 我以為您會出席，擔任我的嘉賓。 |
| 迪爾朵 | 哦…不，我不能丟下這裡的責任。 |
| 甘茲先生 | 那麼如果找雪莉曼森，社團的總務股長，也是我最好的學生之一，請她陪同前往呢？ |
| 迪爾朵 | 好，就這麼說定了。 |

## 補充單字

**notation** [no`teʃən] (n.) 譜號，標記
**astounding** [ə`staʊndɪŋ] (a.) 使人震驚的
**phenomenal** [fə`namənəl] (a.) 傑出非凡的
**chaperone** [`ʃæpə͵ron] (v.) 陪同，監護
**treasurer** [`trɛʒərə] (n.) 財務總務長

### *Tongue-tied No More*

**take turns 輪流**
Dan and I usually take turns to cook. 丹和我通常輪流煮飯。

**it's settled (then) 就這麼說定**
It's settled then—we're going to Hawaii for Christmas this year.
就這麼說定了，今年聖誕節我們要去夏威夷度假。

# 震驚西洋棋界

〔貝絲贏得第一場錦標賽後，她與養母艾瑪一起吃早餐。〕

Alma     *[reading from the paper]* "The world of Kentucky chess was [11]**astonished** this weekend by the playing of a local girl who [12]**triumphed** over [13]**hardened** players to win the Kentucky State Championship. Elizabeth Harmon, a student at Fairfield High, showed a mastery of the game **unequaled** by any female, according to Harry Beltik, whom Miss Harmon [14]**defeated** for the state crown." *[holds up check]* And a hundred dollars. You won this.

Beth     I wanna open a bank account. But you have to go with me, because I need a parent or a guardian.

Alma     I just didn't ❶ <u>have the faintest idea</u> that people made money playing chess.

Beth     There's tournaments with bigger prizes than that.

Alma     How much bigger?

Beth     Thousands of dollars.

Alma     **Goodness**.

Beth     So, can we go to the bank today after school?

Alma     Certainly.

©Shutterstock.com

## Vocabulary

11. **astonish** [əˋstɑnɪʃ] *(v.)* 使驚奇，震驚
12. **triumph** [ˋtraɪəmf] *(v./n.)* 勝利，巨大成功
13. **hardened** [ˋhɑrdənd] *(a.)* 頂尖的，強硬的
14. **defeat** [dɪˋfit] *(v./n.)* 擊敗，打敗
15. **leaf through** *(phr.)* 快速翻閱
16. **calculate** [ˋkælkjə͵let] *(v.)* 計算

### 補充單字

**unequaled** [ʌnˋikwəld] *(a.)* 無與倫比的
**goodness** [ˋgʊdnɪs] *(int.)* 天啊！

艾瑪     〔朗讀報紙〕「這個週末肯塔基的西洋棋界為之一驚。一名當地女孩戰勝數名頂尖棋士，贏得肯塔基州冠軍。伊莉莎白哈蒙是費爾菲爾德高中的學生，根據哈利貝提克所言，她的精湛棋藝沒有任何女性可及，哈蒙小姐打敗了他，摘下州賽之冠」。〔拿起支票〕還有百美元獎金。妳贏了這筆錢。

貝絲     我想去銀行開戶，但妳必須陪我去，因為需要家長或監護人陪同。

艾瑪     我完全不知道有人用下棋來賺錢。

貝絲     還有其他錦標賽，獎金比這個更多。

艾瑪     更多是多少？

貝絲     好幾千元。

艾瑪     天啊。

貝絲     今天放學後，我們可以去銀行嗎？

艾瑪     當然可以。

# 信心十足

〔當天稍晚，艾瑪開始為貝絲下一場錦標賽做計劃〕

Alma | I've been [15]**leafing through** this chess magazine. It says here that there is a tournament in Cincinnati, and the first prize is 500 dollars. I ➊ <u>took the liberty</u> of calling.

Beth | What about school?

Alma | I could write a medical excuse claiming **mono**. It's ➊ <u>quite the thing</u> in your age group, according to the *Ladies Home Journal*.

Beth | Where would we stay?

Alma | At the Gibson Hotel, in a double room for 22 dollars a night. The tickets would be $11.80 **apiece**, plus the cost of food. I've [16]**calculated** all of it. Even if you only won second or third prize, there would still be a profit.

Beth | I'll win.

Alma | I ➊ <u>have every confidence</u>.

---

艾瑪 | 我一直在翻閱這本西洋棋雜誌。上面說辛辛那提有一場錦標賽，第一名的獎金是 500 美元。我主動打了電話。

貝絲 | 學校怎麼辦？

艾瑪 | 我可以幫妳請病假，說你有單核白血球增多症。根據《婦女家庭雜誌》 這個年紀的孩子經常得這種病。

貝絲 | 我們要住哪裡？

艾瑪 | 吉布森飯店，雙人房一晚 22 美元。巴士一張票 11 元 8 角，再加上餐費。我都計算過了，就算妳只得第二或第三名，還是有賺頭。

貝絲 | 我會贏的。

艾瑪 | 我對妳有十足信心。

---

**mono** [ˋmɑno] *(n.)* 傳染性單核球增多症，mononucleosis 的簡稱

**apiece** [əˋpis] *(adv.)* 每人，每個

## *Tongue-tied No More*

### not have the faintest idea
完全不知道

I don't have the faintest idea what you're talking about. 我完全不懂你在說什麼。

### take the liberty (of)
擅自，自作主張

I took the liberty of asking Bob to join us for dinner. 我擅自邀請了鮑伯加入我們的晚餐。

### (quite) the thing 滿流行的

Short skirts are quite the thing this summer. 今年夏天短裙還滿流行的。

### have every confidence
有十足的信心，深信

We have every confidence that you'll make the right decision. 我們有十足的信心你會做出正確的決定。

©Shutterstock.com

全文朗讀 ♫ 072　　單字 ♫ 073

Shutterstock.com

## Vocabulary

1. **spark** [spɑrk] *(v.)* 激起，引發
2. **timing** [ˋtaɪmɪŋ] *(n.)*
   時間的選擇，時機
3. **confine (to)** [kənˋfaɪn] *(v.)*
   限制，禁閉
4. **distract** [dɪˋstrækt] *(v.)* 消遣，娛樂
5. **dust off** *(phr.)* 擦去灰塵
6. **purchase** [ˋpɜtʃəs] *(v.)* 購買
7. **website** [ˋwɛb͵saɪt] *(n.)* 網站

### 補充單字

**craze** [krez] *(n.)* 熱潮，瘋狂
**runaway** [ˋrʌnə͵we] *(a.)* 爆紅的，躥紅的

## The Queen's Gambit[1] Sparks Chess Craze
## 《后翼棄兵》效應 西洋棋熱潮激起

When **runaway** Netflix hit *The Queen's Gambit* debuted in October 2020, the [2]**timing** couldn't have been more perfect—at least as far as the chess world is concerned. With much of the world [3]**confined** to their homes due to the global pandemic, people needed an activity to [4]**distract** themselves. Inspired by the fictional prodigy Beth Harmon, who discovers chess in the basement of her orphanage, many fans of the show [5]**dusted off** their old chess sets or [6]**purchased** new ones. In fact, one U.S. company reported that sales of their chess sets were more than 1,000% higher than the previous year! And the popular [7]**website** Chess.com has seen millions of new users create accounts to play online. If you enjoyed *The Queen's Gambit*, why not join the craze?

Netflix 於 2020 年 10 月首度推出爆紅的《后翼棄兵》播出時機再完美不過了——至少就西洋棋世界而言。 由於全球疫情，全世界大部分地區的人都被關在家中，人們需要一項活動來娛樂消遣自己。 劇中的虛構天才神童貝絲哈蒙在孤兒院地下室中發現西洋棋，許多影迷都受到她的啟發，揮去積塵重拾舊西洋棋，或是購買新的棋組。事實上，一家美國公司指出，他們的西洋棋組銷量比去年高出 1,000% 以上！熱門網站 Chess.com 已經有數百萬新用戶註冊帳號，線上下西洋棋。如果你喜歡《后翼棄兵》，何不加入這波熱潮呢？

# The Queen and the Crown: A Virtual Exhibit
## 《后翼與王冠》線上虛擬時裝週

全文朗讀 ♪ 074　單字 ♪ 075

© 擷取自 thequeenandthecrown.com

The two recent Netflix series *The Crown* and *The Queen's Gambit* feature some [1]**stunning** examples of fashion from the mid-20th century. In a virtual [2]**exhibit** hosted by the Brooklyn Museum, fans of these shows can get a 360° view of the [3]**outfits** worn by actresses Anya Taylor-Joy, Claire Foy, Gillian Anderson and others. **Curated** by Matthew Yokobosky, the exhibit also includes other pieces in the museum's [4]**collection** related to the two series, such as an ancient blue ceramic game board used to play senet, an Egyptian **precursor** to chess. But the costumes, like the **glamorous** I'm Chess Dress and the **floral** print Australia Tour Two Piece, steal the show. Visit thequeenandthecrown.com to get a look before it's too late!

Netflix 近期的兩部影集《王冠》和《后翼棄兵》以 20 世紀中令人驚艷的時尚代表服飾為特色。 在布魯克林博物館主辦的虛擬展覽中，影迷們可以 360 度零死角欣賞安雅泰勒喬伊、克萊兒芙伊、吉蓮安德森等女演員所穿的服裝。該展覽由馬修約克博斯基策劃，展品還包括與這兩部影集相關的其他博物館收藏，例如現代西洋棋的前身——古埃及塞尼特棋的古老藍色陶瓷棋盤。但魅力動人的「我是西洋棋洋裝」和花印「出訪澳洲兩件式套裝」諸如此類的戲服搶走了活動焦點。 趕快上以下網址觀看，以免為時已晚！ thequeenandthecrown.com

## Vocabulary

1. **stunning** [ˋstʌnɪŋ] (a.) 驚艷的，出色的
2. **exhibit** [ɪgˋzɪbɪt] (n.) 展覽，展品
3. **outfit** [ˋaʊt‚fɪt] (n.) 全套服裝
4. **collection** [kəˋlɛkʃən] (n.) 收藏（品）

### 補充單字

**curate** [ˋkjʊret] (v.) 精選策展
**precursor** [‚priˋkɜsə] (n.) 前身
**glamorous** [ˋglæmərəs] (a.) 魅力動人的
**floral** [ˋflorəl] (a.) 花卉的

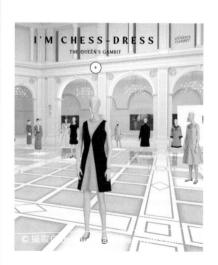

© 擷取自

# GOSSIP GIRL

©Wikicommons

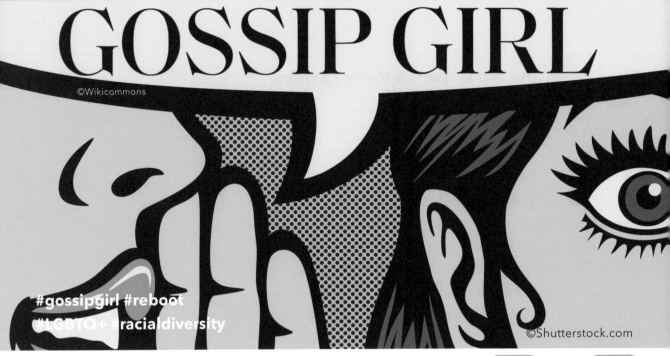

#gossipgirl #reboot
#LGBTQ+ #racialdiversity

©Shutterstock.com

全文朗讀 🎵 076　單字 🎵 077

## *Gossip Girl* 《花邊教主》
### 多元種族性別　重啟八卦女王的鬥爭

HBO GO

**Vocabulary**

1. **diverse** [dɪˋvɝs] (a.)
   多元的

2. **elite** [ɪˋlit] (a./n.)
   菁英階級的；菁英

3. **mischievous** [ˋmɪstʃəvəs] (a.)
   淘氣的，調皮的

4. **narrate** [ˋnæret] (v.)
   講述，旁白

Watch out, because everyone's favorite (and most feared) ˙socialite ˙blogger is back, only this time "she" has an Instagram account. The new *Gossip Girl*, which began streaming on HBO Go in July 2021, is a ˙reboot of the popular teen drama of the same name, which aired from 2007-2012. While the new *Gossip Girl* introduces viewers to a brand new cast of characters that is more racially 1)**diverse** than the original, the setting is the same 2)**elite** private high school on Manhattan's Upper East Side. And fans will immediately recognize the 3)**mischievous** voice of Kristen Bell, who returns to 4)**narrate** all the ˙scandalous activity that takes place in the reboot.

小心唷，大家最愛（也是最怕）的社交名流部落客回來了，只是這次「她」有了 IG 帳號。 新版《花邊教主》於 2021 年 7 月開始在 HBO Go 串流播出，該劇重新開拍 2007 年至 2012 年播出熱門同名青少年戲劇。 雖然新版《花邊教主》向觀眾呈現比原版更多元種族的全新角色，但背景依然是紐約曼哈頓上東

區的同一所私立菁英高中。 粉絲們會立即認出克莉絲汀貝爾淘氣的聲音，她回來講述新版影集中發生的一切醜聞。

The *Gossip Girl* premiere opens with students returning to school as the COVID-19 pandemic eases. We meet Julien Calloway (Jordan Alexander), a fashion model and [1]**influencer** who **T** <u>calls the shots</u> at school, and learn that she's secretly **T** <u>pulled strings</u> to get her half-sister Zoya (Whitney Peak) admitted on a scholarship. **G** As quickly as Julien brings Zoya into her social [5]**orbit**, however, their relationship starts to [6]**deteriorate**. A [2]**compromising** photo of Zoya with Julien's boyfriend Obie (Eli Brown), posted by the mysterious Gossip Girl on Instagram, suggests there's something going on between them, and leads to Zoya being [7]**harassed** by Internet [3]**trolls**. In addition, the [8]**anonymous** blogger attempts to reveal the [4]**machinations** that led to Zoya's scholarship.

▲ Kristen Bell 就是「 XOXO Gossip Girl」的配音旁白

《花邊教主》首集開場，隨著新冠肺炎疫情減緩，學生都回到了學校。 我們看到茉莉安卡洛威（喬丹亞莉珊卓 飾），她是時尚模特兒，也是一位在學校呼風喚雨的網紅，她偷偷動用權力走後門，讓她同母異父的妹妹卓婭（惠特妮匹克 飾）獲得獎學金入學。 然而，就在茉莉安將卓婭帶進她的社交圈之際，她們的關係開始惡化。 神秘的花邊教主在 IG 上發布了一張卓婭與茉莉安男友奧比（伊萊布朗 飾）的不雅豔照，暗示他們間有曖昧關係，導致卓婭受到網路酸民的騷擾。 此外，這位匿名部落客還試圖揭露卓婭獲得獎學金的詭計。

5. **orbit** [`ɔrbɪt] *(n.)*
   勢力圈，星軌

6. **deteriorate** [dɪ`tɪrɪə͵ret] *(v.)*
   惡化

7. **harass** [hə`ræs] *(v.)*
   騷擾

8. **anonymous** [ə`nɑnəməs] *(a.)*
   匿名的

## Grammar Master

### 「一⋯就馬上⋯」表達法

原句 "As quickly as Julien brings Zoya..., their relationship starts..."，使用到 **as quickly/ soon as...**「一⋯就馬上⋯」句型，可用 **no sooner... than**（發生時間沒有比較快）替換 "Julien no sooner brings Zoya⋯than their relationship starts⋯"，若將 no sooner 置句首，則需倒裝將助動詞移至前方 "No sooner <u>does</u> Julien bring Zoya⋯than their relationship starts⋯ "

例：<u>As soon as</u> I saw those cockroaches, I screamed in fear.

= I had <u>no sooner</u> seen those cockroaches <u>than</u> I screamed in fear.

= <u>No sooner</u> had I seen those cockroaches <u>than</u> I screamed in fear.

我一看到蟑螂，就嚇得大叫。

▲ 原版《花邊教主》海報

9. **torment** [ˋtɔrˏmɛnt] (v./n.)
折磨

10. **revive** [rɪˋvaɪv] (v.)
重啟，復活

11. **crush** [krʌʃ] (n.)
迷戀，暗戀

12. **manipulate** [məˋnɪpjəˏlet] (v.)
操控，操弄

### 補充單字

**socialite** [ˋsoʃəˏlaɪt] (n.) 社交名流
**blogger** [ˋblɑgɚ] (n.) 部落客
**reboot** [ˋriˏbut] (n./v.)
新版影集，重新啟動
**scandalous** [ˋskændələs] (a.)
醜聞的，誹謗的
**influencer** [ˋɪnfluənsɚ] (n.)
社群媒體影響者，網紅
**compromising** [ˋkɑmprəˏmaɪzɪŋ]
(a.) 桃色的，有損名譽的
**troll** [trol] (n.) 網路酸民
**machination** [ˏmækəˋneʃən] (n.)
陰謀詭計
**intriguing** [ɪnˋtrigɪŋ] (a.)
有趣的，耐人尋味的
**subplot** [ˋsʌbˏplɑt] (n.) 次要情節
**straight** [stret] (a./n.)
異性戀的，直男直女
**watchful** [ˋwɑtʃfəl] (a.)
密切注意的，監視的

While the Gossip Girl's identity remained a mystery for much of the original series, it's revealed early on in the reboot that a group of [9] **tormented** teachers has [10] **revived** the account. Chief among them is Kate Keller (Tavi Gevinson), an English teacher who is regularly bullied by Julien's friends Luna (Zion Moreno) and Monet (Savannah Lee Smith). Another **intriguing subplot** involves Audrey (Emily Alyn Lind) and Aki (Evan Mock), who are a couple but both develop a [11] **crush** on their classmate Max (Thomas Doherty). Indeed, the reboot has more characters who identify as **LGBTQ+** compared to the "**straighter**" original.

雖然花邊教主的真實身份在原版影集中一直是個謎，但新版《花邊教主》一開始就透露了，一群飽受折磨的老師重啟這個帳號。 其中以凱特凱勒（妲薇蓋文森 飾）為首，一位經常被茱莉安的閨蜜露娜（席恩莫雷諾 飾）和莫奈（薩凡納李史密斯 飾）欺負的英語老師。 另一個有趣的次情節圍繞著奧黛莉（艾蜜莉艾琳林德 飾） 與阿奇（伊凡莫克 飾），他們是對情侶，但兩人都迷戀上了他們的同學麥克斯（湯瑪斯達赫蒂 飾）。 確實，與比較「直男直女」的原版相比，新版有更多多元性別身份的角色人物。

▲ Jordan Alexander 飾演 Julien　▲ Whitney Peak 飾演 Zoya　▲ 新版《花邊教主》海報

Because it's on a streaming service, the new *Gossip Girl* can ⓣ <u>push the envelope</u> further than the original did on cable. While the focus is still on the glamorous lives of wealthy New York City teens, the reboot has them exploring more adult situations than before. But at the same time, they remain under the **watchful** eye of a **Big Brother** figure who tries to [12] **manipulate** them by exposing their behavior. To learn what happens to Julien and the group, catch *Gossip Girl* streaming on HBO Go now!

因為新版《花邊教主》在串流平台播出，尺度更勝有線電視播出的原版。 雖然新版影集仍然聚焦在富家紐約青少年光鮮亮麗的生活，但卻比以前探索了更多成人情境。 但同時，他們仍處於一位「大人物」的監視之下，透過揭露行為試圖操控他們。 要了解茱莉安和好友圈發生的事情，請立即收看 HBO Go 串流影集《花邊教主》！

---

### Tongue-tied No More

**call the shots 主宰一切，有決定權**
Who calls the shots in your department? 你的部門誰主宰一切？

**pull strings 利用權力關係，走後門**
The concert is sold out, but I may be able to pull a few strings and get us tickets.
演唱會售完了，但我可能可以利用關係，讓我們拿到票。

**push the envelope 挑戰尺度，挑戰極限**
Kids like to push the envelope and see how much they can get away with.
小孩喜歡挑戰極限，看他們能夠叛逆到什麼程度。

---

## EZpedia

**LGBTQ+ 多元性別**
女同性戀者（lesbian）、男同性戀者（gay）、雙性戀者（bisexual）與跨性別者（transgender）、酷兒多元性別總稱（queer），或對其性別認同感到疑惑者（questioning）的英文首字母縮略字。後面的 plus+ 包含所有性別認同光譜上的多元性別，如：泛性戀者（pansexual）、無性戀者（asexual）、非二元性別者（non-binary）……等。

**Big Brother 惡霸老大哥**
出自 1949 年英國作家喬治歐威爾（George Orwell）出版的反烏托邦小說《一九八四》。故事時間設於 1984 年，為當時作者對未來的虛構想像。該作品諷刺蘇聯領導人史達林（Joseph Stalin）假社會主義之名，行極權統治之實。他在小說中創造詞彙「老大哥」（Big Brother），暗指極權政府老大哥無所不在地監控著公民。英文中由他的名字衍生出的單字 Orwellian 歐威爾式的，指「極權獨裁的，高壓統治的」。

〔紐約菁英高中開學，老師們完全拿時下年輕學生沒輒〕

Kate　This school produced great people—Caroline Kennedy, Colson Whitehead, Nate Archibald. It's why I wanted to teach here.

Rebecca　It's not like Nate Archibald was such a 1)**saint** when we started.

Kate　You went here, Rebecca?

Rebecca　Class of '09. Back when we still respected authority. Now, they can't be controlled because we've 2)**ceased** to matter. Who needs an education when you're famous for putting on your 3)**makeup**?

Kate　But you said Nate....

Rebecca　When I was a student, we lived under constant threat. People were ❶ <u>scared straight</u>. It was this thing that started 4)**freshman** year, called itself "Gossip Girl." Kind of like an ***Orwellian** Big Sister. Kept tabs on students it 5)**deemed** important.

---

## Vocabulary

1. **saint** [sent] *(n.)* 聖人，道德崇高的人
2. **cease** [sis] *(v.)* 停止
3. **makeup** [ˋmek.ʌp] *(n.)* 化妝品
4. **freshman** [ˋfrɛʃmən] *(a./n.)* 一年級（生）的；一年級生
5. **deem** [dim] *(v.)* 視為

### 補充單字

**Orwellian** [ɔrˋwɛliən] *(a.)* 極權的，歐威爾式的

**fucking** [ˋfʌkɪŋ] *(adv./a.)* （用於強調）他媽的，該死的

凱特　這所學校培養了偉大的人才——卡羅琳甘迺迪、科爾森懷特黑德、內特阿奇博爾德。 這就是我想在這裡教書的原因。

瑞貝卡　我們一開始，內特阿奇博爾德並不是這樣的聖人。

凱特　妳在這裡讀書嗎，瑞貝卡？

瑞貝卡　2009 年那屆，以前我們仍然尊師重道的時候。 現在，學生都不受控制，因為我們已經不重要了。 如果你化化妝就可以成名，誰還需要教育？

凱特　但你說內特……

瑞貝卡　當我還是學生時，我們一直活在威脅中。 人們都被恐嚇從善。高一開始就有個東西，自稱「花邊教主」 有點像惡霸大姐頭，她認為重要的學生，就會密切關注。

## 學生主宰

〔茱莉安與卓婭在學校廁所私下見面〕

Julien　I can't believe you're really here.

Zoya　I know, I thought no **fucking** way my dad would go for moving. But when I got the scholarship…. I can't believe we ⓣ <u>pulled this off</u>.

Julien　That's not what I meant. I…I can't believe you're really here. You look just like her. [*hugs Zoya*] I have this whole plan to incorporate you into our friend group.

Zoya　Are you sure you can't just….

Julien　This'll be easier. They'll like you for you and not because you're [6] **related** to me. Met steps at eleven.

Zoya　I was told freshmen don't have open campus [7] **privileges**.

Julien　We own this school. They work for us.

---

茱莉安　我不敢相信妳真的在這裡。

卓婭　對呀，我以為我爸怎樣都不肯搬家。 但當我獲得獎學金時…… 我不敢相信我們成功了。

茱莉安　我不是這個意思。 我……我不敢相信你真的在這裡。 妳長得和她一模一樣。〔擁抱卓婭〕我有一個完整的計劃，要把妳加入我們的好友圈。

卓婭　妳確定妳不能只是……

茱莉安　這會更容易。 他們會因為妳而喜歡妳，而不是因為妳和我有血緣關係。 十一點大都會藝術博物館門口台階見。

卓婭　有人告訴我新生沒有出校的權利。

茱莉安　我們擁有這所學校。 他們為我們工作。

## Vocabulary

6. **related** [rɪ`letɪd] (a.)
   有親戚（或親緣）關係的

7. **privilege** [`prɪvəlɪdʒ] (n.)
   特權，權利

### *Tongue-tied No More*

**scare sb. straight 恫嚇某人從善**
Our son was caught taking drugs, so we sent him to military school to scare him straight.
我們的兒子被抓到吸毒，所以我們送他去軍校恫嚇從善。

**pull off 成功達成，完美表現**
I didn't think we'd win the case, but our lawyer pulled it off.
我原以為我們無法贏得這場官司，但我們的律師辦到了。

©Shutterstock

# 重磅八卦

〔老師們聚在一起討論重啟 Gossip Girl 帳號〕

**Kate**　　We need to center someone people are actually [8]**drawn** to, like Julien. Not only is she famous, people actually like her.

**Wendy**　Julien has no [9]**rival**.

**Kate**　　Who knew what Blair and Serena's relationship was actually like? Gossip Girl's [10]**perception** was reality. So we create our own. Who do we think Julien might....

**Wendy**　Wait, we might not have to make up anything. You know about her sister, right?

**Kate**　　I was on her [11]**admissions** [12]**panel**.

**Wendy**　But do you know how she got there? *[shows others laptop]*

**Jordan**　Is that real?

**Kate**　　The old Gossip Girl knew how to ⓣ tease things out. She got their attention first, and then ⓣ went in for the kill. So we do the same.

©Shutterstock.com

---

## Vocabulary

8. **draw (to)** [drɔ] *(v.)* 吸引
9. **rival** [`raɪvəl] *(n.)* 競爭對手
10. **perception** [pə`sɛpʃən] *(n.)* 看法，感覺
11. **panel** [`pænəl] *(n.)* 評委小組
12. **admission** [əd`mɪʃən] *(n.)* 招生入學

### 補充單字

**DM** *(n.)* 私訊 = direct message
**mythical** [`mɪθɪkəl] *(a.)* 神話般的，虛幻的

---

| 凱特 | 我們需要聚焦真正可以吸引大眾的人物，比如朱莉安。 她不僅有名，還受大眾歡迎。 |
| 溫蒂 | 茱莉安完全沒對手。 |
| 凱特 | 誰知道布萊爾和瑟琳娜的關係到底是什麼樣的？ 花邊教主說得算。 所以我們創立我們自己的花邊教主。 我們覺得茱莉安會向誰…… |
| 溫蒂 | 等等，我們可能不必編造任何東西。 妳知道她妹妹的事，對吧？ |
| 凱特 | 我是入學評委之一。 |
| 溫迪 | 但是妳知道她怎麼進來的嗎？ [ 給別人看筆電 ] |
| 喬丹 | 那是真的嗎？ |
| 凱特 | 舊的花邊教主知道如何套出八卦。 她先引起他們的注意，然後準備徹底擊敗對方。 所以我們也這樣做。 |

# 名利改變了她

〔大雨淋濕奧比與卓婭，奧比帶卓婭回家換上乾淨衣物，便開始聊天。〕

Obie     Sometimes it just feels like we're not even dating anymore. Really, like I'm just this actor, and I'm playing her boyfriend in her story. When we first got together though, it was totally different. That was way before she got into any of that stuff. She wanted to 🔊 <u>make her mark</u> on the world. And now she just, like, tells me what to wear and where to be and what to say. She's making her mark, for sure. 🔊 <u>Don't get me wrong</u>. I mean, she's got a lot of influence. You know, it's just it's her world, it's not ours.

Zoya     OK, two years ago, on my birthday, I got this **DM** from someone who I'd only ever heard of. She'd been **mythical** to me, and then suddenly, she was real. We DM'd and talked pretty much every single day since then. The Julien that I got to know on the other end of those phone calls? Yeah, she's different from the one that I met today.

---

奧比     有時感覺就像我們根本已經沒在交往。真的，我就像個演員，在她的故事中扮演她的男朋友。不過我們一開始交往時，完全不是這樣。那是她開始接觸那些東西很久之前。她想聞名於世，然後現在她就只叫我穿什麼、去哪裡、說什麼。她的確成名了，別誤會我的意思，我是說她有很大的影響力。妳知道，只是這是她的世界，這不是我們的世界。

卓婭     好，兩年前我生日那天，我收到一則簡訊，那個人我依稀只聽說過，她對我來說就像故事中的人物，然後突然間，她真實存在。從那以後，我們幾乎每天聊天。電話那頭我認識的茉莉安？是的，她和我今天遇到的不一樣。

Kathy Hutchins© Shutterstock.com

▲ Eli Brown 飾演 Obie

## Tongue-tied No More

**tease sth. out**
**套出（八卦，秘密）**
It wasn't easy, but I finally teased the truth out of Mark. 一開始並不容易，但我最終從馬克那套出真相。

**go/move in for the kill**
**準備徹底擊敗對方**
After a couple of body shots, the boxer went in for the kill. 拳擊手擊出幾個軀幹拳後，準備擊敗對方。

**make one's mark 成名**
Jonas Salk made his mark by developing the polio vaccine. 喬納斯沙克開發小兒麻痺疫苗而成名。

**don't get me wrong 別會錯意**
Don't get me wrong—I'd love to come, but I'm just too busy. 別會錯意，我很想去，但我就是太忙了。

# 2

# 串流解憂雜貨店

## Stress Relief Streaming Series

在家防疫是否有時心情會有點沈悶,有些人還會 #doomscrolling 暗黑狂刷壞消息,或是 #FOMO(fear of missing out)狂追社群媒體,深怕自己會錯過任何最新動態。在新版《花邊教主》Gossip Girl 我們看到網路霸凌對 Zoya 的傷害,《黑鏡》Black Mirror 看到科技濫用帶來的暗黑結局。深呼吸給自己休息一下,讓這三部串流正能影集幫你放鬆解憂。

《怦然心動的人生整理魔法》Tidying Up with Marie Kondo

日本斷捨離達人近藤麻里惠的心動整理妙招

《冥想正念指南》Headspace Guide to Meditation

靜心冥想消除壓力的正能英文動畫

《安眠指南》Headspace Guide to Sleep

放鬆閉眼一覺天亮安眠英文動畫

# TIDYING UP

### WITH MARIE KONDO
### 近藤　麻理惠

**#mariekondo #tidyup**
**#konmari**

©Wikipedia

全文朗讀 ♫ 080　　單字 ♫ 081

## *Tidying Up with Marie Kondo*
### 《怦然心動的人生整理魔法》

**NETFLIX**

日本斷捨離達人近藤麻理惠心動的整理妙招

### Vocabulary

1. **shrine** [ʃraɪn] *(n.)*
   神社，聖殿

2. **philosophy** [fə`lɑsəfi] *(n.)*
   哲學

3. **consultant** [kən`sʌltənt] *(n.)*
   顧問，consult 諮詢

4. **gender** [`dʒɛndə] *(n.)*
   性別

Tokyo native Marie Kondo developed an interest in organizing at a young age. At home, she enjoyed cleaning her **siblings'** rooms, and at school she was put in charge of tidying the bookshelves. Kondo worked as an assistant at a Shinto [1]**shrine** in her teens, an experience she says helped shape her organizing [2]**philosophy**. She began working as an organizing [3]**consultant** while still in college, and even wrote her **thesis** on a related topic: "Tidying Up as Seen from the Perspective of [4]**Gender**." Kondo's consulting business was so successful that she soon had a six-month waiting list, so she decided to write a book, *The Life-Changing Magic of Tidying Up*. The book was a **bestseller** in Japan and then Europe, and sold so well in the U.S. that Kondo moved her business—and her family—to Los Angeles in 2016.

出生於東京的近藤麻理惠小時候就對整理產生興趣。 在家裡她喜歡清理兄弟姐妹的房間，在學校她負責整理書架。 近藤十幾歲時在神社擔任助手，她說這段經歷幫助她形塑奠定整理哲學。 她在大學期間就開始擔任整理顧問，甚至還撰寫相關主題的論文：「從性別的角度觀察整理」。 近藤的顧問事業非常成功，很快就累積了六個月的預約等待名單，於是她決定寫一本書《怦然心動的人生整理魔法》。 這本書先後在日本和歐洲暢銷，在美國也賣得超好，以至於近藤在 2016 年將她的事業與家庭搬到洛杉磯。

It was probably [5]**inevitable** at this point that Kondo would end up on TV, and she did just that with the Netflix reality show *Tidying Up with Marie Kondo*, which premiered in January 2019. In each episode, Kondo, along with her [6]**interpreter** Marie Iida, visits an American family and guides them in using the KonMari method to organize and tidy their home. But before she visits her first family, the Friends, Kondo explains her method. "The KonMari method is unique," she says, "because I organize by category rather than by location." In the KonMari method, [7]**household** items are tidied in the following order: first, clothing; second, books; third, papers; fourth, *komono* ([8]**miscellaneous** items from the kitchen, bathroom and garage; and fifth, [8]**sentimental** items.

▲ 日本整理達人 Marie Kondo

5. **inevitable** [ɪnˋɛvətəbəl] *(a.)*
無可避免的

6. **interpreter** [ɪnˋtɜprɪtɚ] *(n.)*
口譯者

7. **household** [ˋhaʊsˌhold] *(n.)*
家庭

8. **sentimental** [ˌsɛntəˋmɛntəl]
*(a.)* 感情的，多愁善感的

近藤到了這個成功點，最終會上電視大概也是無可避免地， 她的 Netflix 實境秀《怦然心動的人生整理魔法》於 2019 年 1 月首播。在每一集中，近藤與口譯飯田真理惠一起拜訪一個美國家庭並指導他們使用 KonMari 方法整理打掃他們的家。 但在她拜訪第一個家庭（弗蘭德夫婦）之前，近藤解說她的方法：「KonMari 方法是獨一無二的，因為我是按類別整理，而不是按位置整理。」在 KonMari 方法中，居用品按以下順序整理家：首先是衣服、 其次書籍、 第三文件、 第四小物（廚房、浴室和車庫的雜物）、第五情感物品。

## Vocabulary

9. **residence** [ˈrɛzədəns] (n.)
住所，居住

10. **assess** [əˈsɛs] (v.)
評估

11. **dresser** [ˈdrɛsə] (n.)
斗櫃

12. **overflow** [ˌovəˈflo] (v.)
湧出，溢出

13. **strew** [stru] (v.)
撒滿，散佈

14. **ritual** [ˈrɪtʃuəl] (n.)
儀式

15. **discard** [dɪsˈkɑrd] (v.)
丟棄，拋棄

### 補充單字

**sibling** [ˈsɪblɪŋ] (n.) 兄弟姐妹
**thesis** [ˈθisɪs] (n.) 論文
**bestseller** [ˈbɛstˈsɛlə] (n.)
暢銷作品
**miscellaneous** [ˌmɪsəˈlenɪəs] (a.)
混雜的，多樣的
**clutter** [ˈklʌtə] (n.) 雜亂，凌亂

©Shutterstock.com

Arriving at the Friend [9]**residence**, Kondo and Iida meet Kevin and Rachel, a married couple with two young children, four-year-old Jaxon and two-year-old Ryan. Busy with work and taking care of the kids, the couple is struggling to keep their house tidy. They also feel the **clutter** is affecting their relationship, and hope to spend more quality time with each other and the kids. But before the tidying can begin, Kondo needs to [10]**assess** the damage. They start in the kids' playroom, which also has a closet and [11]**dresser** filled with Kevin's clothes, and move on to the master bedroom, where both closets are [12]**overflowing** with Rachel's clothes. Next is the kids' bedroom, which is so [13]**strewn** with clothes and toys that Rachel trips and falls! ☏ <u>Needless to say</u>, the rest of the rooms aren't any better—the kitchen sink is piled with dishes, and the garage is cluttered with junk.

近藤和飯田到達弗蘭德夫婦的住處，與夫妻凱文和瑞秋見面，他們有兩個年幼的孩子，四歲的賈克森和兩歲的瑞恩。 這對夫妻忙於工作和照顧孩子，很難保持家裡的整潔。 他們也覺得雜亂影響了他們的關係，並希望與彼此和孩子們度過更多美好時光。 但在開始整理之前，近藤需要評估雜亂程度。 他們從孩子們的遊戲室開始，有一個衣櫃和斗櫃都裝滿凱文衣服，然後移動到主臥室，兩個衣櫃堆滿瑞秋的衣服到要滿出來。 接下來是孩子們的臥室，裡面的衣服和玩具到處亂扔，還因此絆倒瑞秋！ 不用說也知道，其餘的房間也好不到哪裡去——廚房水槽裡堆滿了碗盤，車庫裡亂七八糟的雜物。

After Kondo guides the Friends through a "greet the house" [14]**ritual**, it's time to get to work. She has them gather all the clothes in the house into piles and then teaches them the most important part of the KonMari method: going through the items one at a time and keeping those that "spark joy"—she compares it to holding a puppy—and [15]**discarding** those that don't. Next, Kondo teaches Kevin and Rachel her special folding method, which makes clothing much easier to organize and store. Now that they ☏ <u>have the hang of</u> things, the couple spends the next few weeks—the whole process takes about a month—working through the rest of the categories. So what are the results? On Kondo and Iida's last visit, the house is neat and tidy, and the couple is happier and more relaxed than they've been in years. Yes, the KonMari method works!

在近藤引導弗蘭德夫婦完成「迎接房子」的儀式後，是時候開始工作了。 她讓他們把房子裡所有的衣服都聚集成堆，然後教他們 KonMari 方法中最重要的部分：一一檢查物品並留下會「激起喜悅」的東西——她比喻成像抱著一隻小狗——並丟棄那些沒有激起喜悅的東西。 接下來，近藤教凱文和瑞秋她特殊的折衣法，這使衣服更容易整理和存放。 現在這對夫婦掌握了重點，在接下來的幾週裡（整個過程大約需要一個月）處理其餘的類別品項。 那麼結果如何呢？ 近藤和飯田最後一次造訪時，房子整理得井然有序，夫妻倆比過去幾年更快樂、更放鬆。 是的，KonMari 方法真的有效！

---

### Tongue-tied No More

**needless to say 不用說**
Needless to say, they won't be inviting me over for dinner again.
更不用說，他們再也不會請我到他們家吃飯。

**have/get the hang of 學會，上手**
A: Did you ever get the hang of using that program? 你學會那個程式了嗎？
B: Yeah. It took me a while, but I have the hang of it now. 有，很花時間，但我現在上手了。

---

〔瑞秋與凱文講述結婚五年來家裡的變化〕　　　　　全文朗讀 ♫ 082　單字 ♫ 083

| | |
|---|---|
| Rachel | Kevin's like a natural romantic and he's super thoughtful. What I love about him is that if I'm really [1)]**passionate** about something, he's ❶ <u>on board</u> with me. |
| Kevin | Rachel always has one thing on her mind and that's enjoying her life. She's super **quick-witted**. We have two great kids. Four and two. Jaxon and Ryan. |
| Rachel | We had wanted kids, we planned for them. But...kids and work, ever since that, things are hard to do. |
| Kevin | I feel like our house is a home, but I feel like it's a constant struggle to be. |
| Rachel | We find there's just kind of so much stuff, and we end up getting [2)]**frustrated** about it. |
| Kevin's | [3)]**definitely** cleaner than I am. When it comes to throwing my clothes over here and letting them ❶ <u>pile up</u> and leaving laundry for a while, that's me. |

## Vocabulary

1. **passionate** [ˋpæʃənɪt] (a.)
   充滿熱情的
2. **frustrated** [ˋfrʌˌstretɪd] (a.)
   感到挫折的
3. **definitely** [ˋdɛfənɪtlɪ] (adv.)
   確實地，的確地
4. **absolutely** [ˌæbsəˋlutlɪ] (adv.)
   絕對地，當然地
5. **chaos** [ˋkeɑs] (n.) 混亂
6. **resolution** [ˌrɛzəˋluʃən] (n.)
   解決，解答
7. **perfectly** [ˋpɝfɪktlɪ] (adv.)
   十全地，完美地

| | |
|---|---|
| 瑞秋 | 凱文天生浪漫，他也超級體貼。我愛他每當我興致勃勃要做一件事，他都會陪我瘋。 |
| 凱文 | 瑞秋腦裡總有一股念頭，那就是享受生活。她超級機智。我們有兩個很棒的孩子，四歲跟兩歲，傑克森與萊恩。 |
| 瑞秋 | 我們想要小孩，他們在我們計劃之內。不過…孩子和工作，自此之後，事情很難處理。 |
| 凱文 | 我覺得這棟房子是我們的家，但我一直都覺得好像很難維持這個家。 |
| 瑞秋 | 我們發現我們有太多東西，我們最終為滿屋雜物感到氣餒。凱文絕對比我愛乾淨。說到把衣服亂丟，任由它們堆起來，把髒衣服丟在一旁不洗，那個人是我。 |

## 討厭洗衣

〔近藤與飯田來到瑞秋與凱文的房間看到衣櫃〕

Iida　　Can she [Kondo] look inside?

Rachel　**Absolutely**. You can do whatever you want.

Iida　　So, how do you separate them? In categories, or...?

Rachel　Um, I think…so, I don't do it. We have someone help us do it, like a laundry person. 'Cause I hate doing laundry.

Kevin　We fight about laundry. It ☎ <u>pisses me off</u> a lot. It's not because she doesn't do the laundry, it's because we hire somebody to come do it.

Rachel　It's freaking ⁵⁾**chaos**. My kids are just like running around and being crazy and we never get anything done. So I think to myself, "What's an easy ⁶⁾**resolution**?" If we don't have enough time, then maybe we can pay somebody to do these things, and that way we have more time.

Kevin　It's because we're ⁷⁾**perfectly** capable of doing those things.

---

飯田　　她（近藤）能看衣櫃裡嗎？

瑞秋　　當然可以，妳們什麼都可以自便。

飯田　　妳怎樣分門別類？以種類，還是…？

瑞秋　　呃，我想…我沒有分類。我們僱用別人幫我們處理…一個洗衣工，因為我討厭洗衣服。

凱文　　我們因為洗衣服而吵架，非常惹我生氣。不是因為她不洗衣服，而是因為我們僱了人來洗衣服。

瑞秋　　一切超級混亂。我的孩子跑來跑去，瘋狂不受控，我們什麼家務也做不了。所以我想「有什麼簡單的解決方法？」如果我們沒有足夠的時間，那或許我們可出錢僱人做這些事，那這樣我們有更多時間。

凱文　　問題是我們完全有能力做這些事。

### Tongue-tied No More

**on board (with) 贊同，在同陣線**
Is everybody on board with Elizabeth's proposal? 大家都贊同伊莉莎白的提案嗎？

**pile up 累積，堆積**
If the bills keep piling up, I won't be able to pay them. 如果帳單繼續累積堆疊，我無法付清。

**piss sb. off 使某人生氣**
Brad's rude behavior really pisses me off.
布萊德無理的行為很令我生氣。

# 神奇寶盒

〔近藤與飯田帶著小禮物到來〕

**Rachel**　Come in, come in.

**Kevin**　Good to see you, good to see you.

**Rachel**　What is this, and why are you holding a box?

**Kondo**　I figured that today, you'd need to store little things.

**Kevin**　Oh ⓣ <u>my goodness</u>. What is this?

**Iida**　We'll be taking care of the [8]**storage** of miscellaneous items, so I thought these might ⓣ <u>come in handy</u>.

**Kondo**　Miscellaneous items include everything except clothes, books, [9]**documents** and sentimental items. I always use boxes when tidying miscellaneous items. By using boxes, you can **compartmentalize** the drawers neatly.

---

## Vocabulary

8. **storage** [ˋstorɪdʒ] (n.) 儲藏，存放
9. **document** [ˋdɑkjəmənt] (n.) 文件
10. **motivate** [ˋmotə͵vet] (v.) 激勵，激發
11. **mentality** [mɛnˋtælətɪ] (n.) 心態，想法
12. **relaxation** [͵rilækˋseʃən] (n.) 放鬆
13. **totally** [ˋtotəlɪ] (adv.) 完全地，整個地

### 補充單字

**quick-witted** [ˋkwɪkˋwɪtɪd] (a.) 機伶的
**compartmentalize** [͵kəmpɑrtˋmɛntəlaɪz] (v.) 劃分，分隔
**insane** [ɪnˋsen] (a.) 瘋狂的

瑞秋　請進，請進。

凱文　很高興見到妳，很高興見到妳。

瑞秋　這是什麼？妳為何拿著個盒子？

近藤　今天我認為⋯你們需要存放一些小東西。

凱文　天啊，這是什麼？

飯田　我們要處理存放各種雜物，所以我認為這些盒子可能會派上用場。

近藤　雜物包含所有非衣服、書籍、文件或情感物品的物品。當我整理雜物時，我都會使用盒子。透過盒子，你就可以把抽屜分隔得有條有理。

©Shutterstock.com

## 改變生活

[ 近藤最後拜訪時，凱文與瑞秋聊使用 KonMari 方法的成效 ]

**Kondo**　Both you, Rachel and Kevin, worked on your entire house this time. You had quite the experience.

**Kevin**　Thank you. It was a lot of work, but it was [10]**motivating** knowing what the end was gonna be.

**Iida**　And you finished.

**Rachel**　Yeah, which is crazy. With two young kids, it's crazy.

**Kondo**　I'm so happy.

**Rachel**　Marie, she changed my life. It's just [11]**insane** how, like, my [11]**mentality** has changed.

**Kevin**　There's a sense of, like, [12]**relaxation** and...just doing all the things we need to do. If it's laundry, OK, we do it. If there are dishes, we just do it.

**Rachel**　Even if things do pile up, it's like, "Nope, we got this. I could [13]**totally** do this."

**Kevin**　There is more time to just ❶ <u>hang with</u> the kids, especially for me, when I come home from work. We're just looking forward to living this way for the rest of our lives, hopefully.

---

近藤　瑞秋和凱文你們兩人，這次努力整理整棟房子，這是相當辛苦的體驗。

凱文　謝謝，有很多事要做，但知道最終成果很有激勵性。

飯田　你們完成了。

瑞秋　沒錯，太瘋狂了，跟兩個小孩一起完成，很瘋狂。

近藤　我太開心了。

瑞秋　麻理惠改變了我的生活，我也改變了我的心態，太狂了。

凱文　有一種像放鬆的感覺，做我們需要做的所有事情。如果要洗衣服，好，我們就洗。如果有碗盤，我們就洗。

瑞秋　即使事情堆積如山，我們會說「不怕，我們做得到，我可以完全做得到。」

凱文　有更多時間和孩子一起玩，特別是我下班回家後。我們期盼餘生都以這方式生活，但願如此。

### Tongue-tied No More

**(oh) my goodness/gosh
我的天啊！**
Oh my goodness, what a busy day I had today! 我的天啊，今天真是忙碌的一天！

**come in handy 有用，派上用場**
A pocket knife can really come in handy on a camping trip. 口袋折刀在露營時真的可以派上用場。

**hang (out) with
和⋯一起玩，共度時光**
I usually hang with my friends after school. 我下課之後通常會和朋友們混在一起。

headspace

©Wikicommons

#meditation #relax
#headspace # AndyPuddicombe

©Shutterstock.com

全文朗讀 ♫ 084　單字 ♫ 085

# *Headspace Guide to Meditation* 《冥想正念指南》
## 放鬆身心 冥想正能解除生活壓力

In our modern world of social media and smartphones, everyone's lives are filled with [1]**distraction** and [2]**stimulation**. And the pandemic, which has caused so many people to lose their freedom, their jobs and even their lives, has added fear and stress to the mix. But what if there were a way to slow things down, for our minds to [3]**unwind**, for our bodies to let go of that stress? When was the last time that you stopped, that you were still, that you put down your phone, that you got rid of all the distractions around you? When was the last time that you did nothing? These are the questions that former [4]**Buddhist** monk Andy Puddicombe asks in the new Netflix series, *Headspace Guide to Meditation*.

©Wikicommons

▲ Headspace 創辦人 Andy Puddicombe

ZEN

## Vocabulary

1. **distraction** [dɪˋstrækʃən] (n.)
   分心，娛樂消遣

2. **stimulation** [ˌstɪmjəˋleʃən] (n.)
   刺激

3. **tragedy** [ˋtrædʒədi] (n.)
   悲劇

4. **grief** [grif] (n.)
   悲傷

5. **devote** [dɪˋvot] (v.)
   將…奉獻給，致力於

在現代社會中，社群媒體和智慧型手機讓每個人的生活充斥著干擾與刺激。 而武漢肺炎疫情導致眾多人失去自由、工作甚至生命，交雜更多恐懼和壓力。 但如果有辦法放慢速度，讓我們的心靈放鬆並讓身體釋放壓力呢？ 你上一次停下來、沈靜、放下手機、擺脫周圍所有干擾是什麼時候？ 你上一次什麼事都不做是什麼時候？ 這些是前佛教僧侶安迪帕帝康在 Netflix 新影集《冥想正念指南》中提出的問題。

But who is Andy Puddicombe? Born in London and raised in Bristol, Andy was a 22-year-old studying sports science when [3]**tragedy** struck. In a few short months, several close friends and relatives died in accidents. Unable to handle the [4]**grief** he was experiencing, Andy dropped out of university and travelled to the Himalayas to study meditation. After spending a decade in Thailand, Burma, Nepal and India, he was **ordained** as a monk at a Tibetan **monastery** in northern India. He then returned to the West and [5]**devoted** his efforts to spreading the meditation message. Andy taught in person at first, but wanting to reach more people, he started a company called Headspace in 2010, and created a smartphone meditation **app**, which now has 40 million users around the world.

FellowNeko © Shutterstock.com

但誰是安迪帕帝康？ 安迪出生於倫敦，在布里斯托長大。他 22 歲就讀運動科學時，遭受一場悲劇。 短短幾個月內，幾位親朋好友在事故中喪生。 安迪無法處理他所經歷的悲傷，從大學休學，前往喜馬拉雅山學習冥想。 在泰國、緬甸、

6. **anxiety** [æŋˋzaɪətɪ] *(n.)*
   焦慮

7. **stroke** [strok] *(n.)*
   中風

8. **hormone** [ˋhɔr.mon] *(n.)*
   激素，賀爾蒙

9. **soothing** [ˋsuðɪŋ] *(a.)*
   撫慰人心的

10. **animation** [.ænəˋmeʃən] *(n.)*
    動畫

11. **scan** [skæn] *(v./n.)*
    掃描，檢查

12. **enlightenment**
    [ɪnˋlaɪtənmənt] *(n.)*
    開悟，啟蒙

---

**Tongue-tied No More**

**take up** 開始從事

I'm thinking of taking up skiing this winter. 我想今年冬天開始學滑雪。

Mind
Body
Soul
© Shutterstock.com

---

© Shutterstock.com

尼泊爾和印度度過了十年之後，他在印度北部的藏傳佛寺受戒為僧。 之後他便回到西方致力於推廣冥想正念。 安迪起初親自授課，但為了傳授更多人，他於 2010 年創辦了一家名為 Headspace（心境） 的公司，並開發了一款智慧型手機冥想應用程式，目前在全球擁有 4000 萬用戶。

With so many people ☏ taking up meditation, there must be a lot of benefits, right? On the mental side, meditation can help you manage stress, reduce [6]**anxiety** and develop peace of mind. And there are less obvious benefits as well. One study showed that a month of meditation with the Headspace app can improve mental focus by 14%, and another that just a single session reduces mind wandering by 22%. The physical benefits of meditation come mainly from its ability to reduce stress. Over time, stress can cause high blood pressure, which increases the risk of heart attacks and [7]**strokes**. By relaxing the body and mind, meditation actually lowers stress [8]**hormone** levels and improves our health. According to a University of California study, people who meditate produce less stress hormones than those who don't.

這麼多人學習冥想，肯定有很多好處吧？在精神方面，冥想可以幫助你管理壓力、減少焦慮並讓你安心， 也還有一些不是那麼明顯的好處。一項研究顯示，使用 Headspace 應用程式進行一個月的冥想可將精神專注度提高 14%，而根

據另一項研究，單次冥想可以減少 22% 的注意力分心。 冥想對身體的好處主要來自它能減輕壓力。 隨著時間過去，壓力會導致高血壓，從而增加心臟病發與中風的風險。 透過放鬆身心，冥想實際上可以降低壓力荷爾蒙分泌並改善我們的健康。 根據加州大學一項研究，冥想的人比沒有冥想的人產生更少的壓力荷爾蒙。

So how do you learn meditation from a TV series? In the *Headspace Guide to Meditation*, the [9]**soothing** voice of Andy Puddicombe, accompanied by colorful [10]**animation**, introduces beginners to the basics of this ancient art. In each of the eight 20-minute episodes, a specific meditation technique is covered. Puddicombe spends the first 10 minutes talking about the benefits and science, and the second 10 minutes with a guided meditation that allows you to take each technique for a test drive. After learning how to focus on the breath in the first episode, viewers are introduced to more advanced techniques like visualization, noting and body [11]**scan** meditation. One short season of the *Headspace Guide to Meditation* probably won't take you to [12]**enlightenment**, but it's a good start!

那麼要如何從影集中學習冥想呢？ 在《冥想正念指南》中，安迪帕帝康舒服療癒的聲音伴隨著色彩繽紛的動畫，向初學者介紹這種古老技藝的基礎。《冥想正念指南》共八集，在每集 20 分鐘中，講解特定的冥想技巧。帕帝康會在前 10 分鐘談論好處和科學根據，後 10 分鐘進行引導式冥想，讓你可以嘗試每種技巧。 在第一集中學習如何專注於呼吸後，觀眾將認識更進階的技巧，如視覺化、注意和身體掃描冥想。 短短一季《冥想正念指南》可能無法讓你成佛，但這是個好的開始！

© Shutterstock.com

# headspace

©Wikicommons

**#sleepsoundly #insomnia**
**#headspace #comfysleep**

©Shutterstock.com

全文朗讀 🎵 086　　單字 🎵 087

## *Headspace Guide to Sleep* 《安眠指南》

破解睡眠迷思 擺脫科技　好眠一覺到天亮

### Vocabulary

1. **stumble** [ˋstʌmbəl] (v.)
   跌跌撞撞，蹣跚而行

2. **strain** [stren] (n.)
   壓力，緊張

3. **restful** [ˋrɛstfəl] (a.)
   讓人休息的

©Shutterstock.com

We all know the importance of getting a good night's sleep. When we all enough sleep, we wake up in a good mood and full of energy to face the day's challenges. When we don't get enough sleep though, we [1]**stumble** through the day like a *zombie* and struggle to get anything done. But getting a good night's sleep isn't always easy, and the stress and [2]**strain** of *lockdowns* and working (or learning) from home have made a [3]**restful** *snooze* even more *elusive*. If you enjoyed the Headspace Guide to Meditation, you'll be happy to know that Headspace and Netflix have also put out a guide to help you sleep better. The Headspace Guide to Sleep, which premiered several months after Meditation, is narrated by Eve Lewis Prieto, another *Brit* with a calm, soothing voice.

我們都知道晚上要睡好覺的重要性。 當我們睡眠充足時，醒來心情良好，活力充沛面對一天的挑戰。 然而，當我們睡眠不足時，我們會像殭屍一樣蹣跚而行，且難以完成任何事情。但要睡個好眠並非總是那麼容易，而封城與在家工作（或學習）帶來的壓力與緊張，讓睡好覺變得難上加難。 如果你喜歡《冥想正念指南》，你知道 Headspace（心境）公司和 Netflix 也推出了幫助提升睡眠的指南一定很開心。《安眠指南》於《冥想正念》後幾個月首播，由另一位英國人伊芙路易斯普列托擔任旁白，聲音一樣沉靜而療癒。

4. **professional** [prəˋfɛʃənəl] (n.)
   專業人士

5. **particularly** [pəˋtɪkjələli]
   (adv.) 特別地，尤其

6. **insistence** [ɪnˋsɪstəns] (n.)
   堅決，堅持

7. **recall** [rɪˋkɔl] (v./n.)
   回想，回憶

Back in 2013, Prieto was working as an advertising ⁴⁾**professional**, and reached a breaking point in her life. "It wasn't a ⁵⁾**particularly** good period of my life," she says. "I'd experienced a lot of challenges in my family, I was in a lot of debt, and I was really, really stressed." A friend of hers recommended the Headspace meditation app, and after some ⁶⁾**insistence**, she gave it a try. "I'll never forget my first session," she ⁷⁾**recalls**, describing how she immediately realized she didn't need to feel stressed all of the time. Prieto joined Headspace several months later, and eventually rose to become director of meditation. "I tell my husband that I go to bed with lots of people every night," she jokes when asked what it's like to host the Sleep series.

早在 2013 年，普列托從事廣告專業工作，並達到了人生的轉折點。 她說：「那並非是我生命中特別好的時期，我的家庭經歷了很多挑戰，我又負債累累，我真的、真的壓力很大。」 她的一個朋友推薦了 Headspace 冥想 app，經過一番堅持，她就給它試了一下。她回憶說：「我永遠不會忘記我第一次使用」，並描述自己立刻意識到她不需要一直感到壓力。 幾個月後，普列托加入了 Headspace 公司，並最終升任冥想主管。當被問到主持《安眠指南》是什麼感覺時， 她開玩笑說：「我告訴我的丈夫，我每晚都和很多人上床睡覺。」

8. **myth** [mɪθ] (n.)
錯誤觀念，迷思

9. **application** [ˌæpləˈkeʃən] (n.)
應用，適用

10. **grip** [grɪp] (n./v.)
控制，緊抓

11. **addict** [ˈædɪkt] (n.)
成癮者

12. **rhythm** [ˈrɪðəm] (n.)
節奏，韻律

©Shutterstock.com

Before getting into the use of **mindfulness** techniques to improve sleep, the first episode of the Headspace Guide to Sleep starts by exploring some sleep-related [8)]**myths**. One of the most common is that everyone needs eight hours of sleep a night. The <u>sweet spot</u>, it turns out, is somewhere between seven and nine, and can vary from person to person. Another **misconception** is that exercising before bedtime is bad for sleep. But several studies have shown the exercise can actually help you sleep, as long as you give yourself an hour to <u>wind down</u> first. How about alcohol and coffee? Some find that a **nightcap** can help them fall asleep, but as alcohol can affect the quality of your sleep, it's best not to drink before bedtime. The same applies to coffee, but you don't have to **abstain** completely like some believe—a few cups a day is fine as long as it's before 5 p.m.

在講解使用冥想正念技巧來改善睡眠前，《安眠指南》的第一集首先探討了一些與睡眠相關的迷思。其中最常見的之一就是每個人每晚都需要八小時的睡眠。事實證明，最佳時間落在 7 到 9 小時之間，並且因人而異。另一個誤解是睡前運動不利於睡眠，但幾項研究顯示，運動實際上可以幫助您入睡，只要你先給自己一個小時的時間放鬆下來。那酒和咖啡呢？ 有些人發現睡前小酌可以幫助他們入睡，但由於酒精會影響你的睡眠品質，因此最好不要在睡前喝酒。這同樣適用於咖啡，但你不必像某些人認為的那樣完全戒咖啡——只要在下午 5 點之前，一天喝幾杯還可以。

## The Perfect Night's Sleep Starts Before You Get Into Bed

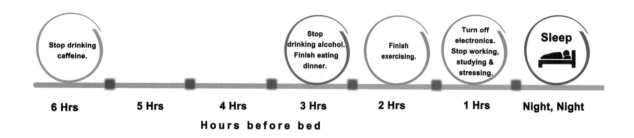

With the myths <u>out of the way</u>, Prieto turns to the [9]**application** of mindfulness techniques. In Episode 1, she starts with a deep breathing exercise to help you wind down. Next, she has you visualize warm sunlight pouring into your body to create a sense of stillness, and then has you count backwards from 1,000 to zero. "If you're still awake and interested in learning more," she concludes, "check out the next episode in our series, where we will focus on how our devices keep us up at night and what we can do to break out of technology's strong [10]**grip** on our sleep." If you're a smartphone [11]**addict** like so many people these days, you won't want to miss Episode 2. And if you're still having trouble sleeping, you'll want to catch the remaining five episodes as well, which cover topics like sleeping pills, [ ]**insomnia** and finding the perfect sleep [12]**rhythm**.

隨著迷思的破解，普列托轉向正念技巧的應用。 在第一集中，她從深呼吸練習開始，幫助你放鬆。 接下來，她讓你想像溫暖的陽光湧入身體，創造一種寧靜感，然後讓你從一千倒數到零。 「如果你仍然清醒並且有興趣了解更多，」她總結說，「請收看我們的下一集，我們將重點介紹我們的裝置如何讓我們夜不能寐，以及我們如何擺脫科技對我們睡眠的強烈控制。」 如果你像現在很多人一樣智慧型手機使用成癮，你不能錯過第二集。如果你仍然無法入睡，你也會想看剩下的五集，其中涵蓋了像安眠藥、失眠和找到完美睡眠節奏等主題。

©Shutterstock.com

---

### Tongue-tied No More

**sweet spot 最好的時機，最強的打擊點**
Autumn is the sweet spot for me when it comes to comfortable weather.
說到舒服的天氣，秋天對我來說是最好的時機。

**wind down 放鬆，鬆懈**
Kelly likes to wind down with a hot bath after a long day at work.
凱莉整天工作之後喜歡泡熱水澡放鬆。

**out of the way 破解，解決**
Now that midterms are out of the way I can finally relax.
現在期中考結束了，我終於可以放鬆。

# 串流 KOLs 訪談

## Interviews with Content Creators

除了我們熟知的國際串流平台，台灣許多影音產業也投入發展本土串流平台，
YouTube、Podcast 也提供素人創作發表的空間。本期《總編嚴選》也採訪了本
土串流平台 GagaOOLala 創辦人杰德影音 CEO 林志杰、瑞典 YouTuber Jonas.

杰德影音 CEO 林志杰原本是矽谷的律師，回到台灣創立杰德影音從事國外頻道代理，2014 年發起台灣國際酷兒影展（Taiwan International Queer Film Festival），創立本土最大串流 GagaOOLala 以 LGBTQ+ 多元性別題材，並以多國合作推出原創影集，拓展全球版圖。大家熟悉的「哈哈台」、「DramaQueen 電視迷」都是杰德影音旗下業務。

瑞典 YouTuber Jonas 原是綠能太陽能板工程師，在與 Charlie 相戀多年後，來台結婚定居。他告訴我們瑞典教育注重環境保護與性別平權的價值，並分享他在台灣的跨文化婚姻生活。

# 本土最大串流平台
# GagaOOLala 創辦人林志杰

## 故事 是最好的同情心製造者

採訪撰稿／邱鈺玲

©杰德影音提供

串流平台是現代人不可或缺的重要娛樂管道，就算你不愛追劇，至少也曾使用串流平台消磨時光。相信大部分的人平常都習慣使用海外的串流平台，但其實台灣也有一個串流平台正努力地「逆輸出」台灣的創意文化。

本次我們專訪杰德影音的執行長林志杰，邀請他分享台灣最大串流平台「GagaOOLala」的現在、過去與未來。

### 一頭栽進影視行業的矽谷律師

GagaOOLala 是暴雨中的一把傘，讓許多無助的同志酷兒得以依靠，暫時忘卻長期遭受的不平待遇。撐起這把傘，並努力不讓傘開花的人，叫做林志杰，一個曾在美國矽谷工作的執業律師。

林志杰很早就展露對影視的興趣，大學期間，他邊讀書，邊經營B2B 電影代理事業。同時兼顧課業事業，蠟燭兩頭燒的結果，就是把健康燃燒殆盡，他因此神經麻痺，足足躺了 6 個月。

在鬼門關走過一遭，體悟到人生可能隨時歸零，他便開始思考究竟要以何為人生志業。痊癒後，在矽谷擔任執業律師的他，遇到一名來自新加坡的客戶，問他是否有意願到自己的影視公司擔任法務，於是他一頭栽入影視業，至今已 16 年。

### 走出櫃子 用影像為同志發聲

2005 年林志杰決定自立門戶，一開始以動畫起家，因不敵市場無情和高昂成本，索性轉型設立「杰德影音」，改作頻道發行和代理。

轉型雖成功，但穩定意味著停滯，所以只能另闢蹊徑。「其實那時候就是無聊加上皮癢，想做自己的東西。」林志杰打趣地說。

誰都想做自己的東西，但想成功，就得找到利基市場。除了繼續原來的事業，他還在 YouTube 創立「Gaga 台」、「Lala 台」、「DramaQueen」，和「哈哈台」觸及海外市場，並不惜走出躲了 40 年的櫃子，只為了順利將公司多年來積累的經驗與資源，藉由「酷兒影展」回饋給社會。

好在影展佳評如潮，為延續這股正面能量，他在 2017 年開設台灣最大串流平台「GagaOOLala」，嘗試以原創故事，提升同志議題的能見度。

### 就算被檢舉 也盼成為 世界之窗

目前全球已有 100 多萬註冊會員的「GagaOOLala」，在創辦初期因適逢台灣同婚法通過，獲得海外大量的關注，但他們後來在對同志不友善的地區，就得面對其他串流平台未曾想像的阻礙。

「我們常被擋」，林志杰推推眼鏡苦笑：「我們只是在臉書上PO 男男牽手的照片，就會被檢舉，所以我們一天到晚要處理頻道被鎖的狀況。」他再補充：「我們在網路上投放廣告也常常被擋，像是南亞、印度、印尼等地，我們都沒辦法像一般公司那樣下廣告，只能靠口碑行銷。」

面對困境，林志杰選擇以溫柔回擊，透過故事回應外界的異樣眼光。他邀請導演拍攝《同愛一家》，紀錄台灣不同世代同性伴侶爭取婚姻平權的故事。近期更致力於海外跨國合作，聯手推出原創強檔合輯《同志音樂愛情故事》，找來 10 位導演、10 位唱作人，用創作的力量，訴說 10 個屬於 LGBTQ+ 的愛情樣貌。林志杰也將自己找代理孕母得子的故事翻拍成〈酷蓋爸爸〉。「像我知道很多人對我的家庭有不同的想法，所以我就直接拍一部〈酷蓋爸爸〉給他們看。」他說。

林志杰說，這次採合輯形式，不只是為了測試市場喜好，也希望結合影視與台灣華語音樂的能量，替作品創造更多賣點。

不過多年來促使他努力奔走的，仍是破除大眾對同志族群的偏見。作為非主流族群，同志生活樣貌向來缺乏能見度，但越不理解就有越多誤解。

而好電影有著使觀眾投射自己的魔力，所以他希望藉此讓觀眾明白不同族群的掙扎與苦樂，學會尊重不同的人生。

「因為我相信故事是最好的同理心製造者。用同理心化解誤會、形塑共識，就能推動改革，讓社會慢慢接近理想的樣貌。」

好故事能使人學會同理，也能開拓視野，林志杰認為，在後疫情時代，串流平台已不再是單純的觀影管道，而是取代旅行，探索不同文化的方式。

「未來我們會持續採購好劇本，打造更國際化的介面，努力成為帶大家走向全球的『世界之窗』。」

# 串流自媒體 KOL
# 瑞典 YouTuber Jonas

## 外國女婿情定寶島台灣

採訪撰稿／許宇昇

來自瑞典的 Jonas 三年前追愛來台，與戀愛長跑六年的台灣女孩 Charlie 結婚，夫妻倆目前定居台灣。從事自營媒體創作的他，在鏡頭前幽默風趣，總是能夠侃侃而談，你一定沒想到他在瑞典可是一位太陽能板工程師！曾在韓國與美國柏克萊大學擔任客座研究員。

位於北歐的瑞典，擁有良好的教育政策、高度生活品質。國家注重環境保護、人權自由，能夠包容多元文化、接受來自世界各地的移民。去過北歐國家的人一定覺得當地人民英語普及率遠高於其他歐洲國家。這期《總編嚴選：串流追劇宅英文》介紹了語言學習、跨國文化溝通、綠色替代能源、性別平權等議題。因此，我們邀請 Jonas 分享他在台灣豐富的生活，以及瑞典在各方面成功的經驗。

### 定居寶島台灣

三年前，兩人決定先來台短期居住。沒想到台灣的一切這麼方便，人民親切友善、食物美味、自然環境都深深吸引了 Jonas。隨著 YouTube 頻道得到觀眾迴響，夫妻倆一待就是三、四年。

### 語言學習溝通最重要

Jonas 開朗健談的個性，讓他在台灣交到很多朋友，中文的聽說能力因此進步神速。但他覺得中文困難的點在於聲調，例如：「睡覺；水餃」、「馬；媽」。如果是單一詞組，聽者可能誤會他的意思，但如果用整句話說明，對方自然而然可以理解。其實學習語言重點在於溝通，如果某個字不會說，你可以

用另一種解釋的方式表達。被問到瑞典人英文為什麼都這麼好時，Jonas 首先說瑞典語跟英語很相似，不過重要的是瑞典人能夠接受外來文化。例如，其他歐洲國家習慣看配音電影，他們都看原音，透過影劇來激發學習英文的動機。

### 跨文化婚姻的驚喜火花

當我問到夫妻倆來自不同成長背景，會不會因為價值觀差異而吵架。Jonas 認為正因為彼此不同的文化碰撞，才能激發創意火花。他簡單舉例台灣人永遠把青菜拿來炒，西方人習慣吃沙拉，但紅蘿蔔加熱過營養才會釋放，因為 Charlie 他才能品嚐異國料理，學習不同觀點。即使在一起六年，Charlie 總為他帶來驚喜，外表看似堅強，其實是個心思細膩的女孩。不過他也說道，跨文化戀情能夠結成正果，很大感謝雙方家長從小自由開放的教育方式。

### 瑞典教育 思考與價值

北歐國家的教育重視學生的批判思考能力，學生必須分析整體事件，並提出自我觀點。課程融入環境保護，性別平等的價值。老師、父母不會給學生課業壓力，而是注重每個孩子性向特質發展。在瑞典法律保護兒童，父母不能以管教為由打小孩。曾經一位義大利父親在瑞典因打小孩而犯法。Jonas 開玩笑地說 Charlie 以前總是打屁股教訓寵物貓，嚇壞了他跟母親。而現在 Charlie 也會用鼓勵與心平氣和的方式教導貓咪。

### 工作與生活平衡

Jonas 認為台灣人普遍工作積極勤奮。在與台灣廠商合作時，若週末晚上 9 點傳訊息，台灣人往往一兩個小時內馬上回覆。他認為這是台灣經濟成功的原因，但長期工作壓力可能對身心造成負擔。瑞典人工作講求效率，並能適時休息。Fika（點心時間）是瑞典人聞名於世的生活哲學，企業每天早上 10 點與下午 3 點有各 30 分鐘的 fika，同事一起喝杯咖啡，品嚐瑞典肉桂捲，不談公事，短暫的休息讓工作思緒更加清晰。另一方面，因為瑞典冬季嚴寒、日照較短，大家會希望趕快把工作完成，早點下班回家陪家人，在工作與生活之間取得平衡。

### 瑞典企業理念

瑞典企業注重性別平等，任何的行銷廣告一定會包含多元性別、均衡的男女比例。此外，環境保護、自由人權是每個企業的核心宗旨，產品開發會以環境友善、永續發展、公平交易等目標為考量。

訪談的最後，Jonas 表示自己很幸運能夠投入自營媒體創作，為喜歡的事付出，且更有彈性地安排工作時間。近期 Jonas 與 Charlie 計畫回到瑞典，並在 YouTube 頻道上與觀眾分享瑞典的生活。

**EZ TALK**

# 串流追劇宅英文：
# 道地流行用語、火辣影劇議題
# EZ TALK 總編嚴選特刊

總　編　審：Judd Piggott
作　　　者：EZ TALK編輯群，Judd Piggott，Jacob Roth
翻　　　譯：許宇昇
責　任　編　輯：許宇昇
裝　幀　設　計：謝志誠
內　頁　排　版：簡單瑛設
錄　音　後　製：純粹錄音後製有限公司
錄　音　員：Michael Tennant、Leah Zimmermann
照　片　出　處：shutterstock.com

副　總　經　理：洪偉傑
副　總　編　輯：曹仲堯
法　律　顧　問：建大法律事務所
財　務　顧　問：高威會計師事務所
出　　　版：日月文化出版股份有限公司
製　　　作：EZ 叢書館
地　　　址：臺北市信義路三段151號8樓
電　　　話：(02)2708-5509
傳　　　真：(02)2708-6157
客　服　信　箱：service@heliopolis.com.tw
網　　　址：www.heliopolis.com.tw
郵　撥　帳　號：19716071日月文化出版股份有限公司

總　經　銷：聯合發行股份有限公司
電　　　話：(02)2917-8022
傳　　　真：(02)2915-7212
印　　　刷：中原造像股份有限公司
初　版　一　刷：2021 年 9 月
定　　　價：420 元
I　S　B　N：9789860795295